I should have bought a first class ticket and travelled in luxury. But I didn't. If I had, I would have got some sleep. I would have also avoided trouble.

I boarded the train at Kampar, which was about three-quarters of the way from Singapore to its destination. Warm sweaty air assaulted me as I entered the second carriage from the end, which was packed with soldiers heading up country for a holiday, and, from the smell of them, also a bath.

Three hours from morning and the carriages were still set up for night travel—bunks folded down from the sides, a row of three, so that one bench became three beds. Although they were more like narrow luggage racks.

Some guys were awake, most were asleep. Those who watched me move down the aisle were probably worrying about bandits. If the Chinese terrorists attacked a train it was usually at night. Usually from above. The men on the top bunks were most exposed to bullets piercing the carriage's ceiling.

I looked left and right for a space. The only available one was a top bunk. But it wasn't empty because it had someone's kitbag on it.

I placed a foot on the bottom bunk and took hold of the kitbag.

"Oi!"

The man in the middle bed glared at me.

"My bed," I said. "Mind if I move your bag?"

"Piss off. Find another bed." He raised himself on an elbow.

"Can't see any others. I'm taking this one." I pulled his bag off the shelf and held it out for him to take.

"Piss off," he said again, only this time he swung his legs around, stood and squared up to me. He was big, more than two inches taller than my six two. He had a heavy face to match his size. Ugly. A muttonhead.

Then he pushed me. "Take your hands off my kit!"

Now everyone was awake or stirring, some sitting on their bunks, some moaning at the disturbance. The kid who'd been on the bottom bunk slid away.

I dropped the kitbag on the floor and pointed at the empty bunk. "I'll just climb up."

He moved into my path. "No you don't!"

I held up both hands, palms out, and patted the air.

"No need for this," I said calmly. "Let's just—"

"Let's just what?" Muttonhead balled his left hand, his eyes locked on mine, maybe hoping I hadn't noticed. Maybe he didn't care. His lips were pulled back in a kind of snarl. A big man acting the big dog.

I briefly closed my eyes and took a slow long breath. I really wanted some shut-eye before we got to the end of the line. Oh well.

He was bending his knees. Rotating his hips left. The left fist tightened again but he threw his right. A massive blow aiming for my chin. One punch. One knockdown. One lesson—for me—for everyone watching.

A big man throwing a big punch. It'd be slow. Heavy muscle working heavy bones, but that wouldn't matter.

2

SINGAPORE GHOST

Also by Murray Bailey

Singapore 52
Singapore Girl
Singapore Boxer

Map of the Dead
Secrets of the Dead

Black Creek White Lies

I Dare You
Dare You Twice

SINGAPORE
GHOST

Murray Bailey

Heritage Books

First published in Great Britain in 2019 by Heritage Books

16797611

copyright © Murray Bailey 2019

ISBN 978-1-9997954-9-8

Printed and bound in Great Britain by Clays Ltd, Elcograf S.p.A

Heritage Books, Truro, Cornwall

For David, Eric and Stan.
To eternal friendship.

I want us to enjoy, one more time,
Striding out through the woods on a May morning
And up to the ridge, of sheep nibbled turf
Scattered with yellow tormentil and fragments of rock.

With the summit in view in the sunshine,
And our boots gripping the slopes with authority,
Thrusting us upward, over rocky outcrops and grassy cols,
Until, suddenly we are there.

And can look back on the way we have come.
It was a good way, rich and satisfying,
Warm in the sun and in the company of friends,
And no worse for being in the past.

The past is enduring and changeless.
It recedes, but is never erased,
Time runs backwards not forwards
And youth comes after age.

So let us, both together,
Celebrate our shared past,
And find strength in the things that we find there,
And in the bonds of bruderschaft.

Stan Clough 2018

He didn't need much speed with that weight behind the blow.

Which was good.

People said I would have won the Middle East Golden Gloves in 1948 if I hadn't retired from the competition. I hadn't been injured. In fact, I'd won my last bout. My opponent, Scott "Slugger" Stevenson, on the other hand had lost an eye. Accidents happen, but it was bad enough to end my amateur boxing career. It hadn't stopped me training though, and I still considered myself fighting fit.

I read his movement, moved back and right. Enough to know his heavy punch would miss my chin. Enough to leave Muttonhead off balance. I rocked forward and my right hand—my weaker hand—jabbed out. No real force behind it, but lightning fast. And he was moving into it.

Without gloves, I aim for a soft target. The solar plexus was ideal, but he had big chest muscles beneath his shirt. Hit a muscle and my hand would just bounce off. So I aimed for his nose. Just a tap. Jab and recoil. Not too hard. A sting rather than intending any damage. It had the desired effect. He sucked in air, eyes in shock. Then he sat on the bench behind him, like I'd just pushed him over.

He touched his nose, checking for blood. None.

"You could've bust it," he said in a quieter voice.

I ignored him, looked up and down the carriage. I addressed the men, although Muttonhead was the main target audience. "You're on furlough. Enjoy your holiday. Penang is a beautiful and safe island. Don't mess it up by causing trouble."

"You an undercover MP?" someone close behind me asked. I turned, saw all the faces looking at me, nervous, questioning my presence. And then I saw a man standing in the shadows at the end of the carriage. I turned back and looked down at Muttonhead.

"Don't waste your furlough in a jail. Got it?"

The man at the end stepped forward into the light.

"Officer!" someone shouted. Bodies started to scramble from their bunks.

The man barked back: "Easy men. Back in your beds. It's all over in here." Then he pointed to me and beckoned.

In front of the train was a little pilot engine that pulled two weighted trucks. This lead train was empty, except for the driver and stoker. It ran a short distance in front of the main engine, effectively testing the tracks in case they had been disconnected or removed by bandits.

The main train had four carriages that could have been something from the Orient Express, although that's where the similarity ended, because attached to the rear was an armoured truck with two old Lewis guns. The carriage before the gun-truck was first class: half cabins, half Pullman.

I was in the dining section drinking coffee. Through the back window I could see the soldier aiming a Lewis gun into the dark jungle. His presence gave me little comfort. Any attack could be over by the time our chap reacted.

The man opposite, the officer, was an infantry captain.

"I recognize you, don't I?" he said. Since he'd invited me to join him in first class, I knew it wasn't as a result of my little confrontation. He spoke with a public school accent and I figured him to be a couple of years older than me.

He reached across and held out a hand. "Jack Elmhurst," he said.

4

"Ash Carter."

"Ex-captain, ex-MP."

I must have looked surprised at his knowledge because he then explained. "I saw you board at Kampar. I recognize you from the officers' mess. You visited Minden Barracks last year."

"You're based in Penang?"

"That's right."

"And in the middle of the night you saw me board?"

"I'm a terrible sleeper. I blame the coffee. Problem is, the more tired I am, the more of the muck I drink."

I was more of a tea drinker, but the coffee tasted good and I figured I wasn't going to get any sleep now. This guy wanted company and the first class seats were more comfortable than a whole bunk in cattle class.

"Serve in the war?" I asked.

"Briefly. After coming down from Oxford, graduated from Sandhurst then did Berlin. But it was all over by the time I got there. Thank the Lord!"

I'd been to Cambridge, and we joked about the rivalry before talking of our army experiences and postings. I told him I'd resigned a year ago and been based in Singapore since.

He called the waiter and asked for breakfast. It was still before dawn but we were served anyway.

"Mind if I ask why—why you're on the train?" he said, and then shrugged. "Sorry to be nosey. It's been a long journey, and I've been the only person in first since KL."

"Not a problem," I said. "Travelling to Minden Barracks as well."

"We've a new CO."

"Colonel Jim Dexter," I said. "I know. He's the reason for my visit." The truth was it had been time to move on from Perak. Dexter had called me. I'd worked

5

with him in the Middle East and he said he had a problem. He needed my help and I welcomed the opportunity to move on.

Elmhurst's eyes became slits as he considered this. "Is that all?"

"Just visiting. And you? I can't believe you've been enjoying R and R in Johor."

"Long story," he said.

"We have the time."

So Elmhurst told me about a problem in the barracks. It wasn't a long story but he managed to spin it out. What it came down to was a concern about some bad behaviour that seemed more than alcohol related.

He said, "We heard that Majidi Barracks in JB had seen a similar problem, so I was packed off to find out about it."

"The CO there's Colonel Underwood," I said, nodding.

"You know him?"

"I was part of the team investigating their problem."

Elmhurst's eyes narrowed, then the expression turned to a frown. "But you said you'd resigned a year back."

"I had."

He waited expectantly for my explanation.

"Working for Singapore's Internal Security," I said, "and also helping 200 Provost."

"Ah. And are you still? Was that why you were in Kampar?"

I shook my head.

Rain suddenly pounded the windows, and a minute later, lightning crackled overhead.

We ate our breakfasts and didn't talk for a long time while the thunderstorm deafened us.

Eventually it subsided, and Elmhurst said, "Blimey! You never get used to them."

I nodded, although I'd spent months experiencing storms worse than that and on most days.

He said, "Since you've been to Minden before, you know about the curse?"

He could see by my reaction that I hadn't. "It's nonsense of course." He laughed.

"Of course."

"But I experienced it myself. Friday 13th, I cut myself shaving. In fact, many of the lads did."

I looked out of the window. Now that the storm had passed, the sky was getting lighter quickly. The jungle had gone and we were travelling through flat land covered with rice and tapioca fields.

"It all started in the war," Elmhurst said, leaning forward to get my attention.

"What did—the shaving cuts?"

He laughed again. "No, that's just a silly example, but you know that no soldiers got killed on Penang during the war, right?"

I hadn't known that, but I nodded.

"But there were plenty of deaths by accident. It was only when the CO died that people started recognizing the curse."

"And why a curse?"

"Because the barracks was built on a sacred hill. The ancient people of Penang believed the spirits of their ancestors gathered there. The spirits are said to haunt the place on certain nights."

"Like Friday 13th?"

"Right."

I nodded, although it was highly unlikely. The Friday 13th superstition came from action by French King Phillip IV. On Friday 13th 1307, he had many of the Knights Templar rounded up, tortured and burned at the stake. I figured the myth grew because of the link with the date and Judas being the thirteenth disciple and betrayer of Christ.

"So what happened to the CO?" I asked.

"Hit by a cannon ball in a ceremony."

"Unfortunate," I said.

"Very," he said. "But my theory is this: the behaviour is linked somehow. It's not the same as the alcohol problem in Majidi Barracks, I've learned that, but there's some kind of bad spirit. Perhaps it possesses people and makes them go mad."

I was still thinking about what he'd just said about deaths. "Anyone die recently?" I asked.

"Yes, ten days ago, some poor idiot shot his head off."

Ah, I thought, so that's why Colonel Dexter called for me. He suspects a murder and wants me to investigate.

However, I couldn't have been more wrong.

TWO

The branch line ended at a town on the coast called Perai. From there, a ferry would take us across the two-mile strait to the island.

It was a busy little place, half port, half industrial. I could see lots of tongkangs lined up in front of godowns along a wharf. I could see goods being carried down from the warehouses and loaded onto boats. There was a marine police patrol boat out there too.

The strait wasn't busy in comparison to Singapore's harbour, but big ships languished in the deep water while sampans and junks laboured against the current.

I could also see the ferry out there and was told it was about half an hour away.

The soldiers bundled off the train, stretching and laughing. I figured there was a high degree of relief. They'd made it unscathed, without an attack on the train. I spotted Muttonhead and he seemed well behaved, joking with his mates.

A Hurricane fighter plane came in low overhead going to RAF Butterworth a few miles north. The men from the train cheered like it was returning from some great mission saving the British Empire. However, the reality will have been much more mundane; probably just a reconnaissance mission.

After milling around the platform the men gathered like starlings until they trooped off towards the ferry terminal.

Captain Elmhurst joined the other soldiers, while I headed for the market to kill time and also get a sense of location.

I bought a little brass ornament—some kind of Buddhist statue with multiple arms—and had it gift-wrapped. Soon after, a horn sounded just before the ferry docked. But I already knew it was close because I could hear the grunt of lumbering diesel engines.

I joined the queue of about a hundred men and watched the broad, flat-bottomed boat as it crunched onto the concrete ramp.

The transfer of vehicles, goods, people and animals on and off had a military precision and we were soon underway.

The sky was now big and bright and no one headed for the seats inside. Instead, everyone crammed around the railings on the two open decks.

I had a good spot up top and watched the mainland recede rather than the approach of the island. I'd seen Penang before and didn't need the crush of men as they excitedly spotted the wooden huts on the hill overlooking the sea, where many would spend their furlough.

I could see the station and the steam train. Alongside it were various railway wagons and then sheds. On the right were huge piles of coal and aggregates.

To the left of the station was the road and then the market that stretched long and thin beside it. Behind that were Malayan houses and shops in a huge block. By the ferry terminal I could see a cluster of buildings for the workers on the right of the slipway and a harbour police building on the left. Then came a long stretch of quays, offices and warehouses. Finally, they thinned into what looked more industrial, factories maybe. Behind all of this was the jungle, first low and then bobbling into foothills. The colours changed from verdant green to lighter and then bluish. By the time it reached the distant mountains, the jungle looked violet and then pale grey. On a clear day like today, I never tired of looking at the beautiful landscape and colours like they were part of a watercolour painting.

I breathed deeply and enjoyed the view.

And then people started moving, preparing to disembark long before the horn announced we'd almost arrived. I saw people returning to vehicles and the decks clear.

That's when I saw him.

A Middle Eastern-looking man, probably an Arab, looked directly at me from about twenty yards away. I realized I'd seen him before in Perai, while I was walking round the market. Had he been following me?

The ferry thumped onto land and the metal ramp clanged down. The Arab didn't move.

I waited.

Within a minute everyone had gone below to disembark, leaving us alone.

I started walking towards him.

He dug a hand into his gown and pulled out a knife. As it came out, he started running. Straight at me.

I stopped and crouched.

He was three paces away, his eyes wide. I remember them vividly: red-rimmed and crazy. He had one intention. He meant to kill me.

My hand snapped the Beretta from my ankle holster. Whether his mind registered the gun, I'll never know. His pace didn't falter.

Raising the gun, I shot him between those crazy eyes.

THREE

I spent the good part of an hour with the police, providing them with a report. There wasn't much to tell. I didn't know the Arab. I'd only just seen him. He attacked with a knife and I shot him in self-defence.

"Why would a complete stranger do that?" the police chief asked me for the third time.

"I don't know," I said for the third time. However, I had my suspicions I just didn't want to share them with this policeman.

Colonel Dexter's man was waiting for me outside the police station with a Land Rover jeep. He didn't ask me what had happened, but I saw him look at the blood splatter on my shirt.

"Not mine," I said, and he grinned.

We went up the hill out of the port by George Town towards the army barracks. We came to rubber trees where the barracks had been built around a plantation house. After bumping off the tarmac onto cobbles, we passed under the entrance archway.

There was minimal security, unlike for mainland barracks. They didn't fear a bandit attack here. Maybe they should have. It struck me that the enemy would be smart to target somewhere so vulnerable. However, they never had.

Only the central block had three storeys. Around opposing sides of a square, the other buildings had two floors—offices and accommodations. There were six smaller barrack blocks, all grey concrete, but these were partially hidden by the numerous palm trees in the grounds, so their ugliness didn't detract from the base.

In addition, there was a hospital, a school and married officers' houses.

Beyond, rubber trees surrounded three sides and playing fields on the fourth. Overall, it was an attractive place to be based.

"Not bad, eh?" Dexter said, pumping my hand.

"I thought you liked Cyprus," I said as I took a seat in his office. His window had a good view across the fields. Further north and east I could see white sandy beaches.

"No complaints," he said, "but you know what a mess the Middle East is."

I nodded.

"At least we're out," he said, and paused. He knew— at least guessed—what I'd done in Palestine before I resigned and fled to Singapore. I wondered if he'd say something, but then he just smiled knowingly. "At least *you* are out. But a shame you're no longer with the military police."

I took the opportunity to hand him my gift.

"What is it?"

I just raised my eyebrows and waited as he carefully unwrapped it.

"Oh God!" he said, staring at the little bronze statue in his palm.

"I thought you'd like it." I laughed.

"I bloody hate it!" he said. "I hate silly little ornaments."

"I know."

13

Now it was his turn to laugh. "As soon as you're out of my room, Ash, you know that's going in the rubbish bin," he said, putting the statue on the end of his desk.

"Yes, but it was worth it just to see your face."

He laughed again. "Good to see you, Ash."

"You too."

We made small talk and I wondered when he'd tell me why I was really here. However he didn't. Instead, he finally said, "Look, get settled in and we'll have dinner and we can talk about what I need you for."

I was tempted to cut things short and say, "Sure, we'll talk about the recent death that you think is murder," but I didn't. I knew him too well. Let him tell me in his own time. There was clearly no rush.

His man took me to the officers' quarters and showed me my room.

I tossed my bloody shirt in the bin and showered. I had specks of the guy's blood on my neck and a spot on an ear. Dexter had clearly noticed but chosen not to say anything.

When I got out of the shower I found a clean white shirt had been left on my bed, compliments of Colonel Dexter. There was also a message that I'd be collected at six.

In the army you learn to sleep when you can. Despite feeling wide awake from all the coffee I'd drunk on the train, I knew I was short of sleep. So I lay on the bed and shut my eyes.

Afterwards, I strolled around the grounds, looked in at the hospital in case an old flame was still there, but she wasn't. She'd returned to England months ago.

I continued my walk and was passing the communications office when a clerk came out.

"Are you Captain Carter?" he said uncertainly.

When I said yes, he handed me a note.

"You've had a call, sir," he said. "She didn't leave a name but said you'd know who she was. Said it wasn't urgent."

I shook my head. "Any other clues?"

"Oh, yes, she was calling from the Cathay Building in Singapore."

Su Ling, the stunning Eurasian who worked for the owner of the largest Chinese business empire in Singapore. It had to be her, although I was surprised it wasn't urgent. Last time we'd spoken, she'd asked for a way off the island, a way of escaping from her boss, Andrew Yipp. Officially, he was a businessman and philanthropist. Unofficially he was the head of the largest Chinese secret society in Singapore. Unofficially because secret societies were illegal and he would never admit his control and influence and, undoubted, nefarious activities. And proving such activity was another matter.

Since she said it wasn't urgent, I decided to call her after my dinner with Dexter. I also knew she was more likely than her boss to be in the office late at night.

Over dinner, Dexter was full of stories from the past but didn't mention Palestine until the dessert arrived. After the waiter had left, Dexter glanced around as though making sure no one could overhear. We were in an exclusive restaurant in George Town with only four other tables and partitions between them. We couldn't see the other patrons, they couldn't see us and I was sure they wouldn't hear a hushed exchange either.

"He was an Arab," Dexter said quietly. "The man you shot."

"The police at the harbour wouldn't tell me anything about him."

"That's because they don't know. He had no identification papers on him. All they found was a mugshot of you and his vicious-looking knife."

I hadn't registered the type of knife at the time. Now I visualized it and saw an elegant, curved blade.

"Ceremonial killing knife," Dexter said. "Probably meant to gut you."

"Nice."

"Do you think—?"

"Must be," I said knowing he'd figure out the connection. It didn't take much consideration. I'd been on assignment in Palestine. The Peace Commission of the United Nations was meeting in Jerusalem and I'd been chasing down leads. We'd been fighting the terrorists on both sides for years and my informer knew a specific cell planned to attack the peace meeting.

I said, "I can still see what they did to Malik and his family." I took a breath. "It still makes me sick to my stomach."

Dexter nodded. "And you did what you had to."

I figured he knew or at least guessed what I'd done, but I told him anyway. "I found who they were. The Palestinian authorities had no motivation to arrest them. So, yes, I did what was necessary and got away as soon as I could."

"And now they've found you."

I shook my head. I'd been thinking about that too. "I think it was opportunistic. They're looking for me and one of them spotted me. He was alone. What he should have done is call it in. Get reinforcements. Instead he went for the glory and suffered the consequences."

"Well, thank God," Dexter said.

We ate dessert and he finished a bottle of wine.

"And so you're here."

"Because you asked," I said, hoping he'd finally tell me about the case.

"You've heard about this silly curse," he said.

I was surprised. "Only this morning. On the train."

He said nothing.

"I thought this was about a potential murder, Jim."

He shook his head. "No, this is about the curse and a reporter. I have a babysitting job for you."

FOUR

As Dexter's driver pulled away from the restaurant, I noticed a girl playing on the street. About six years old, she had a hoop and was trying to get the knack of spinning it around her waist. It fell immediately and she tried again.

"I'll walk," I said.

The driver stopped.

"You're annoyed," Dexter said.

I climbed out and looked back at him. "More like disappointed."

"I thought you'd like the work... and you're someone I can trust."

"But not enough to investigate a murder."

He shook his head. "Ash, if I thought the chap had been murdered, I'd have had the MPs investigate, not an independent. No, I need you to make sure this reporter doesn't come up with any wild theories."

"We'll talk tomorrow," I said, and shut the door.

I watched the car drive down the road before turning back and strolling through the streets of the capital. Sodium and neon lights burned in the darkness and the evening pub activity had just begun. Soldiers tumbled into the town looking to spend their meagre army wage on the usual.

No fewer than four prostitutes approached me and I bade each one a good night before continuing on my way. I reached the harbour and kept walking until I reached a sea wall. There were fishing boats moored for the night with nets and pots on the path. The smell of rotten fish and seaweed was strong.

I kept going until the air smelled better and I came to another harbour wall. I sat on it, legs dangling over the edge, and looked across the dark shimmering expanse.

The only lights came from the ships out on the water. A light wind whipped a fine mist in the air, refreshing on my face.

The little girl outside the restaurant had reminded me of Malik's daughter, Ishtah. She'd been ten. Big dark eyes, trusting and happy despite the hardship and troubles. I'd given her a spinning top on the first occasion we'd met. She'd been grateful but said next time she'd like a hula hoop.

Malik had scolded her for her rudeness but I liked her, and a few days later she had her hoop. My eyes pricked with tears as I visualized her and her little brother playing in their yard. Thank God I hadn't witnessed the atrocity that Malik had known. Four men had found him and made him watch as they slit his son's throat. Then they raped and murdered little Ishtah before slitting his son's throat and then raping and brutalizing Malik's beautiful young wife.

I could hear their screams. I could feel his desperation, unable to protect his family, his outrage, his abject horror and his gut-wrenching realization that he could do nothing to save them from this hell. The gang made him watch before they gouged out his eyes.

"In your mind, you will see this again and again for eternity," they had told him.

19

I knew all of this because an old woman relative had been hiding in another room. She said that, when they cut his bonds, Malik had lashed out like a crazed animal. The four men had just laughed at his blind flailing. Then he'd scrabbled around, his body slick with his family's blood until he found each of them. The old woman said his howling had been more terrible than the screams.

I pictured him, clutching their lifeless bodies, his own life totally destroyed, until he could take it no more. I couldn't imagine taking my own life, but as soon as he had a knife, Malik hadn't hesitated. He'd died with his arms around his loved ones.

And it was my fault. I'd recruited him. I'd persuaded him that we could protect him and his family. I was wrong, and I'd never make such a promise again.

Malik had gained information about an assassination attempt. The Palestinian terrorists were going to murder the Palestinian UN representative and blame it on the Israeli Zionist group called Lehi. After all, they had been responsible for the murder of the UN Security Council mediator a few years earlier.

With Malik's information, security had been tightened and the attack never happened. But before that, the Palestinian police investigated the destruction of Malik's family and concluded it was a personal or random incident. I knew they wouldn't take action, and when I approached the British Army, I met with the same brick wall. It was too sensitive.

So that's when I resigned my commission and made my plans to get away within two weeks after revenging Malik and his family's deaths; revenging the brutalization of pretty little Ishtah.

I shouted against the wind and threw a stone hard into the darkness.

* * *

20

My skin and clothes were damp from the sea spray as I walked into a shop advertising a telephone service. Once on the phone, I asked the operator to connect me with the Cathay Building in Singapore and got put through to Andrew Yipp's office.

Su Ling wasn't available but she'd expected my call and I was asked to wait so that she could call me back.

As I waited, I stood outside on the street and watched the activity in a pub opposite. Men spilled out of the door and after a bit of pushing and bating, two soldiers started taking swings at one another. My ingrained MP's nature made me want to intervene but I didn't want to miss my call, and as I watched, I decided there wouldn't be too much damage. It didn't look like growing into a full-scale brawl.

As quickly as it started, it was over, with both men nursing swollen faces. Everyone trooped back into the pub, no doubt to make amends over another pint of beer.

The telephone rang inside the shop.

"How are you, Captain Carter?" Su Ling asked in her soft, slightly husky voice. I pictured her with her hair up and wearing a cheongsam that would show off her great figure.

"Is this the call?" I asked.

She'd wanted me to help her escape the island, escape from Yipp when the time came.

"No," she said, understanding me. "I wanted to ask a little favour."

I said, "You knew I was in Penang."

"That's why I would like your help," she said. "I want you to find my mother."

21

FIVE

I listened to the hiss on the line before Su Ling spoke again.

She said, "You see, my aunt lives in Penang," like it explained everything.

This was the first I'd heard her talk of any other relatives. She called Andrew Yipp her uncle, although I'd learned that this was just an expression. She had a Chinese mother and British Army father. She'd never known her father and her mother had left her during the war. Yipp had become her guardian.

After another pause she said, "I found some letters from my mother."

"To you?"

"Yes. She wrote to me after she left." I heard sadness in her voice now and realized it explained the awkwardness of the conversation. She continued: "She wrote on special dates. She wanted me to know she was all right and that she loved me. She said she'd come for me when she could."

"What's her name?"

"Miao Wei. Miao Wei Yong."

"You said you *found* the letters…"

"Andrew had them. I found them in a box. He had them, Ash, and he never showed them to me." Her voice had a catch in it. I imagined her beautiful eyes brim with tears.

She took a breath. "All these years, I thought she didn't care... but she did."

"Did you confront him—Yipp?"

"Of course. Andrew said he was protecting me." There was now scorn in her voice, so I figured she didn't believe him.

I said, "You don't know where she is, do you?"

"No."

"And you want me to ask your aunt."

"If she is still there."

She gave me the woman's name: Li Ping Lui. I knew Su Ling never travelled further north than Johor state. Yipp wouldn't let her because his own travel was restricted, according to Su Ling. He feared being branded as a traitor and refused re-entry into Singapore. It had happened to his greatest rival and he didn't want to give the Singapore government that same opportunity with himself.

But I suspected there was another reason Yipp didn't want Su Ling to travel. He was afraid she'd escape.

Su Ling said, "You will try, won't you?"

"I'll do my best," I said, and ended the call.

Talking to Su Ling had snapped me out of my melancholy state. I'd stopped thinking about Malik's daughter, Ishtah, and was now picturing the beautiful Eurasian woman I'd briefly had a relationship with. Although delicious and exciting while it lasted, it would never have worked. I had been employed by the government and she worked for Andrew Yipp. I represented the law and he was undoubtedly crooked. Su Ling had virtually told me that he was the head of the Chinese secret society. And secret societies meant black market trade and other illegal activities. The police knew,

23

they just couldn't obtain evidence. These were politically sensitive times in Singapore, unless someone was suspected as a communist, and Yipp was not.

The air was warm and the cicadas in full voice as I arrived at my room feeling refreshed and ready for whatever tomorrow would bring—even if this was just a babysitting case.

"It's bloody ridiculous!"

I was sitting in the foyer of the Palisades hotel opposite a woman called Hannah Quinn.

The reporter.

"It's ridiculous," she said again.

I shrugged.

"And who the hell are you anyway?"

We'd already done introductions so I figured it was a rhetorical question. She was tall, maybe five ten, with good bone structure that was somewhere between attractive and hard. Her cold eyes said it was more of the latter.

I said, "Tell me about the curse. Why are you so interested?"

She studied me for a moment, perhaps assessing me, deciding whether I was worth talking to.

I said, "Without me you aren't doing any investigating, so we may as well accept the situation."

She picked up on my slip.

"We? You said *we may as well accept the situation.*"

"Sure," I said, "I'm accepting this too. You don't think I'm happy about babysitting a journalist, do you?"

"All right, why?"

"Why what?"

"Why are you doing this?"

I'd caught Jim Dexter for breakfast and talked it through again. He wanted someone he could trust and, in return, I asked him for a favour. I didn't tell him the background, but I gave him Li Ping Lui's name and asked him to use his resources, his contacts, to find her. He'd grinned and we'd shaken on the deal.

"Well?" Quinn said, jutting her chin forward. It was a gesture I would become accustomed to.

I said, "The CO and I go way back. I owe him. Anyway, better it's me than some tight-lipped clerk accompanying you."

"Two reasons," she said softening a little and answering my original question. "I'd rather have reported on Korea, but I've missed that boat. And two, my brother was billeted here for a while and experienced the curse first hand."

"What happened?"

"He fell off a ladder."

I said nothing.

"Twice."

"Accidents happen."

"More accidents happen at Minden than anywhere else. Three of his mates got hit by a car. It randomly swerved off the road and hit them. No serious injury but the driver couldn't explain it. It was like the car had taken control all on its own."

"And deliberately targeted the men."

"That's how it seemed."

I nodded, unconvinced. "Here are the rules: you don't have total free rein because there are sensitive areas. And before you jump to the conclusion that there's something going on, all barracks have sensitive areas. I'm told to ensure everyone is as open with you as possible, but anything that is militarily sensitive is out of bounds."

She said nothing, studying me with those hard eyes, but I figured she accepted Dexter's rules.

"Also," I said, "I'm the lead on this. I start with the questions and I decide when an interview is over. You get to ask whatever you want, but if you are out of order, I will shut down the interview. Understand?"

Still with the hard eyes, she said, "I'm not happy about this."

"What's your alternative?"

"I approach people without your authority and control." She emphasized control like she thought she'd be my puppet on strings, moving whichever way I wanted.

I said, "I don't need a puppet. I've nothing to prove or hide. That's why it's better you have me as your guide."

"Babysitter," she said, throwing my own expression back at me.

"Secondly, you won't get specific access without me. If there's someone we want to talk to, then we can— providing it's not sensitive, as I said."

She clenched her teeth, looked away and then back at me. "All right, Ash Carter, let's put that to the test. Let's start with the man who got killed—who shot himself— just over a week ago."

SIX

The medical officer had a room in the main block. "Shouldn't we be meeting at the hospital?" Hannah asked as we waited outside the MO's office. The brass plaque confirmed his name as Major Scott Dawson.

The door opened and a man with a balding head and kindly face beckoned us inside and pointed at two chairs opposite his desk. He sat and smiled, first at me and then Hannah.

"So you are the reporter," he said with a mild Scottish lilt. I casually wondered whether there were any other countries in the world where a man could have the same name as his nationality.

"Hannah Quinn of the *Manchester Guardian*."

Dawson nodded, and smiled as though impressed.

He waved a hand at the room, which was pristine. Neat rows of books on shelves, grey metal filing cabinets, hand-written labels on the drawers and spines on folders.

He said, "We're meeting here because this is my office—where my files are." He smiled again. "Did you expect a meeting in the morgue, my dear?"

I noticed Hannah twitch at "my dear", but she otherwise masked her feelings.

"Thank you for seeing us," she said, and held up a notebook. "Do you mind if I jot down some notes as we speak?"

I was still looking around the room. Dawson had nothing personal on display, not even a medical certificate. There were no loose papers on his desk, which was clear with the exception of a blotting pad, an inkpot and pen. The room smelled of old paper, the way a library does.

Hannah said, "We'd like to talk about Corporal Tanner." Then she glanced at me and gave me an ironic smile. Our first meeting and she'd already broken the rule. However, Major Dawson had been primed. He knew why we were here.

He reached into a drawer and placed a paper file in front of himself. "Corporal John Tanner, 1st Royal Hampshire Regiment. Died 13th May 1953. Nineteen."

I asked, "Cause of death, Major?"

Dawson smiled. "No, no. Please call me Scott. Since Miss Quinn here is a civilian and we're talking officer to officer. A captain, weren't you? There's no need for formality."

"All right. How did he die, Scott?"

"Fatal gunshot wound to the head." He tapped the folder then slid it over to me. "Bullet entered under the chin. Just here"—he demonstrated—"and came clean out of the upper left cranium. A hole with a diameter of three and a half inches. Death would have been instantaneous."

I looked at the autopsy report. I also noted the personal items on the deceased: a few coins, a piece of string and a tiny doll-like object.

"The bullet?" Hannah asked. "What size would it have been?"

"Calibre," Dawson said, explaining like he would to a child. "We call it the calibre. Anyway, the bullet was a 303."

That surprised me. I thought they'd all switched over to the new standard .22 calibre rounds.

Dawson must have noticed because he said, "We've some old stock Lee Enfields. You know, the old faithful—Rifle Number One—used for training and local guard duty." He looked at Hannah. "You see, there's no trouble on the island. We don't really need to defend ourselves."

"And yet men do guard duty?" She wrote furiously as she spoke and I noticed she wasn't using the standard shorthand.

Dawson inclined his head and smiled. "They do. That's the army for you, my dear. Sometimes we do things just because they've always been done or the rule book says they have to be done."

I said, "Was Corporal Tanner at the firing range or guard duty?"

"Guard duty. Alone."

"And he shot himself?"

"Yes. Close range." Again with the demonstration, although this time the hand was held like a gun to the soft part under his chin. "Bang!"

I sat back, surprised by the information. This didn't sound like an accident. Not the way Dawson demonstrated it.

I said, "Suicide then?"

"No."

Before I could speak, Hannah voiced my thoughts. "Are you saying he was murdered?"

"No, I am certainly not. It was judged to be a freak accident."

When Dawson didn't elaborate, I said, "Tell us why it wasn't suicide, Scott."

"As I said, the rifle was a Number One. Overall length forty-nine inches. The distance between the tip of the average man's index finger and his chin is about thirty-six inches."

"About the length of the barrel from trigger to muzzle," I said.

"Correct. Although you'd lose at least an inch, maybe one and a half, to flex the finger." He paused and smiled. "You could do it comfortably, Ash. The average man? Well he could just about manage to shoot himself like that."

I said, "You're saying Corporal Tanner wasn't of average height?"

"No, he wasn't. Corporal Tanner was five six. Fingertip to chin was thirty-one inches. I measured it. Like I said, you could have done it, but not our friend John Tanner. He couldn't have pulled the trigger."

"So he was murdered," Hannah repeated.

"No."

Hannah had her pen poised and I waited for the explanation. Dawson enjoyed the anticipation for a minute.

Finally, he said, "Tanner dropped the rifle and it went off. Damned unlucky."

He paused again.

"Two reasons I know this. Firstly, there were no fingerprints on the trigger. Secondly, there were two witnesses."

Hannah looked at her notes. "You said he was patrolling alone."

"Ah, he was. But he was still seen by two other men. One was another corporal on guard duty and the second was a sergeant enjoying a quiet cigarette."

I said, "Could I see the body?"

The MO's demeanour changed briefly. His smile turned to a scowl before he forced the smile back.

"For sure. Once SIB, always SIB?" he said.

"Just interested."

He nodded. "Well, you're lucky. He's due to be shipped back to England in a week and is still in cold storage."

The morgue was in the basement below the hospital. Dawson led us there and we waited while an orderly was sent to get the body. He returned with a coffin on a trolley and lifted the lid for us.

The corpse had almost half his cranium missing, skin folded over the hole. I figured the brain had been removed and something packed in its place, but there had been no attempt to cover the cavity. I was impressed that Hannah didn't blanch at the gruesome sight.

Tanner was indeed around five foot six, and the bullet had passed through the soft tissue below his chin and punched a large hole in the skull.

"Was there burning—gun powder?" I asked.

"Under his chin? You're wondering how close the muzzle was?"

I nodded.

"A small amount. I estimate the muzzle was between eight and twelve inches away. Consistent with being dropped vertically and firing up into his chin."

I indicated that I'd seen enough and the orderly replaced the lid.

Hannah said, "Why would his gun go off? Don't they have safety catches or something?"

I said, "They're bolt action. The bolt has to be drawn and the bullet loaded."

Dawson agreed. "It must have been cocked and ready to fire. I should also point out there was a scuff on the

31

stock consistent with striking concrete. It was ready to fire. It hit the ground and the gun fired." He shrugged. "It shouldn't happen but the gun discharged without anyone pulling the trigger."

"Has it happened before?" I asked.

"Not to my knowledge. But that doesn't mean anything. Just one of those things I suppose."

"Bad luck," Hannah said.

"For sure."

"The curse?"

Dawson looked at her sharply. "I'm a scientist, young lady. I can't comment on the paranormal."

She returned his hard look. "Are you aware of any other paranormal activity?"

He took a breath and I wondered if he was controlling a bad temper or just mild irritation with her. "I repeat: I'm a scientist. I don't believe in any curse or evil spirits. And I'm certain Captain Carter here is of the same opinion."

"Could you let us have the weapon that killed Tanner?" I asked. "Also, the names of the witnesses?"

He seemed to relax and pulled a piece of paper from his pocket. "For sure, I came prepared."

I glanced at it and saw two names.

"And the gun?"

He shook his head. "You'll have to see the quartermaster about that. Ask for number 666."

SEVEN

As we went downstairs, I said, "Remember, let me take the lead."

"Because it's Colonel Dexter's rule?"

"Yes, and because sometimes the military do things in a certain way. Approach someone the wrong way and they might clam up. You must have noticed the major stiffened a couple of times."

She went to argue but I interrupted. "Just let me lead, OK?"

She nodded—or at least raised her chin, which I took to be agreement.

Outside we saw a colour sergeant with a clipboard. He was watching men on the parade ground.

He turned and looked at us as we neared. With grey hair and a craggy face, I placed him at forty or forty-five.

The colour sergeant smiled. "The reporter?"

"Hannah Quinn," she said, returning the smile.

"And you're Ash Carter," he said, looking at me. "Friend of the Colonel. You need any assistance, you come to me."

"Thanks, Colour," I said.

"The name's John Harper," he said. "Can I help now?"

"Heading over to the QM's office," I said.

He fell into step with us. "I'll walk you over."

"How long have you been in?" I asked, knowing he must have served for a long time.

"Twenty-five years in three weeks. And that's enough for me."

"Retiring?" Hannah asked.

He nodded. "Although this posting has been a semi-retirement. Here we are." We stopped outside a shed with *Stores* stencilled over the door and he shook both our hands. "Remember, if you need anything, just come and ask."

I thanked him and we stepped inside and got directed to a separate secure room where they kept the weapons. The air was warm and it smelled of oil and metal.

"What did Dawson mean by *always SIB*?" Hannah asked as we walked over.

"Special Investigations Branch."

"I thought you were an ex-MP."

"I was. SIB is the detective division. Like standard detectives within the police—only specialized in military matters."

"SIB!" a man said with alarm. He appeared from the cage and locked it behind him.

I shook my head. "Not anymore, don't worry. This is Miss Quinn from the *Manchester Guardian*. We're interested in anything that might be linked to the curse."

"Sergeant Lee Cooper," he said. "You're interested in that poor chap Tanner, right?"

"Yes," I said. "You can speak freely, Sergeant. We've nothing to hide."

Cooper didn't immediately speak.

Hannah said, "Rifle number 666?"

"That's the one. The Number of the Beast," Cooper said with a sheepish grin. He turned, unlocked a metal bar door and looked over his shoulder at us. "The armoury," he said unnecessarily before he disappeared into the room beyond. Moments later he returned with a rifle and placed it on the counter. It was a Lee Enfield No.1 Mk III. On the wooden stock "66" was stamped in black. An extra "6" had been crudely scratched in afterwards.

"It was a joke," Cooper said. "The real reg number is sixty-six. Some smart alec added the other six."

"Who?" Hannah asked.

"I don't know. Happened before my time."

I asked, "Had there been trouble with the gun before?"

"Not as far as I'm aware."

I picked up the rifle and held it under my chin. Using my thumb I could have pulled the trigger. I stretched my arm and figured I had about two more inches' gap between muzzle and chin.

"He didn't shoot himself," Cooper said. "Too difficult."

I turned it around and looked at the scuff on the stock.

Cooper said, "It struck the ground and went off."

"You know that for certain?" Hannah asked, scribbling notes.

"No, Mum."

"Please don't call me Mum!" she snapped.

Cooper looked at me and pulled a face. "Oops, sorry, Miss then, I suppose?"

I said, "Is it possible that it would fire when dropped?"

"Yes, sir," Cooper said. "It was tested."

"But the gun is still in use."

"They tested a few and they all do it now and then. Not every time. Maybe one in five times. Looks like the poor bugger was unlucky."

35

"Very," I said. "Mind if we continue this outside in the fresh air?"

Cooper took the rifle back, locked up the cage and led us outside. He set up three chairs in the shade of the building.

Once we were settled, he said, "Unlucky thirteen."

"Dying on the thirteenth," Hannah said.

"And on his nineteenth birthday. He was born on the thirteenth too."

Hannah wrote it down. "It was John Tanner's birthday…"

"Unlucky chap, born on the thirteenth, died on the thirteenth. Although it was a Wednesday not a Friday, which is a shame."

"Why a shame?" I asked.

He shrugged. "Sorry, it was meant as ironic."

Hannah said, "So you think it's to do with luck or the curse?"

Cooper shrugged again. "Don't know, Mu— Miss. Maybe it's the same thing, sort of. Maybe the curse targets people who have bad luck."

"What other cases have there been?"

"No deaths by shooting themselves, if that's what you mean, but plenty of injuries from misfires. And squaddies are forever dropping Bren's on their feet and breaking toes."

"Tell me about some of those accidents. Ones people think might be curse related." Hannah seemed to be in full reporter mode now.

Cooper started recounting stories, some of which he knew personally, but most were second-hand. Hannah prompted and wrote down personal details, making sure she had people's backgrounds as well as the details of the incidents. Human interest angles, I figured.

After ten minutes I found myself tuning him out. The stories weren't anything different to what happened a thousand times at a hundred other barracks. I watched the normal activity of any barracks: people walking smartly to and fro, officers being saluted, no one casually loitering. A squad marched in the parade ground. A Bedford truck picked up a unit and trundled out under the entrance arch. An ambulance trundled the other way, across cobbled stones to the hospital.

I flashed back to Palestine.

The ambulance at Malik's home. The bodies. The blood.

I know it was guilt that had driven me the most. It was my fault that Malik had died and his family murdered. I'd had to find those four men and make them pay. The police and British Army wouldn't do it, so I'd turned vigilante—although I didn't think I was a vigilante at the time. It just felt like Malik and his family needed avenging. I'd needed to make the killers pay. I'd needed to make them suffer.

After the old woman had told me the awful details, I managed to find a boy who had seen the men leave. Initially the kid had been in shock. He'd heard the screams and witnessed the aftermath. Eventually he told me he'd remember what the men looked like.

With Malik's previous help I already knew who the terrorist faction was. I knew where they would meet and plan. And it only took two days to locate the first killer. The boy confirmed it and I followed the man from a market to his home.

I thought he was alone but I was wrong. He had a family. He wasn't much different from Malik but had two girls instead of one. They were younger than Ishtah had been, maybe seven and five, with poor, grubby clothes.

At first I felt sick. How could a man with children of his own rape and murder a young girl? But then it also made me realize, no matter how evil he was I couldn't do what I'd planned. I couldn't torture him, couldn't make him suffer, because of them.

I admit I killed him, but I did it a day later, when he was away from home so that his girls wouldn't see.

Then I moved on to the next man and then the next and found that each of the terrorists had a young family. It's a crazy world where a cause can override human morality, can drive people to do things that would surely be abhorrent in the cold light of day. I had no doubt that these were devoutly religious men too. Somehow they divorced their actions from their daily spiritual lives.

So there was no great retribution, no vengeance except for their executions. And I thought I'd got away with it, thought I'd escaped to Singapore without the authorities, or terrorists, realizing who'd done it.

Which was of course foolish.

They knew because of Malik, and if they didn't know before then they would torture and kill until someone told them about me. I had paid the young boy well and hoped he'd been sensible and got away. I prayed they hadn't got to him.

"Haven't we, Ash?"

I snapped back to the present. Hannah was looking at me.

"We've got enough, haven't we?"

I stood and thanked the sergeant for his time.

"Will I get a mention?" he asked Hannah. "In your article I mean?"

"I'm sure you will," she said, although by now I could tell when she wasn't being totally honest. It was that little lift of the chin.

"Where now, Mr Investigator?" she asked as we walked across the parade ground. The squaddies had left and we were the only ones out in the noon sun.

"The first witness," I said, referring to the first name on Dawson's note. "We go and talk to Private Roy Reeder."

EIGHT

Tanner had died on the boundary of Minden Barracks' grounds. We stood in the trees, the undergrowth trampled by years of men on patrol.

Reeder said, "It was his nineteenth birthday and he'd only been in Penang four months."

The private was a young skinny lad with acne on his cheeks and nose.

We'd found Reeder on his way to the mess hall with his mates. They'd been the squad square-bashing on the parade ground while we were sitting in our deckchairs with Sergeant Cooper. I asked him to delay his lunch and show us where Tanner had died.

The kid looked tired and awkward. Despite this, I sensed he was as hard as nails. He reminded me of a similarly skinny kid I'd scrapped with in school. Each time I'd knocked him down, he'd got up again; didn't know when to quit.

I said, "Tell us what you remember from that night."

"It was dark."

"Right. You were both on patrol."

"Yeah."

"But not together."

"No."

Hannah asked, "Where are you from, Roy?"

40

"Southampton. Born and bred as they say."

"Brothers and sisters?"

He answered easily as she ran through a list of personal questions. Then she moved on to his experience in the army and at the barracks. When she'd finished she gave me a slight nod. My turn. Like we were a tag team.

I said, "You were on patrol that night. Talk us through everything from picking up your gun."

"Oh right," he said, seeming more comfortable now. "There were four of us on night patrol. We picked up our guns from the armoury and were given instructions. John and I had the internal boundary."

When he paused I asked, "What was the number on your gun?"

"I had 56. John got 66, only it had the extra six. You know, the Number of the Beast, 666. Like a joke."

"And you all laughed?"

Reeder took a breath, thinking. "Not really. I remember the QM laughing. I think it was because John looked nervous. You know, it's not nice having 666 on your gun."

Hannah said, "The QM? You mean Sergeant Lee Cooper?"

"Yes."

"You don't like him?"

"Not really."

I shook my head. "And the QM laughed?"

"Yeah, he chose 66 for John and found it funny."

"Because of the curse?" Hannah said.

He shrugged. "Yeah, I suppose."

To move things along, I said, "All right. You collected your rifles and set off on patrol."

"Yeah I did two circuits of the perimeter."

"Did you pass John each time?"

41

"Yeah, well once. The second time was, well you know, when it happened."

"And he was here? In this spot under the trees?" I asked.

"Yeah."

"And this is where you passed the first time?"

"No, we passed further up. I was surprised I hadn't seen him, then a few minutes later I saw him smoking under the trees. He was always bunking off for a quick smoke."

I said nothing.

Reeder felt his collar. Like the rest of his shirt, it was soaked with sweat. It was humid, and I guess he was also hot from the parade ground.

Hannah said, "And that's when it happened?"

"The gun going off? No, it was a few minutes later. I'd carried on and then heard the bang. I ran back and found... found him." His voice quavered, then he composed himself. "God it was awful. I didn't see him at first, not until I shone my torch around and saw his body with his head half blown off. I knew he was dead. Straight off. I didn't need to check for a pulse or nothing. I just ran back to the guard house and reported it."

"When you heard the shot, didn't you immediately worry about bandits?" I asked.

"Not really. It's safe here. The patrol's just for the sake of it really."

"But it could have been."

"I suppose."

I said, "How do you think it happened—the gun going off?"

"He must have dropped it."

"It was cocked ready to fire."

"I suppose."

42

I said, "That's against regs."

"Yeah, but some of the boys do it, just in case."

"In the jungle, yes," I said, "but we're talking about a patrol that's just a formality. *Just for the sake of it,* as you said. There was nothing to fear."

The private looked uncomfortable.

"What?"

"Well, I suppose he was worried about the curse and the Number of the Beast."

I said, "So because of the number on his gun, he put a bullet in the chamber."

"I suppose."

"Did you?"

"I didn't have number 666."

Hannah said, "Would you have loaded your gun if you'd had 666, Roy?"

"I suppose. Maybe."

"Are you afraid of the curse?"

He shrugged then looked at me. "There's nothing else I can tell you."

"You know the names of the other two on guard duty that night?" I asked. "You said there were four of you."

"Yes, though they weren't anywhere near." He gave us two names and Hannah wrote them down. I could have got them from a number of places, not least from the colour sergeant we'd met. He knew who was assigned where. But I wanted to judge Reeder's reaction and read nothing except the facts.

When he saw she'd finished writing, Reeder said, "Can I get my lunch now?"

I inclined my head and we started walking back towards the buildings. We stayed with him.

Hannah persisted: "Has anything happened to you, Roy?"

"What—to do with the spooks?"

43

"Anything at all?"

"A few scares, that's all. Just jumpy rather than any real evidence of spooks or anything, if that's what you mean."

"And was John Tanner... *jumpy*?"

"Very, especially lately—I mean just before the accident."

We walked back to the buildings. We were like an arrowhead, Reeder in the middle and a step ahead of us, like he was uncomfortable being too close.

I said, "Do you know the other witness?"

He took three paces before replying.

"Sergeant Cox, I think."

"You think?"

"Sorry, I know. Yes, Sergeant Stewart Cox."

Hannah said, "Is he one of your mates?"

"A sergeant?" He scoffed. "Not likely. Anyway he's a sapper."

"A sapper?"

"Royal Engineers." He stopped and looked at her quizzically. "Are you going to interview him too?"

"Should I?"

He raised his eyebrows. "I don't know. But I suppose they have had a lot of trouble. They say their hut's haunted, so if you want to talk about a curse, I suppose he's as good as anyone to talk to."

"Then yes, I'll talk to this Sergeant Cox."

Reeder nodded, turned and started walking again. "You should know you'll have to wait."

"What do you mean?" I asked, although the answer immediately came to me.

"They headed out this morning. Some bridge down or something. They'll be gone for a while."

I remembered seeing the Bedford truck leave the barracks while we were outside talking to Sergeant Lee

44

Cooper from the armoury. I briefly wondered about chasing after them but figured they'd be on the ferry, maybe already on the mainland by now.

"That's a shame," I said. "We'll talk to him when he gets back then."

When Hannah said she'd head for the hotel and write up her notes, I was relieved. I really wanted to talk to Cox alone—assuming he returned this afternoon.

I'd been thinking about what Reeder had told us in the woods, about what he'd seen. It was something I didn't want to share with a reporter. Something about Private Reeder's story that didn't add up. And I hoped Cox could clarify.

NINE

However, instead of going back to the hotel, Hannah seemed to change her mind. She asked me to have lunch with her first. We'd followed Reeder back to the main buildings and she said she was suddenly hungry. I offered her the officers' mess, but she wanted to go into the general mess hall. And I discovered lunch wasn't her main objective.

We queued and collected food, but while I ate she scooted around and asked soldiers about their experience of the curse. At first she appeared to have difficulty getting people to talk, but then she struck lucky. She sat next to a guy and took frantic notes. After that, they were virtually queuing up to give her their stories.

She came back to my table grinning.

"It went well then?" I said.

"Lots of material." She sat down and took a forkful of food that was surely stone cold by now. I offered to get her some more, but she was content to pick at it.

She glanced at me a couple of times and I think she was disappointed that I didn't immediately ask for a summary of what she'd learned.

"I got three interesting stories," she said eventually, and then paused. Again, I think she was prompting my interest.

I took a sip of tea and waited.

She said, "The motor pool seems to have had more than their fair share of incidents."

I said nothing.

"Damaged vehicles, blown tyres, that sort of thing."

"Sounds normal," I said.

"All right, but more than normal apparently, so much so that people say the garage is haunted."

I must have shown my incredulity because she frowned at me.

"You don't believe in ghosts and ghouls then?"

"No."

She shook her head. "Well, another common theme was the assault course."

"What, lots of accidents there too?"

"Now you're mocking me."

I said, "Of course things go wrong on assault courses. People fall off equipment, they slip, they make fools of themselves. It seems like an easy option."

"What does?"

"Blaming some kind of supernatural force. It's less embarrassing."

"I'd like to see it anyway."

I shrugged. "Your choice."

We walked out into a torrential downpour. In the army, you get used to it. Rain doesn't stop play. You ignore the weather and carry on.

Hannah on the other hand wasn't in the army. She scooted back inside the mess hall.

"How long will it last?" she asked.

"Twenty minutes."

"Really?"

"I have no idea. I'm not a meteorologist. In the rainy season it can rain all day and for days on end, however, I expect it's just a cloudburst. So twenty minutes."

47

We sat at a table near the exit and watched as the rain pounded the windows. The room emptied until there were just a handful of us remaining.

I caught her watching me.

She said, "Did you always want to be an MP?"

"Not specifically."

She leaned forward. "What does that mean?"

"That I didn't really plan it."

"And you went into the"—she glanced at her notebook, which she'd opened just before speaking—"Special Investigations Branch."

"I did."

She paused. "Any exciting investigations?"

"Not that I can talk about."

"Anything you can talk about?"

She had intelligent eyes, and I could feel them trying to read mine.

I said, "You like to get information on people."

"Of course. That's what journalists do."

"I thought journalists wanted the story—the facts."

"People are the story—well, most often. It's about human interest. The facts, on their own, don't make for a great read."

"When you chatted to some of the lads in here, did you get facts or human interest?"

She smiled. "Both. I always capture personal details, just in case."

I nodded. "The rain's stopping."

"Twenty minutes, give or take. Maybe you are a meteorologist."

We went outside into the sunlight. There were steaming puddles everywhere.

"The motor pool?" I asked.

"The assault course," she said.

* * *

48

The assault course was a mile outside Minden Barracks on the edge of a wood. It had probably been a big jungle once but had now been cleared down to a few acres.

Hannah wore sensible shoes but they were soon splattered with grey mud as we walked the last hundred yards along a track.

The arrangement of the assault course looked fairly standard, with climbing walls and towers, rope swings and rope walks, car tyres and tunnels. It was half in the open, half through the trees, using them for the higher activities. Besides the quickly drying pools left by the rain, there was a big splash pond at the end of the rope swing. It looked difficult to clear and I guessed everyone got their feet wet, probably much more. That was the idea. This wasn't meant to be fun.

Our approach scattered some birds, but besides that, I saw no sign of life, no one in training.

I could tell Hannah was frustrated as she walked along the route through the course. She looked at the equipment but her head had dropped with disappointment.

"This'll only get used once a day at most," I said.

"What's the point?"

"Of the assault course? To ensure the men are fit enough. To put them through their paces."

"And weed out the weak ones?"

"That does happen. Men have to be tough and prepared. I know it's called the Malaya Emergency, but it's a war out there. You can't wear kid gloves fighting any enemy. Put a man in the field without preparation and you reduce his chance of survival."

"You sound like a propaganda leaflet."

I shrugged and we walked some more without speaking.

After the splash pool, that I now saw was more mud than water, she said, "The men said the woods are haunted."

I stopped and stared into the densest part. "They don't look haunted."

"What does haunted look like?"

I smiled and shook my head. "I wouldn't know."

"They said it was at night."

I saw no sign of lights. Training here at night could be dangerous rather than spooky, but I said nothing.

She started walking again, heading for the muddy track. "We'll come back—when someone's here," she said. "Now I'd like to see the haunted motor pool."

TEN

I did introductions. Sergeant Matt Walsh, in charge of the motor pool, had a thick neck and sloping shoulders. In fact, it was hard to see where his neck ended and the shoulders began.

"Yes, it's haunted," Walsh said.

The motor pool was also outside of the barracks and down the hill from the assault course woods.

"Because of the curse?" I asked.

"I don't know what it's from, but there was something here."

Hannah had her notebook out. "What was it, Sergeant?"

Walsh glanced at me, probably checking it was all right. I nodded.

"Something evil," he said, his voice firm and honest. "I haven't got a better name for you."

"Here in the garage?"

"In the garage, in the compound. All about, but mostly here in the garage."

"Could you talk me through some examples—Matt, wasn't it?"

"Yes, it's Matt." He walked us over to a new-looking ladder. "The first time I saw it, it was at the top of this ladder."

"Could you describe what you saw, Matt?"

"I'd like to say it was a headless horseman or an old woman, but I can't. It was just the suggestion of a shape. Like white smoke. Wispy. It sort of flickered and evaporated."

I looked at the ladder, which ascended to a platform that covered half the garage.

Hannah placed her foot on the lower rung.

"Careful," the sergeant said. "Perhaps I should go first, Miss Quinn."

We followed him up, one at a time. He held the ladder for Hannah and then helped her onto the platform.

It was a storage area with wooden boxes, barrels, ropes and cans.

Hannah said, "You wanted me to be careful."

"In the past, we've had a ladder rung break—"

I said, "The ladder's new."

"Replaced it," Walsh said. "Anyway, we had another fall... or maybe it was pushed away."

"Pushed away?"

"There was no one up top," he said. "Except the thing."

"There's no other way down from here?" I asked.

"No. You're thinking someone was up here, that it wasn't the ghost, but there wasn't. First time, that's what I thought. I was furious, but I checked and there was no one up here."

He took us back down and again offered Hannah assistance. She took it, despite needing none.

"What else, Matt?" she asked. "You said there were incidents inside here and in the compound."

"Lots," he said. "We've had vehicles break down and things go wrong. A first I thought it was a practical joke, like someone was having fun with us, but now I don't think so. Not after seeing it."

Hannah asked, "Has anyone been hurt?"

"We've had lots of injuries. From objects falling on men to trucks rolling over feet."

I must have looked unconvinced because he added: "Moving without a driver!"

Hannah asked him to walk us around and provide specifics, and as he spoke she dropped in questions, such as the names of people involved. When she could, she also asked more personal questions, and I imagined her building her personal interest elements.

When there was a lull in the conversation, I said, "Earlier you said *was*. There *was* something in the garage. Has it gone now?"

Walsh looked awkward. "We got rid of it."

Hannah said, "What does that mean?"

"Exorcism."

She raised her eyes, suddenly more interested. "Tell me more!"

Walsh swallowed. "We used a local witch doctor. He came, did a song and dance, covered the place with holy water." He swallowed and implored me with his eyes. "Look, I was shaken, right? I saw something up there that scared me shitless. So I'd try anything to get rid of it."

"And it worked?" I asked.

"Yes. Mostly."

"Mostly?" Hannah said.

"Well we haven't seen this wispy smoke thing since, but stuff still happens. So I figure it's still haunted. Maybe we just can't see it anymore."

Hannah asked some more probing questions that sounded like padding for an article, and we were just

53

about done when a clerk entered the motor pool compound. He walked straight for us, looking at me.

"Captain Carter?" the young man asked.

"Yes?"

"The CO would like a word, sir."

Colonel Dexter was standing with his back to me as I entered his office. When he turned around I was surprised by the expression on his face.

"What the hell?" he snapped.

"Jim?"

"Where is the reporter now?"

When we'd parted at the motor pool, Hannah agreed to return to her hotel. The plan was for me to collect her in the morning and we'd find the instructor from the assault course. In the meantime I hoped to speak to Sergeant Cox of the Royal Engineers—the other witness.

"She's at the Palisades hotel," I said.

"I trusted you to handle her."

"I am handling her."

"Is that what you call it?"

"Look," I said, irritation edging my own voice. "You asked me to do this babysitting job and I'm doing it."

His anger didn't lessen. "You were supposed to keep her under control."

"If you didn't want her to ask questions, why allow her in?"

"Because I thought you could handle it!"

I shook my head. I'd never seen Dexter like this, not with me anyway.

"It's all getting too personal. Get her to stick to the curse story, that's all you need to do."

"Fine," I said.

He turned his back and looked out of his window and I assumed the meeting was over. I was about to leave when he said, "I've information for you."

"Yes?"

"That woman you're looking for. The police chief thinks he knows who it is, although she's not called Lui anymore. Her surname is now Gao. Lives over in Batu Feringgi."

ELEVEN

I checked just in case the engineers had returned. They hadn't, so I took a taxi out to Batu Feringgi. On my right were beaches and on my left, plantations. Every now and again, I glimpsed colonial houses and plantation bungalows through the trees. They were a stark contrast to the densely packed poor housing that had been on the outskirts of George Town.

Batu Feringgi had poor housing and shops in the centre with affluent housing on the outskirts and higher ground. The address I had been given by Dexter was a large house with views of the sea.

I knocked on the door and was greeted by an elderly lady. Wealthy, but not so rich as to have a butler, I decided.

"Mrs Gao?"

She eyed me uncertainly and looked behind me at my waiting taxi. "How can I help you?"

"Li Ping Gao, previously Lui?"

"Yes." Her voice was quiet, still unsure.

"Please could I come in and talk?"

Again the look at me and then beyond. "Who are you?"

"My name is Ash Carter and I'm here because Su Ling asked me to find you."

She said nothing for a moment and then opened the door wide for me to enter. We walked along a hall with parquet flooring covered with a nice long rug. Then she led me into a spacious room with a conservatory overlooking a golden beach.

"Would you like tea?" she asked, pointing to a chair. Her face was still a mask of confusion, or perhaps that was just the way she looked.

I declined the offer of tea. "I understand that you are Su Ling's aunt."

"I am."

I held my tongue for a moment hoping she'd fill the silence. She did.

"How is my esteemed niece?"

"She is well and would have visited you herself if not for travel restrictions."

The old lady nodded as though she understood the situation. "Is she still with Mr Yipp?"

"She works as his assistant and translator," I said, and again the lady nodded.

"Very good. She was a good girl." She paused and ran a tongue over what looked like false teeth. "How did you say you found me?"

"I didn't say. I have contacts in the army who know the police."

This news resulted in a slight change of expression but no comment.

I asked, "Have you had dealings with the police, Mrs Gao?"

"Through my ex-husband, when he was alive. We had some trouble in a warehouse. A few times. The police helped. I think the stress killed him in the end. Mr Gao was never good with trouble."

I said, "And you are?"

Now there was a flicker of a smile.

She said, "What did you say your connection with the army and police is?"

"I didn't." I smiled reassuringly, I think. "I know a few people in the police and I used to be in the army."

Now she smiled more openly. "Weren't you *all* in the army?"

I assumed she meant since I was white, although she might have assumed the Second World War. I inclined my head noncommittally.

"Anyway, you didn't come here to discuss our old trouble or my husband, Mr Carter. Is there a message from my niece you were to deliver perhaps?"

"Su Ling discovered letters from her mother."

"Discovered?"

I hoped I wasn't out of line in explaining, but Su Ling hadn't given me any restrictions so I said, "Andrew Yipp had them. He'd kept them from her."

"Had he?"

"There are only a few and they date back to more than five years ago."

"What do you know?" Mrs Gao asked me.

"Very little."

"Then let me get you that cup of tea and I will explain," she said.

TWELVE

While I waited for tea with Mrs Gao, I paced the room. A cluster of silver-framed photographs covered a sideboard. The pictures were mostly formal and featured the same man, often with others. I figured this was her dead husband. He wore a suit and looked important. There were no photographs of children or women other than Mrs Gao.

The old lady returned and poured me a cup of green tea.

"My sister is Miao Wei. I used to call her Meow Meow... you know, like a cat."

I nodded.

She said, "Miao Wei was a lot younger than me. After I was born our parents didn't think they could have any more, so Miao Wei came as a surprise."

She took a sip of her tea and I waited for her to continue.

"Su Ling's father was a soldier—she said the man was an officer, although I never met him and I can't speak to the truth of the matter. Of course, our parents disapproved, but they helped Miao Wei raise Su Ling. You see, because my sister worked. She worked for Andrew Yipp."

I must have shown my surprise because the old lady repeated it and added: "Miao Wei was his assistant. Probably the same job that Su Ling has now."

"What happened?" I asked "Why did her mother leave?"

"You must know that the war was a difficult time. After the occupation of Singapore, it became more difficult. At first it was about having enough food to survive. Then it became about survival itself. I'm sure you know about the hate between the Japanese and Chinese people. They would beat us for no reason and kill us if they suspected treachery."

She looked out of the window. "Some people resisted and some collaborated."

I said, "It's always the way."

"Our father was executed for being a member of the resistance. He wasn't, I am sure, but men were killed back then for simply looking at a Japanese soldier."

She sipped tea and looked away, and I was sure she was overcome by emotion for a moment. When she spoke again she said, "Our mother died from lack of food, although she gave up. She stopped wanting to help herself, to live."

"What about Yipp?" I asked.

Her eyes were cold and small as she said, "He took the other path. His business did all right during the occupation."

I nodded. Maybe the old lady felt some recrimination. I felt nothing. Yipp was a survivor, whether under the British or Japanese masters.

I said, "And your sister still had work. She was all right?"

"She was. I suspected something between Andrew Yipp and my sister, although she always denied it. And she was able to support her daughter."

"What happened to her?"

"She disappeared just before the Japanese invasion. One day she went to work and the next she was gone."

I said, "And where were you at the time?"

"Living in Singapore."

This tallied with information from the police. They'd said Li Ping Gao had come to Penang from Singapore during the war.

"And you came here...?"

"Yes."

"Do you know where your sister went?"

"Yes. We helped her escape."

"We?"

"My husband and I—although we weren't married until later. He had contacts in Penang. She came here via Kuala Lumpur and a number of other places. It took her almost a month to get here."

"And then what happened?"

"When we arrived, my husband used his contacts to set up business here."

"To your sister?"

"Miao Wei kept on going. She stayed with us for a few weeks and then left."

"Where next?"

"She continued up to Thailand."

"You know this because?"

She looked at me like I was asking too many questions. "Is there a problem? Where did you say you were from?"

I wondered how good her short-term memory was. Had she already forgotten our earlier conversation? "Su Ling asked me," I said. "She's a friend and I'd like to understand where her mother went and where she is now, Mrs Gao."

She studied me through narrowed eyes for a moment. Then she said, "I don't know where she is."

"Did you know she wrote Su Ling letters?"

"No. She may have written to Su Ling but she didn't write to me. She didn't stay in touch."

"Why didn't she take Su Ling with her?"

The old lady looked confused and rubbed her forehead. "I remember we talked about it. I think the plan was to take her but something went wrong. I think she couldn't get away from Andrew Yipp with her daughter. You know he is her guardian?"

I nodded. "How old was she when this all happened?"

"Su Ling? Nine—or ten, I think."

"What can I tell her?"

The old lady looked uncertain. "Her mother loved her. I'm sure she intended for Su Ling to join her. Maybe she still does."

"But she stopped writing after a few years."

"Perhaps she was unhappy Su Ling didn't reply. Maybe she is still worried Andrew Yipp will find her."

"Why?" I asked. "Why was she so afraid of Yipp?"

Mrs Gao took a long breath and looked out of the window. She turned her focus back to me. "Because Andrew Yipp is a dangerous man. My sister knew his secrets, and later he was responsible for our father's death."

Before I left, she removed a diamond and sapphire brooch from her gown. "Take this," she said. "Give it to Su Ling as a gift from me next time you see her."

"I'll write a receipt," I said.

"No need." She waved me away. "No need at all."

I had found Su Ling's aunt and spoken to her. However, I had no constructive information to pass back to Su Ling. I went to the Communications Room and asked them to place a call to the Cathay Building. Minutes later, Su Ling came on the line.

"I found your aunt," I said. "Her surname's Gao now."

"She re-married?"

Of course, the name Lui hadn't been her maiden name, so Mr Gao was her second husband.

"Yes," I said. "Although the second husband died."

"Two dead husbands... Is she all right?"

"Seemed well. Lives in a big house with terrific views."

"Did she tell you anything useful?" I could hear the desperation in Su Ling's voice, but I had no good news.

"I'm afraid she doesn't know anything. Your mother stayed with your aunt and her husband for a few weeks in Penang before moving on."

"Did she know why my mother didn't take me with her?"

"She said it was too dangerous."

"Too dangerous!" I heard Su Ling suck in air, and when she spoke again, her voice cracked. "I would rather have taken the risk than be left by my own mother. I was only eleven. She just abandoned me."

I remembered Mrs Gao saying nine or ten and figured her memory must be going. I waited a moment for Su Ling to relax before continuing. "She intended for you to join her."

"That's what my aunt said?"

"Yes."

There was just the sound of wires for a long time.

She said, "That means she's dead."

"Maybe not. Your aunt said Miao Wei may have given up. She never got a reply. Maybe she thought you blamed her. Maybe she thought you didn't want to join her."

Again the silence, and I guessed she was processing that.

"One other thing," I said. "Your aunt told me that Andrew Yipp was the reason your grandfather was killed by the Japanese."

"How?"

"I don't know the details."

More silence, then she said, "Thank you," before ending the call abruptly.

Back at my room in the barracks, I found a note under my door. It had the letterhead of the hotel, so I guessed she'd been back there as agreed. I expected to collect her in the morning, but Hannah had other plans.

The note asked me to join her at 7pm because she'd found something.

THIRTEEN

I hurried over to the Palisades hotel and she met me in the foyer with a little bag over her shoulder.

Joking, I said, "I hope this wasn't a trick to have dinner with me."

She frowned. "I've been working. I've been looking into that witch doctor story. They call him a bomoh, and I've been told where to find him."

We hailed a taxi and she asked for a place called Ayer Itam. I was happy to accompany her. This was a good diversion away from the army. I still wanted to speak to Cox, the Royal Engineer sergeant, but he hadn't returned to base yet.

"Have you heard of Kek Lok Si—the Temple of Supreme Bliss?" she asked.

"No."

"Apparently it's the largest Buddhist temple in Southeast Asia. Here on this little island."

We soon arrived at the village of Ayer Itam and were dropped off in a bustling market. The sky was now dark, but multiple lanterns hung from market stalls, scattering coloured light.

We could also see the temple above us on a hill. There were lights all the way up, candles and lanterns.

Then I could see a complex of properties that were staggered up the hill, culminating in a seven-storey pagoda.

We made our way in that direction, moving with a throng of people: vendors, buyers, sightseers and pilgrims. The market stalls continued and we found ourselves climbing white stone steps.

Hannah opened her bag and pulled out a Brownie camera. All around us were people selling food, handicrafts and bric-a-brac of all kinds. There were plates of sliced papaya and other fruit. Pineapples were carved into shapes, many a representation of the pagoda itself.

She snapped a bunch of photographs and put the camera away.

I heard someone say there were two hundred steps. I looked up and figured they were probably right.

Most of the people walked but some restricted and slowed progress by kneeling and praying.

"Isn't it incredible," Hannah said as we wended our way between the devotees and vendors.

I wasn't sure whether she was meaning the general atmosphere or the amazing temple buildings. They seemed an eclectic mix of Chinese, Thai and Burmese.

I asked, "Is this bomoh chap a Buddhist?"

"I don't know," she said, "My limited information is that they can be of any religion and any race. Like this temple, Penang's religions are a blur between Islamic, Hindu and Buddhist, as well as the other Chinese religions like Confucianism and Taoism."

"You have done your homework!" I said as I almost stepped on a woman who had flung herself on the steps directly in front of me. After sidestepping her, I caught up with Hannah.

"That's what reporters do—research," she said.

"Are you thinking this is part of your article?"

"Possibly."

We reached the top, relieved that we hadn't fallen over anyone praying. Ahead was a courtyard filled with statues, at the centre of which was a shrine.

"There are said to be ten thousand images of Buddha in this temple," Hannah said, and she led me onto the flagstones that surrounded a large pond full of colourful carp and turtles. I could see a path that ascended towards the tall pagoda, but Hannah steered us away.

Large crowds were gathered, and in places they were so dense they were a wall of bodies all straining to watch something. We pushed our way through, receiving elbows and grunts of disapproval.

When we reached the front we found an old semi-naked man sitting in a lotus position, a white sheet wrapped loosely around his body. He chanted, his eyes glazed, praying to a dish of incense that gave off smoke that danced before him. After a minute, he looked up and raised his hands aloft. In them he held a metal rod about fifteen inches long.

The crowd hushed as he lowered the rod and aimed it at his stomach, almost as though it was a knife about to be plunged deep within him. Then, to my horror, he actually did it. He slowly pushed the rod into his skin. There was an initial resistance and then it moved smoothly, passing into his body.

Just as I convinced myself that it must be a trick and he'd now retract the rod, I saw the point push against the skin of his back. Then it broke through with a trickle of blood. The crowd gasped and then immediately fell silent.

This was no illusion. Of course, the rod avoided organs somehow. I figured it just passed through skin, but it looked impressive nonetheless.

All the time, the old man was chanting. He released the rod and wafted smoke into his face, took a long breath and raised his head and arms. His eyes met mine and I realized he was in some kind of unseeing trance-state. It made me think about the corporal who'd shot himself. Had John Tanner been under the influence? I felt a niggle in the back of my mind: a thought that wasn't fully formed and I couldn't quite reach it.

The old man dropped his hands and began the inexorable task of withdrawing the rod. It came out bloodied, and yet when the tip was withdrawn, I saw no blood seep from the wound. It was red, but the hole seemed to immediately close up once the rod was out. How was that possible? Again I wondered if there was an illusion here.

Still in his lotus position, the old man collapsed like an exhausted marathon runner who'd crossed the finishing line. There was a gasp from the spectators, but no one moved to assist him. I too felt transfixed by the display.

We waited, and within a few minutes the old man moved and returned to sitting upright. He had stopped chanting and just stared into the distance.

For a long time he sat motionless and the incense burned. People dropped money into a dish and moved away. The crowd thinned until we were virtually the last ones standing there.

Hannah squatted next to the old man and spoke to him. For a long time the bomoh didn't respond.

She turned to me and asked if I had any cash. I placed coins in the dish and Hannah leaned in again and spoke.

He opened his mouth, although I couldn't catch his words.

Hannah stood. "He says we should go to the Chinese cemetery. That's where we'll find the bomoh we're looking for."

"This isn't him?"

"No. There are many. I just knew we'd find one here tonight."

"Where's this Chinese cemetery?"

"Not far," she said, and I thought there was a mischievous glint in her eye.

"OK, what aren't you telling me?"

She raised her eyebrows. "He's at the cemetery to pacify a restless or bad spirit."

We threaded our way through the mass of people ascending the steps and jumped in the back of a trishaw waiting at the bottom.

She spoke to the cyclist and we set off, going south through the village.

"You speak Malay," I said. I hadn't understood what she'd said to the bomoh or trishaw cyclist but I recognized the language.

"Ah, something personal you've learned about me," she said without further explanation.

I didn't press her for more.

After about half a mile we noticed a drum beat filling the air. Then we came to a cemetery on a small hill.

Outside, we stopped and walked under the colourful arched entrance. Flaming torches sent smoke spiralling into the darkness, turning from orange to grey. Inside, we faced graves set in regimental lines. Unlike typical Western cemeteries, each grave had three white walls, like a string of connected, giant stone scoops.

The combined glow from the torches and the sound of the rhythmical drums made the night feel heavy with ancient souls. Incense and burning torches made the air chokingly thick as we moved between two rows of graves towards a crowd and an intense glow.

Everyone we saw wore a white headband and had a red cloth sewn onto their sleeves. In their hands were bamboo sticks that trailed paper streamers.

In the midst of the crowd we saw a wizened Malay. He had a whitewashed face and he danced and jiggled around a central pyre as a handful of assistants beat drums. Unlike the man at the temple, this one met my expectation of a witch doctor. He chanted and swayed and howled as though possessed. The crowd swayed too, as though they were becoming one with the incantation.

I found myself focusing on the chant and could feel it build with the rhythm of the drums. The vibration was like a heavy heartbeat in my body. As the noise grew I saw Hannah sway and realized I was also moving with the beat. In the dark it was hard not to be carried by the swaying mass of people.

Then Hannah closed her eyes, and she looked startled when I touched her arm. I found the contact also helped me break the spell we were falling under.

I said, "It's the smoke."

"Yes," she said, her voice slurred.

I pulled her away so we were further from the display and less under the influence.

The howling built to a crescendo and the drums beat louder and louder, pounding in my chest and making my fingers tingle. Then suddenly the flames of the pyre flared up with a whoosh and a final burst of light. The drums stopped, the witch doctor threw himself on the ground, and the fire went out. A puff of wind blew out all of the torches too.

There was utter darkness and immediate silence—not even the night-time creatures uttered a sound for what seemed like an eternity. Then, gradually, noises returned. The crowd lit their torches and began to file out of the cemetery.

I couldn't see the bomoh. I scanned the people as they left, but he wasn't there. The bomoh had vanished.

Hannah spoke in Malay to a few people but they were Chinese and either didn't understand or didn't want to.

"Where is he?" I asked her.

She held up her hands and shook her head.

We circled the cemetery. There was no way out except through the arch. A few people hung around but no one had a white face and no one was dressed like the witch doctor.

I figured it would have been easy for him to change his appearance in the sudden darkness and guessed he'd slipped out with the crowd as one of them.

"What now?" Hannah asked.

"Quick," I said, after we passed under the archway.

Hannah scooted up beside me.

"What is it?"

"We're being followed." I said. "Keep looking ahead, don't look around. When we came down the temple steps there was a young man behind us. I've just seen him again, watching from the darkness. Ducking behind walls."

"What are we going to do?"

"Walk back towards the market. When we turn, up ahead, I want you to keep on walking. I'm going to wait."

We went down the hill before turning sharp right. I ducked into a doorway hidden by shadow. Hannah continued onwards.

Moments later a man took a step around the corner and hesitated by my doorway. I grabbed him by the throat and walked him backwards until he hit the wall and was pinned against it.

It was a Chinese teenager, scrawny and scared.

71

"Hands on your head!" I barked. The kid complied, taking shallow snorting breaths through his nose.

"Why are you following us?"

The young man said nothing.

Hannah appeared beside me.

"Who is he?"

I said, "Who are you, kid?"

The boy's eyes bulged and watered.

"Maybe you're gripping too hard," Hannah said, concerned. "Maybe he can't talk."

I didn't think so, but I eased my grip.

A flicker of a smile appeared on the boy's lips and then he spoke rapidly in Chinese. I picked up an odd word but couldn't translate.

"Do you speak Chinese?" I asked Hannah.

"No."

I must have eased my grip too much because, as I spoke, the kid swivelled and squirmed out of my hands and darted away.

I had to sidestep Hannah to avoid barging into her. By the time I started running, the young man was rounding the corner. And when I got there, he'd vanished into the darkness.

I ran forward a few paces before giving up. There were too many places to hide or turn, and without a light, it was pointless giving chase.

Again Hannah came up beside me.

"Did you understand any of what he said?" she asked.

"One thing," I said. "He said a name. I think it's who he works for."

"And?"

"He said something like 'Doctor Sullyman'."

FOURTEEN

We walked back to Ayer Itam village. I looked out for the Chinese boy but didn't spot him, and I was sure we were no longer being followed.

"Eat with me," Hannah said, pointing to a restaurant.

I hesitated.

She added: "Come on, you must be hungry, and I don't like eating alone." She didn't wait for a reply and I followed her inside.

After ordering food, she said, "For a minute then— when I asked you to join me—you looked terrified."

I shook my head.

She said, "Which kind of explains why you made a joke of it when we met this evening."

I shook my head again. She was mistaken but I didn't want to say that I'd rather get straight back to the barracks in case the Royal Engineers had returned.

"I don't bite, you know," she said, smiling.

"I'm sure you don't."

"Oh? I could take that as an insult. I can be tough if I need to be."

I nodded. I'm sure she could. She was a confident woman and on her own. As a reporter, I figured she'd have a certain amount of steel.

She said, "Mind if I ask what Colonel Dexter wanted to see you about earlier?"

I didn't bother explaining about Su Ling's aunt, but then that hadn't been the main reason. I said, "He was cross that I wasn't keeping you under control."

She raised her eyebrows. "Why?"

I thought about it for a moment. Should I confess?

But before I could decide, she said, "You're suspicious John Tanner's death was more than an accident."

Damn! I said nothing.

She said, "You're a detective. I could tell by the questions. You can't stop your mind processing the information and asking pertinent questions."

"It's already been ruled as an accident."

"What does your gut tell you?"

I shook my head. "It's not my job here. I'm accompanying you in our investigation into this so called curse."

"But—"

"But nothing, Miss Quinn. It's precisely why Colonel Dexter was cross. We are not questioning people about Tanner's death. Understood?"

The food arrived and we ate a while, a tension between us.

Eventually I broke the silence. "So you don't speak Chinese but you do speak Malay. What's the story behind that?"

For a moment I thought she wouldn't answer, but she took a drink, flashed an easy smile, and I figured she accepted that I wouldn't challenge the army's ruling on Tanner's death. Not with her anyway.

"I'll trade," she said. "I'll tell you about Hannah Quinn if you'll tell me about Ash Carter."

"I can't talk about any investigations."

"I don't want any of your secrets."

"Really?" I said with disbelief.

She placed a hand on her heart but her eyes said otherwise.

She said, "I wasn't always a reporter."

"No?"

"I began my career in London—the City—working for a trading firm."

I said, "I don't know nothing about that type of life."

"I hated it. High pressure, misogynists... no, that's being polite. They're a bunch of sexist pigs."

"All of them?"

"Most of them. It's a way of life and not for me."

I detected suppressed annoyance, maybe anger in her tone, but didn't pursue it. After a moment I prompted, "So you became a journalist?"

"You're turn. We'll come back to me later," she said, switching the charm back on. "You said you didn't want to be an MP..."

"That's not what I said."

She smiled. "Why did you become one then?"

"I expected to join the army. After all, the war didn't end until I left university. I came from a long line of military men, so it seemed natural anyway."

"Anyone I would know?"

"No," I lied. There weren't many people who knew I'd changed my name because of my father, and most people knew of the strategist involved in the Dresden bombings. I certainly wasn't going to let a journalist into my secret.

She asked some more questions about my background before switching to her own.

"I'm here to prove myself," she said. "As an investigative journalist, that is."

"Why here?"

"As I told you, I was too late for Korea."

"And your brother was here."

"Right."

"That doesn't explain the language."

She took a breath. "I had a boyfriend who was half Malayan."

I waited. When nothing more came, I said, "He worked at your firm, didn't he. Was he a City trader?"

"He was my boss." She shrugged. "Let's just say it didn't end well."

"And that's why you switched careers."

"Yes."

We chatted some more, and by the time we left, the tension about John Tanner's death and my opinion had totally dissipated.

"What next?" I asked in the taxi back to her hotel.

"In the morning: the sergeant from the Royal Engineers and someone from the assault course."

I said, "And you'll let me lead."

"Of course."

"Remember, this isn't an interrogation. Your article is about ghosts."

She raised her chin and smiled.

On the hotel steps I declined the offer of a nightcap.

She said, "We didn't talk about the witch doctor."

I shook my head. It had been an interesting diversion but not really my concern.

"I'm going to find that bomoh again and interview him."

"Good," I said. "You don't need me for that."

"Are you so sure?"

I said nothing.

"Doctor Sullyman," she said. "Why did he have you followed? Is he afraid of something?"

I shook her hand. "Goodnight, Miss Quinn," I said, and walked away. She'd been right. This Doctor Sullyman bothered me. How did he fit in and could I find him?

FIFTEEN

Su Ling finished in the bathroom, making sure her image was immaculate. But instead of slipping away through the side door like she normally did, she waited for Andrew Yipp to come out of the bedroom.

His eyes flared. "Why are you still here?"

"I want answers."

He straightened his suit, buying time, then looked into her eyes. "What do you need to know, esteemed niece?"

"More about my mother."

"I told you all I know. She sent those letters and I kept them from you—to protect you."

"Protect me?"

He sat and pointed to the floor in front of him. "I will discuss this only if you remain calm."

"I am calm."

"Sit and breathe."

He waited until she was sitting opposite, her body less tense.

"Now," he said, "what can I tell you?"

"Why did she stop writing?"

"How can I answer that?"

"Tell me honestly, did she do something wrong?"

Without hesitation he said, "Yes."

"Did you find her and...?" She couldn't finish the sentence but the question was clear. If her mother had wronged him, he'd have killed her. No one offended Andrew Yipp and lived.

"I did not find her."

"Did you look?"

"Yes."

She forced herself to say it: "And you didn't have her killed?"

"I did not. Not me, nor someone for me."

"Would you have killed her?"

He said, "I cannot say. It has been many years," but she read his unspoken thought. Yes, he'd have killed or at least punished her. And then the realization struck Su Ling.

"You kept me as punishment."

Yipp didn't respond.

"You kept me and you kept her letters to me. You let me think she didn't care and had abandoned me." She took a breath. "Was that because you wanted me for yourself? God, I was only eleven."

He shook his head, sadness in his dark eyes. "That came later... I never intended..."

"What did she do? What did my mother do that was so bad?"

"She stole from me."

"How much?"

"A lot... and I trusted her."

Su Ling noticed she was speaking to him like she'd never dared before. And he was responding. Anyone else—maybe any other subject—and he wouldn't have tolerated it. Which told her something else.

"Was she your lover too?"

He looked away.

"Answer me!"

"Yes, she was in my bed. I looked after her. I looked after you." His normal tone returned. "Su Ling, your mother never married. You had no father and I offered protection and security."

"Tell me what happened."

Yipp stood. "Walk with me."

"Out the back way?"

"No. Let's walk out of the front."

"What if your wife…"

Yipp didn't respond. He was already walking to the stairs.

When she fell in step behind him he said, "Remember this was before the war. Times were hard even before the Japanese invasion. I had a thriving business before the war and the British started restricting activity. Without our secret channels, I would have been destroyed."

"How does that explain anything?"

"Your mother was my personal assistant and she had access to my accounts."

"All right…"

They came out onto a busy street in Chinatown. People knew him, and if anyone thought anything of Andrew Yipp appearing here with anyone other than his wife, no one acknowledged it. No one would dare say anything.

He continued to talk as though Su Ling was the only one around. "We knew it was only a matter of time before the Japanese came. I never thought the British could stop them and they foolishly thought the attack would come by sea.

"We had to protect the business, which involved making sure it would survive no matter who was in charge. The first thing I needed to do was hide the money."

"And she took it."

"She hid it and then disappeared."

"How much?"

"Enough to buy a new life. Not enough to cripple me."

"Why did she do it?"

He missed a step and she almost collided with him.

"Andrew?"

He faced her and there was the sadness again. "I don't know. You think I'm a hard man, Su Ling, but I loved your mother and I thought she loved me."

SIXTEEN

I had breakfast with Dexter in the officers' mess.

"Sorry I chewed your head off yesterday," he said. "You're doing me a big favour."

"Apology accepted."

"Did you find that lady—the Chinese one you were looking for?"

"Yes."

"Any use?"

I shrugged. "Probably not, but I needed to speak to her as a favour for another friend."

"Perhaps you should make a career out of helping people."

"I'm not sure that will put food on the table."

Dexter laughed, because as soon as I finished speaking, the waiter placed a full English breakfast before me.

"It works sometimes," he said. Then his smile faded as he read something in my face. "What is it?"

"I'm a detective. I can't help it."

"Can't help what?"

"Being suspicious about Tanner's death."

"Ash, Ash, Ash." He shook his head.

"What?"

"Investigating his death would be a waste of time. In addition, I wouldn't want a reporter questioning his death unnecessarily. You know how they can spin things."

"Can I hear a *but* coming?"

"But I do have a problem."

"The behaviour problem."

He looked at me, startled.

I said, "I met Captain Elmhurst on the train here. He told me he'd been sent off to find out if other barracks had similar problems."

Dexter cleared his throat. "He shouldn't have told you."

"Don't blame him, Jim. I knew most of the story anyway. I knew about the problems in Johor, but it's not the same, is it?"

"No."

"And that's the real reason I'm here."

"Bad spirit," he said, lowering his voice. "Has anyone used that term?"

"Of course. I've heard your men refer to the ghost or ghosts as bad spirits—or was it evil spirits."

"What if it's linked? What if it's literally about spirits—you know, alcohol rather than ghosts? What if the curse is just a cover story?"

"Is that what you think?" I asked.

"Well, personally, I don't believe in ghosts."

"Me neither."

We ate a few mouthfuls before he spoke again.

"What have you learned about Tanner's death?"

"He allegedly dropped his gun and it went off."

"And?"

Did Dexter really want to know what I thought? I took a sip of tea before responding. "The effect has been tested, and evidence suggests, when loaded, sharp

83

contact with the ground can cause a loaded rifle to discharge."

Dexter said nothing.

"All right," I said. "I don't like it because Tanner was in the woods. I looked at the ground where he allegedly stood. It was soft. I didn't even see a stone it could have struck."

Dexter leaned back and then forward. "Right," he said. "You haven't spoken to Sergeant Cox yet?"

"The Engineer."

"Hear his version and tell me what you think."

"I will," I said. "Although I saw him leave yesterday. Some kind of bridge incident."

"He's back. Came in during the night."

"OK." I nodded. "And there's one more thing you can do for me."

"Find someone else for you—as a favour?"

"In a way." I told him what happened last night, about going to the temple and cemetery and being followed. "The skinny kid said a name that sounded like Doctor Sullyman. Does that name ring a bell?"

"No, but I'll ask around. How do you think it's connected?"

"I have no idea," I said, shaking my head. "But I do know you don't have someone followed for no reason."

SEVENTEEN

The reporter and I were on our way to the Royal Engineer's hut when I noticed a man leaving. He had a neck that ran into sloping shoulders: Sergeant Walsh from the motor pool.

I changed direction to intercept him. Hannah hurried to keep up with me.

"Sergeant Walsh," I called as we neared.

"Ah," he said, missing a step. "I was looking for you."

"In the sapper's hut?"

"I knew you were headed there. Obvious you'd speak to the witnesses. Guessed you'd be here first thing but it seems not."

I didn't bother explaining my meeting with the CO before collecting Hannah from her hotel.

I just smiled and nodded.

"How can I help?" I said.

"I remembered something. Something I forgot to tell you yesterday but remembered when I realized you'd speak to Geordie."

"Geordie?" Hannah asked. On the way, I'd again reminded her to let me lead the discussion and figured this question didn't violate our agreement.

Walsh said, "Sorry, I mean Sergeant Cox."

"OK," I said. "What is it?"

"Well, you're asking about the squaddie who shot himself—accidentally mind—because of the curse." He looked at Hannah, "You're interested in specifics... well that incident specifically."

"Right," she said.

"Well, I didn't tell you about those woods. I told you about the ghost I saw in the garage and all the other things there but didn't say I'd also seen something in those woods."

"Near where Corporal Tanner died?"

"Precisely."

"What did you see?"

"I saw a ghostly image one night. It sort of flitted between the trees and then vanished. Not on that night, you understand. I wasn't there then, but I saw it before."

"When before?" I asked.

"Maybe a week. Other men have seen it too... at other times."

Hannah had her notebook out and was scribbling furiously. "And you're sure it was a ghost?"

Walsh rubbed his neck down the slope to his collar. "I know it sounds foolish but yes, more of a ghost than the thing in the garage loft. Shadowy, if you know what I mean."

"And the thing at the motor pool was more like smoke?"

"White wispy smoke," he said.

"OK, thanks, Sergeant." I looked at Hannah. "Any more questions?"

"No, not now, but maybe later."

We separated, Walsh heading across the grass towards the road. I realized it was a short cut to the motor pool. We continued towards the Engineers' hut.

There was a man outside, watching us as we approached. Sergeant Cox, I guessed, and was right.

"I've been expecting you," the sergeant said in a north-east accent—Geordie. "Do I salute or shake your hand?"

I offered him my hand and held his meaty palm briefly. The guy was taller than me but thinner, so his thick hand felt strange in comparison. Years of manual labour, I guessed.

Hannah introduced herself and said, "You're from Newcastle, Sergeant?"

"Sunderland," he said, and his tone told us he didn't appreciate her guess. But Sergeant Walsh had called him Geordie.

I said, "You're nickname isn't Geordie." A statement not a question, but he answered like it was one.

"No, why would I—?"

"Sergeant Walsh called you Geordie."

Cox nodded. "He was messing with you—me too. He knows I hate being called a Geordie or from Newcastle."

"Sorry," Hannah said.

"So you want to talk about the curse?"

"And the incident you witnessed."

I saw his jaw tense. "What?"

"I've witnessed many incidents, Mr Carter," he said. "I've been here a long time. I've seen units change and COs come and go, and so, yes, I've seen a lot."

Hannah pointed to a row of deckchairs outside the hut. "Mind if we sit?"

He nodded and we moved the seats so that we formed a triangle, Hannah leaning forward, notebook and pen at the ready.

"Let's start with the Corporal Tanner incident," I said. "I understand you were a witness."

"Aye."

"What did you see?"

"You know it was dark, right?"

"What time?"

"What time did it go dark or what time did I see him?" He pulled a smile. "Just before midnight. Maybe eleven fifty."

I waited.

He said, "I was out walking and saw the two squaddies doing their patrol." He smiled again. "You know it's all ridiculous, don't you? There's no need to patrol the barracks, and if the bandits did attack then a handful of kids with no experience aren't going to do diddley squat to stop them."

I said, "You saw both of them?"

"Aye."

"Who did you see first, Tanner or Reeder?"

"The other kid. Forgot his name, but yeah, Private Reeder."

"Did you speak to him?"

Cox snorted. "You bet. I didn't want one of those scared kids shooting me. So yes, I introduced myself."

Hannah said, "Anything else? What did he say?"

"I don't remember. Nothing maybe."

"OK," I said, "then what?"

"I kept walking and came up to the woods. I saw the other kid, Tanner. He asked for a smoke."

"Did you have one?"

"Aye. He knew because I was smoking."

"What brand?" Hannah said, writing.

"Player's, Miss. Everyone smokes Player's."

A couple of men came out of the hut, saw us, hesitated and went back inside.

"What then?" I asked.

"I gave him a smoke, lit it from mine like you do, then carried on. Didn't think anything of it. Later, he was still there, only the second time, he was twitchy."

"What time is it now?" Hannah asked, beating me to the question.

"Maybe ten past midnight."

"Why twitchy?" I asked.

"Because he had his gun up this time. This time I thought he was going to shoot me. But it turned out he thought he'd seen the ghost."

"The ghost?"

"The one that lives in the woods. The one they call the Shadow."

"Have you seen it?" Hannah asked.

"Aye."

I said, "What about that night?"

"No. Maybe. No, I can't say I did. You know there are always things in the dark and the trees, noises and the like. No, I can't say I saw it that night."

I should have kept quiet, but my investigative brain was on full tilt. I thought, *what the hell*, and said, "Tell us more about what Tanner was doing."

"He was searching, you know, sweeping his gun around like he'd seen something. I told him to calm down, that it was nothing like. And that's when I noticed it."

"Noticed what?"

"He had no shoes."

Hannah and I looked at one another. This wasn't something we'd been told before.

Cox shrugged and waited for us to comment.

I said, "What did you make of that?"

Cox shrugged again. "Crazy kid, was what I thought. I'd heard of people thinking the ghost couldn't get you without shoes."

89

"Why?" Hannah asked.

"I've no idea. I don't know how these things work. It's like superstitions, isn't it? No one really knows why. Like why is it bad luck for a black cat to cross your path? From right to left. Maybe we know these things because there's some truth in it." Again he shrugged. "I'm no expert."

"It's lucky in Ireland," Hannah said.

"What is?"

"Seeing a black cat."

Cox laughed. "There you go. Like I said, I'm not an expert."

I said, "So what happened next?"

"I probably poked fun at him. You know, made a jibe about him being scared before I left him there."

"And then?"

"A few minutes later I heard him scream and then the gun went off. I went back and found him dead. By that time the other kid patrolling had already seen him."

"Private Roy Reeder," Hannah said.

"Aye. I heard him running off."

I waited a beat and then said, "Weren't you suspicious?"

"What, of the other kid?"

I nodded.

Cox frowned and pulled a scornful face. "Nah. He was too scared. And he didn't have the time."

"You were the last to see Tanner alive," I said, again asking more questions than I should have in front of the reporter. "Why weren't you the first back? Why did Reeder get there first?"

Cox pulled the same face. "Maybe he'd been approaching. I was walking away. Also, I didn't run back. I was cautious, you know? I didn't know he'd shot himself. He might have been shooting at the ghost." Cox chuckled. "Crazy kid. Might have shot at me out there in the dark."

I nodded and waited in case Cox would say anything else. He didn't.

I turned towards the Engineers' hut and glanced up. There was a face at the window. Whoever it was moved back out of sight. Like a shadow.

It was warm. Cox's breathing was loud. Maybe it was a deviated septum. I'd known someone who'd had surgery to reduce the whistle.

Hannah stopped writing notes and looked at me.

"We done?" Cox asked.

I said to her, "Give us a minute, please."

For a second I thought she'd complain, but then she levered up out of the deckchair and walked a few paces. Out of earshot I hoped.

I focused on Cox and lowered my voice. "What's your theory, Sergeant?"

"Just man to man. I think it was an accident. The kid was scared. He had a bullet in the chamber. It was set to fire and he dropped it. It was an accident."

I waited and again checked Hannah wasn't too close, although she was looking at me, a question in her eyes. Cox didn't move, except for his middle finger picking at his thumbnail.

I said, "That's the official version, but what's your theory? Honestly."

"Like I said, it wasn't the other kid, if that's what you mean?"

"No," I said, and let the silence grow between us.

The nail picking became more rapid and I raised my eyes.

He said, "Aye, I have a theory."

I said nothing.

"If I tell you then it didn't come from me, right?"

"All right."

"His arms were too short to pull the trigger, right?" He looked into my eyes to confirm that I'd come to that conclusion. "The bare feet. He could have pulled the trigger with a big toe. Maybe he actually shot himself."

EIGHTEEN

Hannah wanted to watch an assault course exercise and we had three hours before the next one. After visiting Sergeant Stewart Cox, I walked her to the exit. She asked what Cox had told me.

"Just between us," I said.

"You asked if he had a theory—a different theory—whether the death wasn't an accident."

I shook my head. "Miss Quinn."

"I had to ask," she said with a cheeky smile.

I didn't say anything for a few paces, our shoes click-clacking on the cobbles until we reached the mess hall.

"What are you thinking now?" she asked, stopping.

I was thinking about Cox. Just gut-feel, but I sensed there was something he wasn't telling me. As an MP I experienced it all the time, although normally it was someone keeping a secret. This guy ended our conversation suggesting there was another explanation for Tanner's death. And yet my gut still felt uncomfortable.

Hannah was waiting for a response.

I said, "It'll rain again in a couple of hours."

"Ah, my weather forecaster." She laughed. "What are you really thinking?"

"I was thinking about the assault course. We have a few hours before there's an exercise out there."

"Can we interview the other two on guard duty?" She took out her notebook and read out their names.

"I've set that up for two hours' time. Before the assault course."

She started walking again, only this time heading for the mess hall.

"We've lots of time. I'll go back to the hotel but before that, have a quick cuppa with me," she said.

I opened the door for her then followed her in. We sat near the door opposite one another and a lady poured us thick stewed tea into china cups followed by a splash of milk.

"Next time let me take you to the officers' mess," I said.

She took a sip, pulled a face and agreed.

"I know you don't want me involved in questioning Tanner's death but can I ask you a question?"

"You can ask, but I may not answer."

She nodded. "OK, would there be a problem accepting suicide?"

I think she read my reaction. Had she overheard Cox after all? I took a breath.

"Possibly."

"Why?"

"Because suicide would look bad. There's no proof either way, so the CO opted for the least painful explanation."

"For the barracks? For the army?"

I shook my head. "For his parents."

She thought about it and took another sip of the stewed tea.

"Don't write about it," I said. "Same reason."

"Unfair to the parents?"

"Right."

"But what if it was suicide?"

"Just speculation. As far as I'm aware, investigative journalism isn't speculation."

"Then you'd be surprised."

"At the expense of people's feelings?"

She raised her eyebrows and then nodded.

"Don't do it," I said.

"Then tell me what a bee sting means?"

I frowned. "Apart from the obvious?"

"Last time we were here, a few men mentioned bee sting like it was a taboo thing. Could it be connected, do you think?"

"No."

She was studying me. "You know what it means, don't you?"

"Beasting," I said. "It's an army term for teasing someone."

"Teasing?" She raised her eyebrows, not believing me.

"More like punishment," I said.

"It sounded like bullying," she said.

I shook my head. "I'm sure it's not sanctioned here, Hannah." I realized it was the first time I'd called her by her first name, and it made her smile.

She said, "But think about it. Beasting and the Number of the Beast. It could be connected."

"Don't!" I shook my head. "This is about a curse, maybe a ghost. It's not about teasing or punishment. All right?"

She looked at me for a long time without speaking. Finally she said, "All right."

We left the rest of our tea and headed under the arch towards the main road outside the barracks. Along the road was a row of wooden huts with palm leaf roofs.

One was a café of sorts called Tucker's Bar and Grub. I'd eaten there in the past. With my friend from the hospital. But I wasn't looking at the café. There was a Morris there—a taxi. I waved to the driver and Hannah climbed in.

"See you later," she said. "Or join me for lunch, Ash?"

I said, "Right," but I was distracted. Not because it was the first time she'd used my first name but because of the trishaw riders hanging about waiting for customers. "Sorry, what did you say?"

"Lunch?"

I shook my head. "Things to do. I'll see you in an hour and a half."

The taxi drove away and I stayed beside the road, looking at the trishaw riders. One young man stood apart. He was looking at me. Brazenly.

The kid from the Chinese cemetery.

Would he run if I approached? I took a step in his direction and then another. He was about twenty paces away and didn't move.

I kept going and closed the gap quickly. His eyes were fixed on me and he looked nervous, so much so that I saw his hands shaking.

"Yes?" I said, stopping face to face.

"Come." He pointed to a trishaw and took rapid steps to it, me following.

He climbed onto the bike seat and nodded at the bench behind him. He said something else, but I didn't understand, and he tried a nervous, reassuring smile.

I sat on the bench in the shade of the awning and said, "OK, let's go."

The kid grinned, more confident now, and we lurched into motion as he stood up from the seat and pounded the pedals.

As we passed the other trishaw riders, I noticed frowns on their faces. This wasn't an official taxi and I figured they thought he'd stolen business. I could also see that the kid didn't have a weapon, whereas I had the Beretta in my ankle holster.

I had an inkling of why the kid had picked me up. It would be to meet this Sullyman chap, and I'd find out why we'd been followed to the cemetery last night. So I sat back and relaxed, enjoying the fresh air in my face as the kid raced down the hill towards George Town.

We went through the town to the docks and then a short distance along the front. After the godowns there were office-like buildings. We stopped outside one with a faded green sign. The lettering said it was the Souter and Hancock Shipping Company. The name meant nothing to me although it seemed familiar. Now I thought about it, I recalled seeing a similar green sign on a warehouse on the mainland.

There was a single door and the kid used his head to tell me that was where I should go. I got out and he scooted away, like he was relieved to have done his part of the job.

I stood outside for a moment, assessing the three-storey brick building. It looked maybe a hundred years old. All of the buildings did, although this one had aged worse than most. The windows were dusty and white paint peeled from window frames.

I placed my hand on the doorknob, turned it and opened the door. Inside, to my surprise, the paint was fresh and clean, the floors had been recently swept and I could smell polish.

There was a room to the right, a staircase in front of me, and behind that I saw another door. People were working in the rooms. I could see benches and boxes.

A man in the room on my right looked at me.

"Doctor Sullyman?" I asked.

"Upstairs please," the man said, pointing as though I needed no further advice.

I nodded and took the stairs. Again to my surprise, it had a smart runner and stair rods that were in contrast to the faded exterior.

At the top I saw more rooms and people. These were sitting, heads down. I judged the operation was downstairs and the accounting and administration on this floor. There was one closed door, with frosted glass and a name etched on it: Dr Suleiman.

I knocked and entered.

A Middle Eastern man in an elaborate gown looked up from his desk and removed his round glasses.

For a second I froze. My mind screamed: Palestinian! Was this man a member of the group that was looking for me?

He stood, smiled and extended his arms in a gesture of welcome.

"I apologize for the cloak-and-dagger, Mr Carter," he said in an accent that could have passed him for British aristocracy. This was no Palestinian terrorist, and I chided myself for the foolish first impression.

He stepped from behind his desk, a tall man who moved with elegance and finesse. He waved his hand to a chair before easing into its neighbour.

"Can I offer you anything to drink?" he asked, still smiling.

I sat, conscious that my gun was now within easy reach should he have a knife concealed beneath his gown.

Suleiman said, "You are wondering why I wanted to meet you, yes?"

"And why you followed me last night."

"Ah, yes. I apologize if it worried your young lady. You see, I was intrigued, and I am a man who values information."

"Who are you?"

"Just a businessman. You on the other hand are not just a tourist, are you, Mr Carter? You work for the Singapore government, do you not?"

I shook my head. "Not anymore, and, Dr Suleiman, you are clearly more than just a businessman. What business are you in?"

"Import and export," he said, which is what I suspect most of the businesses near the port did.

"And what does that mean exactly?"

"Let's talk about you, if we may? Or at least your young lady? I understand she is called Hannah Quinn. What can you tell me about her?"

Suleiman clearly knew quite a bit about Hannah so I just said, "She's from the *Manchester Guardian*. A reporter interested in the curse at the army barracks here."

"And you, Mr Carter? Why are you here?"

"I'm her chaperone," I said.

"I like the word chaperone. It has a nice ring to it, don't you think?" He smiled. "Now, how do you take your tea?"

I shook my head. "I'm fine, thank you."

"Why are you Miss Quinn's chaperone?"

"As a favour to the CO of the barracks."

He thought for a moment. "Interesting," he said after a few seconds, perhaps hoping to prompt more from me. Perhaps guessing that Jim Dexter and I were friends.

I said nothing.

He said, "And why were you in Ayer Itam last night?"

"Looking for the witch doctor—the bomoh—who performed an exorcism at the barracks."

He nodded and waited.

I said, "And why did you have us followed?"

"To see where you went of course, Mr Carter. And what about earlier? You paid a visit to a house in Batu Feringgi. That wasn't with your reporter, so it was something else, correct?"

"Another favour," I said.

He smiled, and I judged it to be genuine. His eyes creased with warmth. "You are being very cryptic, Mr Carter."

"Tell me something more about yourself. Help me understand why I should talk to you, Dr Suleiman."

"Like I said, I value information. To spell it out, Mr Carter, you help me and I can help you."

"How can you help me?"

"The lady you visited in Batu Feringgi, for example. Her name is Li Ping Gao, formally Lui."

I nodded.

He said, "Her husband set up Gao Carpets Import and Export during the war but unfortunately died a few years ago. He wasn't a good businessman and made a lot of foolish mistakes."

"What are you telling me?"

He smiled kindly. "No hidden meaning. I'm not suggesting his death was suspicious or linked to his poor business skills. I just know a lot about him, that is all. If there is anything—"

"I am interested in finding Mrs Gao's sister."

"Her name?"

"Miao Wei Yong."

"It is not a name I know, but I can enquire. Why are you looking for this lady?"

"She's my friend's mother. She came to Penang before the war and then is believed to have travelled to Thailand. My friend would like to find her."

"I will do what I can. And in return I would like to know if you have heard about the bad spirit."

I said, "This is not the same as the curse, is it? When you say bad spirit, you don't mean ghosts."

"That's right."

"People talk about it as though they are one and the same, although the CO of the barracks is concerned that men are under the influence of something. Either alcohol or drugs." I watched Suleiman's eyes and saw them flash at the word drugs. I leaned forward. "Does bad spirit refer to bad drugs?"

"Mr Carter"—he stood and offered me his hand. As he moved I saw a bejewelled kukri knife at his waist—"if you find the source of the bad drugs, I will be indebted to you."

NINETEEN

"I found Dr Suleiman."

Colonel Dexter raised his eyebrows. We were in his office and I'd gone straight there after the meeting at Suleiman's office.

"Suleiman. Jeez, that's a Middle Eastern name. He's not—?"

"One of the Palestinians? Unlikely. He's a local and struck me as similar to Andrew Yipp in Singapore: a businessman who has connections and thrives on information. Which means he's either a politician or dodgy. Maybe both."

"What sort of information?"

"He used the term bad spirit, but he was talking about the behaviour problems. I think he knows more than he's telling, but the implication is that bad spirit is linked to bad drugs."

Before I'd left, I'd questioned Suleiman about his interest and I could see Dexter wondering now. Why did Suleiman care?

I said, "He trades in many things, including medicines. He said there were rumours of bad batches of morphine."

Dexter looked thoughtful. "I'll check with Major Dawson. See if he knows anything. It'd certainly make more sense than some voodoo nonsense, which quite frankly I've never bought into."

I agreed. I didn't believe in ghosts despite the stories I'd heard. I couldn't explain them, but then I hadn't witnessed the sightings.

"About Hannah Quinn..." I said.

"What about her?"

"Why allow her in—a reporter looking into some bullshit curse?"

"Not my decision. It's a new world, Ash. We actively encourage the media now."

I must have looked surprised because he continued: "Plus I think there's a connection somewhere. Maybe her father knows someone in the ministry or maybe the government."

Behind him I could see the sky darkening. Rain was coming in fast.

I returned my focus to Dexter and said, "She asked me about beasting this morning."

Dexter's face froze momentarily, then he looked angry, then he got his emotions under control.

"I got reports of her talking to the men in the mess hall," he said.

"That's right, but it was about ghost stories."

"You're sure?"

I wasn't. I'd let her roam around while I ate lunch yesterday. And then I remembered Dexter bawling me out for not keeping Hannah under control.

I said, "You'd already heard she asked about beasting?"

"No, but it's suspicious. I won't tolerate that here, Ash. I'm sure you know that."

"I do," I said. "She was also asking about the Number of the Beast, because of the 666 on Tanner's rifle."

He pondered that for a moment. "You think they misunderstood?"

"This morning, she asked me. She didn't know what it meant, so yes, I'd give her the benefit of the doubt."

"It's one thing having a reporter looking into a stupid story. It's quite another having one poke around and cause trouble," Dexter said. "You are in control of her, aren't you Ash?"

"Don't worry," I assured him. "I spoke to her about it and she promised to behave. I think we can trust her."

Rain pelted the cobblestones as I waited under the entrance arch of the barracks. Exactly ninety minutes after I'd said goodbye to her, a taxi arrived and Hannah stepped out into the deluge.

I put up an umbrella and jogged over to her. Then, together, we scuttled back to the shelter of the archway.

"You were right about the rain," she said, flicking away water that had dripped onto her cheek. "Where are we going first?"

"I have an office to interview the two guards."

"Hold on a minute, it may stop."

We watched the rain sweep across the parade ground. I saw three men dash between buildings, but apart from that everyone else waited.

I said, "We could wait. The rain should ease soon."

"No, let's go." She ducked her head, ran for the main building and I hurried at her side holding the umbrella.

Both privates were standing at ease by the room I'd been given and I took one at a time.

Neither of them had seen the incident since they'd both been patrolling outside the grounds. Both had heard the single gunshot and been concerned, but they continued their patrol per orders. It wasn't until their guard duty ended that they discovered what had happened.

"Did the QM—Sergeant Lee Cooper—laugh when he gave Tanner his gun?"

Both privates confirmed he had. Both knew it was because of the Number of the Beast and were both relieved they hadn't received it.

One said, "It was because it was Tanner's birthday."

The other said, "The QM is a nasty piece of work."

Hannah asked, "Do you think Sergeant Cooper knew the gun could discharge?"

I was uncomfortable about her question, because it was one I would have preferred to ask them without her presence. However both men gave no suggestion that Cooper intended that John Tanner would get hurt.

"He just likes scaring us," the second man said.

We talked some more and Hannah covered her personal angles and asked about their experiences of ghosts.

I didn't find the interviews useful since neither man had really been involved and I kept checking my watch. Eventually I told Hannah that the assault course would now be in use. She was happy to end the second interview and when we got back outside the downpour had eased and would soon end.

"Let's go," she said.

"OK."

I held the umbrella over our heads and we walked virtually shoulder to shoulder, both leaning in to keep the drips from our heads.

Other people came out now, and despite the rain, normality had returned as we crossed the parade ground. The hospital was on our left and then we came to the scattered rubber trees and the huts beyond, where the Engineers had their base. I glanced that way but saw no sign of Sergeant Cox. After the huts we came to the woods and the path. To the left, down the hill, would take us to the main road where the motor pool was. Ahead we'd come to the spot where Tanner had died. To the right, following the line of the woods, we'd come to the assault course.

"They'll definitely be there, won't they?" Hannah asked, looking at her shoes. "My feet are wet."

"They'll be there," I said, and even as I spoke, we heard the shouts of an instructor demanding the men try harder.

Where we'd seen nothing but quiet, dark woods yesterday, now we saw a riot of activity. Men were charging up and over apparatus, falling into puddles, dropping into the dirty pond. I did a quick count of twenty men and four instructors.

We found a sheltered spot under the trees and watched. Eyes looked our way but we were otherwise ignored.

"Get that lardy arse moving, boy!" an instructor shouted at a soldier who clung to netting. His was the voice I'd heard earlier. Clearly the lead instructor, Sergeant Major Tony Brookes.

Brookes continued shouting as the kid threw an arm up and began climbing once more. He went up and over, became tangled and received more abuse from below.

Men staggered past us, covered from head to toe in mud, looking exhausted.

Brookes switched his attention back to the kid again, who'd fallen into the middle of the pond. "Do it again you pussy!" he yelled.

Head down, the young man splashed out and staggered over to a ladder.

"Faster, boy!" Brookes screamed. "Faster!"

A climb and a walkway later and the young man was at the rope again. He needed to run, leap and grab hold of the swing, giving him enough momentum to clear the pond. Instead, he slipped at the end of the ramp, stumbled, flailed his arms hoping to catch the rope and missed. He belly flopped into the brown water, tried to jump up and slipped in the mud.

Another instructor waded in, grabbed the kid by the collar and dragged him out. He was flung to the ground at Brookes's feet.

"You are a bloody disgrace to the army! A bloody disgrace!" the sergeant screamed. Then he nodded to the junior instructor. "Get him back to the start. He's going again and he's going to do it until he can do it right."

Eventually everyone else had stopped and were waiting, soaked through at the finish. The rain stopped as suddenly as it had begun and steam began to rise all around us.

"It's cruel," Hannah said as we watched the kid going again and again, getting weaker and worse with each attempt.

On the fourth attempt he slipped off a raised plank and dropped his rifle. An instructor with a clipboard screamed at him then dragged him to his feet. The kid was covered in mud, his arms limp at his sides, his head down, dejected.

Brookes strode over. "You failed, Private Peters. And because of you everyone in your squad will be here again tomorrow to do it all again. And if you fail tomorrow, you'll come again the next day." He paused then barked, "Stand up and stand to attention."

Peters pulled himself upright and stood as rigid as he could, although his body quaked with exhaustion.

"Get out of my sight, you bunch of pussies!" Brookes said.

The men formed a line, two abreast, and were led, jogging, down the path in the direction of the barracks.

Only Brookes remained. He watched the ragged line disappear around the curve of the woods then turned his attention to us. We left the trees and met him halfway.

He ran a hand through his wet grey hair before offering it to me.

"Sergeant Major Tony Brookes," he said in a voice totally different from the one we'd heard him use earlier. This was softer, friendlier and had a touch of northern England, maybe Cheshire, in it.

I shook his hand and noticed Hannah's body language. Her crossed arms said she wasn't about to do the same.

"Ash Carter," I said, following with my previous rank and regiment. "Here at the request of the CO and accompanying Miss Quinn, who is a reporter with the *Manchester Guardian.*"

Brookes nodded at Hannah and smirked.

"You think I'm too hard on them," he said.

She took a breath, perhaps choosing her words carefully. "It was difficult to watch."

Brookes's smirk vanished and he looked serious. "I have a job to do, young lady. You know, I'm responsible for those men out there. We may call this war an 'Emergency', but it is still a bloody war. I get them coming here thinking it's a holiday camp. Well I'm here to show them it's not. Better to be beaten by Bastard Brookes than a bandit's bullet, that's what I say!"

"Bastard Brookes?" she said.

"It's an image I like to encourage."

The smirk had returned. I'd known a lot of sergeant majors. All were tough men but some seemed to have a nasty streak and I placed Brookes in that category. He was right, of course. The men needed to understand the

108

reality of war. There would be no second chances if these kids got into a firefight with the enemy. They needed to be sharp and prepared for any eventuality.

"Let's walk back," I said.

Brookes fell in beside me and Hannah followed a pace behind.

"You're here about the curse," Brookes said.

"Miss Quinn is writing an article," I said.

"How is it going?" he asked over his shoulder.

"Interesting. What can you tell me about it?"

"Not a lot."

"What about ghosts in the woods?"

"Never seen one."

"The men say there are. They say the woods are haunted and there have been incidents at the assault course."

Brookes stopped and looked into Hannah's face. "Excuses, that's what they are."

We began walking again and I said, "So it's nonsense?"

"Of course. Do you believe in ghosts, Captain Carter?"

Hannah said, "We'd like your opinion."

"Like I said, Miss. No ghosts."

"What do you know about Private Tanner's death?"

As she said it, I realized that she hadn't asked Brookes any personal questions yet. Maybe she wasn't convinced he was any use, but a faint warning light came on in my brain before I dismissed it.

"He died in the woods, not far from here," he said. "It was an accident."

"How do you know it was an accident?"

This time, when Brookes stopped, he looked at me. "What is this? It was ruled as an accident. I'm not a bloody coroner—or investigator."

He started walking again, only this time it was with a longer stride. I heard Hannah's breathing as she hurried behind us.

She said, "What do you know about him, Sergeant?"

"He was a private with the Royal Hants."

"Corporal," I corrected him.

Hannah said, "Did he ever do the assault course?"

"They all do the course."

"When was the last time he did the course, Sergeant?"

Brookes said nothing, although I sensed a subtle hesitation in his step.

Hannah was suddenly in front of us, running and then stopping us in our path.

"Two days before he died," she said in an accusatory way.

Brookes stepped around her. "Is that right?"

I stared at Hannah. She hadn't shared that piece of information with me. However, her next words shocked me even more.

She said, "Beasting, Sergeant. You are guilty of beasting."

TWENTY

Brookes didn't comment and continued to walk away. Hannah started after him but I grabbed her arm.

"What the hell?"

Her face was flushed and I noticed her teeth clench and unclench before she spoke.

"Sergeant Brookes is a sadistic bully."

"Where is this coming from?"

"You saw how he was with that poor kid earlier. And the men told me he's a nasty son of a bitch."

I shook my head. "He has a job to do."

She pulled her arm sharply from my grip and shook her head at me. "It's more than that and you know it."

I shook my head again. "No I don't. I've known worse than Brookes."

"What about the connection with John Tanner? I was told he'd been singled out two days earlier. The men in the mess hall told me about the beasting. They said Brookes had it in for the boy."

And then I got it. I said, "This was never about ghost stories, was it?"

"I'm not going to make it as an investigative reporter by writing about a curse. If I gave my boss an article about ghosts, he'd sack me on the spot."

"So it was a cover."

"There's beasting going on here, Ash. That's the story, and maybe it resulted in a young man's suicide. Maybe it wasn't just Brookes. Maybe the whole 666 thing is part of it. Maybe there's a whole gang of sadistic men here, including Sergeant Lee Cooper. That's what we need to investigate, Ash."

Anger flared inside me. Jim Dexter had been angry yesterday and I'd assured him I had things under control. She'd encouraged me to talk about beasting in the mess hall—even pretending she didn't really know the word—and now she was accusing a Sergeant Major. She'd duped the army into giving her access and she'd duped me.

I said, "It's over, Miss Quinn." I took hold of her arm once more and marched her past the huts, across the parade ground and to the entrance arch. Outside there was a waiting taxi cab and the trishaw men. I let her walk to the taxi alone.

She didn't comment or turn and I didn't watch her drive away.

I apologized to Dexter, who ranted more than he had before, only I knew it was justified this time. However, when he calmed down, he said it wasn't my fault and later took me for dinner at his second favourite restaurant in George Town.

The arrangement with the reporter was over and I said I would return to Singapore.

"You should stay," he said. "There'll be work in Penang for you."

I told him my mind was made up and then between courses I said, "Forgive me, I have to ask."

He nodded, maybe guessing my question.

I said, "Are you sure the reporter was wrong about beasting?"

112

"One hundred per cent. There's always some bullying. You put any bunch of men together and someone falls to the bottom of the pecking order. You know that, Ash."

I did. I'd seen it many times in the army. But, like he said, it wasn't just the military; it was the ugly side of human nature. Beasting, on the other hand, was more extreme, and I trusted Dexter would know whether he had a problem or not.

After the main course had been delivered and we couldn't be overheard, I said, "My other question is about Tanner's death."

"Oh?"

"Miss Quinn said it was suicide. All right, she linked it to beasting, but let's put that aside. When we questioned Sergeant Cox—the witness—he also raised the possibility of suicide."

"The MO said it was impossible."

"Cox said that Tanner wasn't wearing shoes. He could have pulled the trigger with his toe."

Dexter shook his head. "Really? Think about it. If you were going to kill yourself, would you fire a gun with your foot?"

"It depends on my state of mind."

Dexter looked surprised.

I raised my hands. "OK, OK, I agree. It would be highly unlikely anyone would plan that. However, you need to explain how the gun went off. I'll accept that a drop onto concrete could cause it but…"

He shrugged. "Freak accident. Maybe hit a stone or something else hard like a log."

"Were any found?"

"The site was too disturbed." He shrugged again. "I think it's the only feasible explanation though."

The subject changed and we chatted about the past for a while. He was intrigued about the time I'd spent in Malaya.

"Will you go back?" he asked. "Is that your plan?"

"No," I said, having spent the last few hours considering my next move. "I'm going back to Singapore."

"You take care then. If you change your mind about Penang, I'm sure there's work for you here... and I don't mean just doing favours for people."

I couldn't imagine what it was but thanked him for the gesture anyway. I spent a final night in my room at the barracks before heading across the strait to Perai and the nearby RAF Butterworth. Dexter had kindly arranged an indulgence flight to Changi for me and I spent an hour and a half strapped in an airless fuselage with a unit of laconic paratroopers.

I usually spend travelling time like this pondering whatever case I was on. Not this time. Because John Tanner's death wasn't a case. Instead I thought about the tough job Colonel Dexter had. There was the curse and alleged bad behaviour of some soldiers—maybe linked to alcohol. He also had a tough bunch of sergeants. Harper, the craggy faced colour sergeant undoubtedly had control but he was about to retire. Then there were the four who I'd interviewed: Cooper, Brookes, Cox and Walsh. Cooper, the QM, had a wicked sense of humour, possibly even malicious. Brookes—who called himself a bastard—wasn't particularly pleasant, although I realized he played a role. Then there was Cox, the Royal Engineer sergeant with the north-east accent and whistling nose, and his drinking buddy from the motor pool, Walsh. Sergeant Walsh, the man with a thick neck who seemed to think everything was a joke. He liked sarcasm. When he'd

114

talked about the ghosts and men getting hurt he sounded serious, but I think he secretly enjoyed it.

I didn't like any of them, but then again they weren't my problem.

After thinking about Dexter's tough job I started think about my own future. I could return to earning pocket money as a prize fighter, but that was never a long term option. I didn't want to go back to working for the government but maybe I could find a freelance role somewhere between Internal Security and the military police.

However my more immediate concern was the Palestinian gang. Maybe I shouldn't stay in Singapore. Maybe I should move on, always one step ahead of my pursuers. Constantly on the run, wasn't me. Plus there was a good chance that the gang didn't know I'd been seen in Penang. An even better chance they didn't know about Singapore.

After landing, a short taxi ride took me into Singapore city and my apartment on Beach Road. In the past few months, I'd visited only briefly but knew the cleaner would have been and kept the place fresh.

I opened the door, dropped my luggage and stared at the devastation before me. The sofa had been slashed, the furniture broken and glass was strewn on the floor.

TWENTY-ONE

Su Ling met me in the alley behind the Cathay Building.

"Thank you again for visiting my aunt," she said, and kissed my cheek.

"You're welcome." I handed her the brooch. "She wanted you to have this."

She took it, rotated it in the light to see better and then tucked it away.

"Will you return?" she said. "You could give her something—a present—from me."

"I don't have plans…"

"But you're more likely to visit than me."

"All right. No promises of when, but I'll take it."

She nodded, and I could sense her studying me, reading my eyes.

"What is it?" she asked. "Something's bothering you."

"Nothing." I hadn't intended her to see my concern, but she'd caught me thinking about what I'd do and who had wrecked my apartment.

She touched my arm and I felt the thrill of her fingers on my skin. "Ash…"

"Sorry, it's nothing," I repeated.

"Is it bad news about my mother?"

"No. No! It's just…" In that moment I decided to tell her my concerns. "My apartment has been broken into and turned upside down."

She looked shocked. "By whom?"

"I don't know," I said. "Is there any way that Yipp would do it? Does he know you told me about the letters—about your mother?"

Her grip on my arm tightened then relaxed as she shook her head. "No, and even if he did know, it's not his style."

"What is his style?"

A flicker of a sad smile played on her lips before she said, "Something more severe than that."

"Unless it's a warning," I said.

"No," she said emphatically. "It's not him. Is there anyone else…?"

Of course there was. The most obvious people were the Palestinians. If they were looking for me in Penang then they would certainly look for me in Singapore, and plenty of people knew where I lived.

I shook my head. "I suppose I may have some enemies. My apartment may not be safe for me right now."

"Where will you stay?"

"The Queen's Hotel."

She said nothing for a moment, maybe considering. Then she said, "Your enemies—will they find you there?"

I forced a smile. "I hope not, but I'll be prepared."

"Ash, you can't sit in your room with a gun trained on the door in case some bad people turn up."

"That's my plan," I said, and the smile became more genuine.

She shook her head. "You can't stay in a hotel. Not until you know what the risk is."

117

"Maybe I'll stay at Gillman Barracks," I said, referring to the 200 Provost site to the west of the city.

"No," she said firmly, gripping my arm harder again. "I've a place you can stay in. Wait for me here after dark and we'll get you to a safe house."

Four hours later an old Austin 7 pulled up in the darkness and I climbed into the back beside Su Ling. The driver was a young Chinese woman. More of a girl really. I didn't recognize her, but a nod from Su Ling told me I could trust her.

Su Ling pecked me on the cheek and got out. As soon as the car door clicked shut, we were off.

The driver took me north and east into a congested Chinese neighbourhood.

"Where are we going?" I asked.

The car stopped and the girl turned back and looked at me. She flashed me a smile and then indicated we'd arrived. We'd travelled less than two miles and I climbed out of the car on an unlit street. She led me through one building and then another before taking me up a flight of steps to a room. If I'd been hoping for a luxury apartment I was going to be greatly disappointed. It had a bed, a chair and a toilet. Nothing else. A functional bolthole.

"We hope it's all right," she said as I dropped my small bag on the chair. "The bedding is clean."

"Thanks. I can cope for a few days."

"My mistress says you are to stay as long as you need to. Just use this as a base and never come directly here. The family downstairs will feed you—you can trust them. And in case you are wondering, Andrew Yipp doesn't know about this room."

I nodded. She had sparkly eyes and a nice face—not in the same class as Su Ling, but pretty nonetheless. "Anything else?"

"My mistress says there is only one other rule. You don't contact her while you're here."

I thanked her and wondered if this was Su Ling's own bolthole and whether she'd ever used it. She'd said she wanted to escape the island when the time came and I knew this meant escape the clutches of Yipp. I wondered about asking the girl but then figured she might not know.

"Come," she said, and led me back out of the room and downstairs. There I met my hosts, although we exchanged no names. Immediately afterwards, the girl left me with them and I ate a bowlful of noodles they presented before I returned upstairs.

The bed sheets smelled of Su Ling's exotic scent, and I found my mind flitting between thoughts of her and what I would do tomorrow. Should I be conspicuous in the hope that I would prompt a confrontation or should I disguise myself and search for anyone looking suspicious?

I must have fallen asleep because I thought I heard the door clicking shut, and yet I didn't react. It was a dream. The girl had given me a key and said only Su Ling had the other one.

My desire imagined she was there and I could smell her perfume even more strongly. And then I felt her slide into the bed beside me and place her finger on my lips before she kissed me and I realized this wasn't a dream after all.

TWENTY-TWO

She didn't speak and slipped away before light pierced the curtains, leaving me still half-asleep and yet wanting her touch.

I found myself grinning as I realized my apartment being broken into had been ironically fortuitous. If Su Ling came every night, I might be convinced to stay here for a while.

In the morning I realized my limited wardrobe meant I wouldn't go for a run. Nor would it have been advisable, since a white man jogging around the area was sure to attract more attention than I wanted. However, I had decided to be conspicuous once beyond the immediate vicinity. Slinking around just wasn't my style.

After disguising which building I came out of, I cut my way through alleyways with drying clothes strung across the street. Shophouses ran along on both sides of the road and the streets became more congested, lots of people on bikes heading for work at the docks. Then I hit Princep Street, busy with cars. I turned and headed towards the Cathay Building. Its sixteen floors and radio mast on top made it visible over most of the city.

I imagined Su Ling in there. I figured her boss would be in there too, maybe looking my way out of his office with its expanse of glass windows.

Halfway along the road, I stopped at a shop and bought a banana and two apples before continuing towards the tower. At the end of the road was a pavilion with lawn tennis courts behind. Beyond that was the hill and Fort Canning, the army's Southeast Asia headquarters.

The Cathay Building was now on my right and I turned left into Bras Basah Road, the smell of the sea carried on the morning breeze.

Outside a single-storey brownstone building I hesitated. This was what the local military police called Hotel Bras Basah. It was their city office and had holding cells at the back. I'd had the displeasure of spending a night at the "hotel" when I first arrived in Singapore.

There were large windows and open glass doors to let the air in. Five stone steps took me to the door and I looked in just in case I recognized anyone. It was for no other reason than to say hello. However, it was quiet inside, with just a young man behind the reception desk.

He looked up, perhaps hoping for some activity. Maybe he'd been on all night and it'd been a quiet one. That happened occasionally if there wasn't a troop ship in.

I raised a hand in greeting and turned away. I think he called out, asking if I needed anything, but I went back to the street and continued towards the sea. I crossed two thoroughfares, dodging cars and packed electric buses that were powered by the cables that ran the lengths of most major roads.

From there I turned at North Bridge Road and noticed that the arches across the main roads had a new message. They changed all the time, although "Let Singapore City Flourish" was one I'd particularly noticed. Now they congratulated the new queen on her upcoming coronation. "God Save The Queen" was the most common. We were six days away from 2nd June and I figured plans were in place for a pageant that would rival a Chinese New Year celebration.

Over the Stamford Canal I came out at the back of St Andrews Cathedral. Following the canal I reached the esplanade that everyone called the *Padang*. Here, I sat on a bench and ate my fruit.

The sun finally broke through the high cirrus clouds and I leaned back and enjoyed the view. This spot was more relaxed than the frenetic rush to work and congested streets. The left half of the *Padang* was a sports field with a pavilion at the end nearest me and rugby posts set for a match. The far side had another, larger, pavilion, being the Singapore Cricket Club. Strollers walked around the perimeter and along the path bisecting the sections. The appearance of the sun prompted young ladies to pop open their parasols, providing a splash of colour, although red featured the most.

With the sea breeze filling my lungs I lounged there for half an hour, soaking up the sun like a lizard. I almost forgot my worries. That was until I spotted a Middle Eastern man walk past and look at me. I read nothing in his face, no recognition or surprise, and decided he wasn't one of the Palestinian gang. However, it reminded me that I was here for a reason.

I started walking again and did a circuit of the green before passing the Victoria Theatre, Government House on my right, and crossed the Anderson Bridge.

Fullerton Square with the imposing Fullerton Building was next. The exclusive Singapore Club was in there. It was also home to the General Post Office, possibly the most grand in the world. That and a host of offices downstairs meant that the square was packed with parked cars and hustling trishaw riders.

I waved two away before I was clear of the square and walked a short distance towards the docks. Keppel Harbour was up ahead and I saw no sign of a naval ship, which confirmed my earlier suspicion that it had been a quiet night for the MPs.

Anyone looking for me wouldn't expect me to stroll down here, I decided, so I did a loop back to the Singapore River and Boat Quay.

Coleman Bridge was my favourite of the many that spanned the river, less industrial, with more cyclists and no buses. I used to enjoy standing here and breathing in the intoxicating smells that wafted up from the cargo on the boats below. From here, with the sea at my back, I had a good view of the wharves that lined the river and ran inland. I figured that anyone would also have a good view of me—if they were looking.

I stayed for ten minutes, watching the activity from godown to tongkang as wares were loaded and unloaded. Hundreds of men worked these private docks, with labour tightly controlled. Those with a right to work had a special coin with a square hole punched in the middle. They wore it on a chain around their necks. If it couldn't be seen, I knew they'd be challenged. I also knew that there were Customs men along there, checking bills of lading, ensuring duty was paid on arriving goods.

I'd worked with the Singapore government for enough time to know the challenges faced by Customs and the police in preventing smuggling, counterfeiting and the avoidance of taxes. It seemed endemic and culturally acceptable—at least to certain sectors of society. Chinese secret societies were the core of illegal activities, and I knew that Andrew Yipp was the head of one.

I started walking again. Thinking about him made me think about the alluring Su Ling, and I hoped she'd visit me again tonight despite knowing that we were from different sides of the track and had no future.

Hill Street police station and quarters were on the far side, curving around the corner of Hill Street and River Valley Road with good views of the river. I turned left and followed the road around the hill so that Fort Canning was on my right the whole time.

When I was directly north of the police station on the far side, I found a café and stopped for an early lunch. I was now a good stone's throw from the grass tennis courts and the Cathay Building.

On the one hand, I felt like a tourist enjoying the city that I knew so well but rarely spent time to appreciate. On the other, I started to feel frustrated at my lack of a plan. Was I just going to walk around like this every day until I spotted a member of the gang looking for me?

As I headed up Orchard Road I formed a new plan. Each day, I would find a hidden spot near my apartment on Beach Road and watch for suspicious activity. Maybe I wasn't looking for a Palestinian at all.

I took my time up Orchard, browsing the many shops and picking up some fresh clothes. By the time I reached the top and the junction with Scotts Road, I decided to call into my favourite place for a drink.

Goodwood Park was a classy building with a rich history, originally being a private club for Germans. During the war the Japanese used it as a residence for high-ranking officers, and after the war it briefly became a court for prosecuting war crimes. Now it was a club once more, with elegant furniture, a lot of dark wood and shiny brass. I couldn't afford the membership of the Singapore Club and this was a world away from the rowdiness of most of the Singapore bars.

As I stepped inside it was like stepping back in time. There was an ocean of calm, with a grand piano playing softly in the background and staff in white suits gliding between tables.

I nodded to a few familiar faces and received an elderly lady's frown. I figured my suit wasn't up to the standard she expected.

A waiter showed me to a window seat and I ordered a gin and tonic. Barely a second before he left me, another man appeared.

He sat opposite and gave me a thin smile that I recognized. "Mind if I join you?" he said with a German accent.

I knew him as an employee of Chen Guan Xi, Yipp's biggest rival and officially an exile due to suspicions of his communist leanings. He'd left the country to visit China and had been refused re-entry. And yet I'd previously met him, here in the city.

"How are you?" I said.

"Oh I'm exceptionally well," he said as a waiter delivered my drink.

I waited for the German to speak again and took a sip of my gin. I figured he had something to tell me. This wasn't a social visit.

"You've got a problem," he said conspiratorially.

"Really?"

He nodded. "Captain Carter, we have someone who I think you'll want to meet."

TWENTY-THREE

Outside, the German signalled to a trishaw man who I figured was waiting for him. There was no conversation with the driver; we just got in the back.

I knew the cloak-and-dagger routine of Chinese secret societies but I didn't expect the blindfold he handed me.

"Where are we going?" I asked.

"You'll find out," he said, "but it's best you don't know the location."

I accepted and put on the mask as the rider pulled away. At first I had a sense of where we were, but then I figured the route was deliberately circuitous. They didn't want me to work it out, although I listened hard and tried to visualize locations.

After about ten minutes I knew we'd left the city. Based on the wind direction it felt like north or north-west, and we continued for another ten minutes before I noticed the smell of earth and cooler air. Then we stopped.

"You can remove the blindfold now," the German said. "We're here."

I was right. We were outside the city. We were also beyond any village I knew. There was just a low-level building surrounded by forest. On the flat roof and beside a door, men stood with rifles. No one aimed a gun at me, but I felt their eyes boring into me, assessing.

I was assessing too. I started to wonder whether I'd been foolish. Maybe I shouldn't have been looking for a Palestinian. Maybe this was all about Chen Guan Xi. Could I have upset him somehow? Could it have been his men who had wrecked my apartment?

The German nodded towards the door and I followed. Once there, the guards moved aside and we entered the building.

It was dingy and musty and I figured this was a temporary base or hideout. We went along a corridor and then turned into another.

"That way," he said, and took me to concrete stairs that descended into darkness. Then he indicated for me to go first.

"Is Chen down there?" I asked, surprised that the head of the organization would be in such a dank place. I thought about the gun on my ankle. Should I pull it now before the German pulled one on me?

He didn't reply.

I said, "After you," and he pulled his thin smile.

"Don't worry."

"Why not?"

I suspect he was just having some fun, because he said, "You'll see," and then took the stairs ahead of me.

With practised ease, I caught my ankle, slipped the Beretta out and stuck it in my pocket. Just in case.

As we descended, I expected the air to get colder but it didn't. The smell began to change: more stale than damp. Then I thought I could smell sweat.

At the bottom I could see a faint light at the end of a corridor. There were doors on either side as we walked along towards the light, and I saw that it came from around a door.

The German knocked, and as the door opened, I was struck by a smell worse than sweat. It was rank: fear mixed with urine.

A bony Chinese guy with a rifle held open the door and there was another man inside the small room. He was hanging from the ceiling, chains on his wrists. He might have had dark skin but it was impossible to tell because of the red welts that covered his body.

He was alive but barely. His head was down, hair hanging over his face. His body was limp; the only sign of life was the tremor in his bent legs.

I said nothing.

The German waited for a moment, looking at me. Then he signalled to the guard, who stepped over to the prisoner and pulled his long hair until his face rose up.

Blank eyes looked at me.

"Who is he?" I asked, already guessing if not the name, definitely the organization.

"He says his name is Asif Mamood. And I have every reason to believe him," the German said. "He's told us quite a lot. In fact, he's told us more than we could have hoped."

I said nothing.

"He's from Palestine," the German said, and paused. "In fact, he's from a small town in the Gaza Strip, although that isn't relevant. What is relevant is why he is here and why he was looking for you."

I shook my head. "I don't know him."

"But he knows you and told us a very interesting story about how you killed some of his friends. There are a lot of men looking for you, Captain Carter. Fortunately, we picked him up before he told anyone."

"You're sure?"

"That he hasn't told anyone other than us? Of course."

I said, "How long has he been here?"

"Five days."

"And what will you do with him, assuming he's told you everything there is to tell?"

"Oh yes, Captain Carter, there's nothing more to tell. So he is now surplus to requirements, as you English like to say."

Again I said nothing. The guard let go of the prisoner's head and it flopped back down.

The German said, "So the question is, would you like to do the honours?" From under his shirt he pulled a hunting knife.

Self-defence was one thing. Killing the murderers of my Middle Eastern informant, I could justify. However, the idea of stabbing this poor wretch made me hesitate, partly because it was in cold blood. But also because of the power it gave the German and his organization over me.

He must have read my mind. "He'll just rot here otherwise. Possibly live for another week like this."

I shook my head at the knife. I sensed the prisoner watching me through his greasy hair. I looked harder and saw that his eyes were no longer dull and lifeless. For a moment I saw desperation. Not for life, but to end his suffering.

I stepped sideways, towards the guard, but didn't take the knife. Instead, I pulled the Beretta from my pocket, and in a swift motion, I raised it and shot the prisoner through the back of the head.

The German nodded, appreciation in his eyes.

I said, "I'd like to see Chen now."

"Of course."

A few minutes later we were outside once more and I gulped the fresh air, ridding the stench from my lungs

129

but unable to erase the image of the prisoner from my mind.

The blindfold was returned and we set off in the trishaw.

It was a shorter journey, and this time I knew we'd gone from the jungle towards civilization. I heard traffic and breathed fumes and then the smell of cooking vegetables. I figured we were in a Chinese suburb of the city by the time we stopped between buildings and I removed the band from my eyes.

We got out and the German took me through one building and then another, with people working or eating or washing clothes. No one paid us any attention as we passed them despite us standing out as the only white men. I guessed they were used to people passing through, probably told to ignore anyone who may work for Chen.

After some rickety stairs, we crossed between two buildings one floor up and were met by two armed guards who stepped aside. Suddenly the dust and cobwebs disappeared and I was walking on carpet.

A door was opened for us and I stepped into a room and met the man who wasn't here.

TWENTY-FOUR

Unsmiling, Chen Guan Xi regarded me from across the room with one good eye and one milky-white one. I'd met him once before, at a different property but the same décor. The windows had heavy drapes, the carpet deep and luxurious. Crimson, gold and green were the main colours, including a sweeping crimson dragon in the carpet that stretched between us.

Chen sat behind a desk, looking like a typical Chinese businessman in a suit. However, he was anything but typical. He was a political exile and should not have been on the island.

"Welcome," he said, beckoning me.

I took three paces forward, until I was an arm's length from his desk. He didn't stand and I expected no handshake.

Neither of us spoke for a moment and, in that silence, I wondered if he slipped in and out of Singapore or whether he stayed here the whole time. Did he simply move from secret location to secret location, avoiding attention? I was sure the government didn't know he was here, although I wouldn't have been surprised to hear that various policemen knew. When I worked for the government, we were aware of spies within the police communicating with the unofficial secret societies. There was suspicion that someone close to the top of the police force was involved but nothing had ever been proven.

He smiled, although his eyes never moved. "You are well, I see, Captain Carter."

"And you also." I nodded respectfully.

"But it would appear that your health would be in more doubt had my men not intervened."

"I am grateful."

As though I hadn't spoken, he continued: "It would have been most unfortunate should a certain organization discover you were here. I understand that it was also propitious that you intercepted someone in Penang."

Deciding to speak openly rather than play his games, I said, "You heard I was in Penang?"

He smiled. "I hear many things."

I waited, but he didn't elaborate.

"Were you also looking for me, Mr Chen?"

The old man opened a desk drawer, and for a second I wondered if he was about to draw a gun. Instead, he pulled out a pack of cigarettes, tapped one out, and with a languid motion put it between his lips and lit it. He took a slow drag and blew it out before speaking.

"You were investigating in Penang—at the barracks there."

I watched him take another draw of the cigarette. The smoke filtered through the warm air towards me. When I didn't comment, he added: "Would you like a cigarette? I can assure you they are legal."

"Thank you. No."

"And how was your investigation? A success I hope."

The German moved from behind me until I saw him in my peripheral vision. However, I kept my eyes on Chen.

"There was no investigation," I said.

The old man raised the eyebrow above his good eye. "Is that so?"

I was here because of the Palestinian, because Chen knew my secret, and I was becoming increasingly uncomfortable, although the prickle on my skin may have been the heat. The smoke was also starting to claw at my airways.

I said, "I was accompanying a reporter as a favour to a friend."

"Investigating the curse."

"For a newspaper article."

"The *Manchester Guardian*."

I nodded.

He said, "Do you believe in ghosts, Mr Carter?" and I wondered if he knew the irony of his own position; a ghost in a different sense.

"I do not," I said.

"And yet you investigated."

"I accompanied the reporter."

He stubbed out the noxious cigarette with finality then straightened his neck, and I wondered if he was making a decision.

"You were looking for the wrong type of spirit," he said, and this time he smiled genuinely. If he hadn't had the Chinese accent and had added "My boy", I could have imagined him as a kindly uncle.

So this is it, I thought. He's getting to the point. "What sort of spirit should I have been looking for, Mr Chen?"

"Not a ghost," he said. "And I can help you."

"But the reporter has left with her story."

"There is always more."

I said nothing. Did he expect me to return to Penang and investigate something else?

"Quid pro quo," he said, and the hard eyes returned.

I still said nothing. He was asking me to return the favour for capturing the Palestinian, maybe also in keeping my secret.

He said, "You told me you like doing favours, Captain."

"I said the job in Penang was a favour for a friend."

"Am I not your friend?"

"You have done me a great service."

"Precisely," he said. "I am glad you understand."

Then the meeting was at an end as Chen waved towards the German. The other man stepped up and touched my elbow, indicating that we should leave.

Bemused by the meeting, I followed the German out of the temporary office and through the buildings. Before reaching natural daylight, he handed me the mask and I placed it over my eyes once more.

He guided me outside and into a trishaw.

"Where now?" I asked.

The bike pulled away and he said, "Let's talk first."

"All right."

"You have good relationship with Mr Yipp."

"Chen's biggest rival," I said, surprised by the mention of his name. "However, I am hardly his friend."

"And yet we know he talks to you."

"Not for a while."

"And yet you have connections with him."

Now I realized the other man was referring to Su Ling.

I said, "What is the quid pro quo?"

"We would like you to continue your investigation into bad spirit."

"Because?"

"Because Mr Yipp is supplying morphine to the British Army."

That surprised me. I figured Yipp was involved in opium smuggling and distribution but I'd seen no indication that he supplied the army.

He said, "Unofficially."

"And you know this how?"

"We just do."

"If it is illegal then you should report it to the authorities."

I imagined the German shaking his head at my preposterous suggestion. Turn on such an important person—a rival business head? Not openly anyway. Not if you didn't want a war between secret societies. Such battles required subtlety and finesse.

He said, "We would like you to gather information."

"And feed it to you?"

"Deal with it in an appropriate manner."

Ah, so I find the evidence and I report it.

He said, "You can remove the blindfold now."

We were on Scotts Road, the sun in our eyes until the rider turned into the drive of Goodwood Park.

I got out and the German shook my hand.

"Good luck," he said.

I said, "I'm not planning a return to Penang."

"You may not need to, but if you do then gather evidence of the bad spirit. The bad morphine."

TWENTY-FIVE

I returned to the room above the Chinese family's home. There were two motivations for continuing the subterfuge. Firstly, I couldn't be sure that there weren't more Palestinians out there. Sure, Chen's men would be looking out for me, but I had no idea how effective they would be. I didn't admit the second reason until the first morning after. Su Ling didn't visit me again. After two nights, I decided the hiding was over. I gave the family a gift and they bowed deeply and wished me good fortune.

My apartment on Beach Road had been tidied and repaired and I soon slipped into my old routine, despite having been away for many months. My training regime had suffered more recently and I set about improving my fitness, which included spending hours at the boxing gym at the YMCA.

I kept a watchful eye for anyone suspicious and, apart from generally enjoying Singaporean life, I set about looking for the evidence requested by Chen.

My first formal visit was to the government office of Internal Security. Secretary Coates had been my boss for a short time. Like Chen, he had information on me, and like Chen, he never spelled out what he knew. He'd been unhappy when I'd resigned but hadn't used the information against me. I suspect he never intended to.

Chen, on the other hand, was undoubtedly ruthless and manipulative, and I knew I would have a problem with him at some point.

Coates had passed away, I was told by his office. He'd only been fifty-six, although he looked ten years older, probably due to his *good-living* lifestyle and stress. He fretted over the rise of the People's Party and the fear that control over Singapore would be lost to independence. He'd also stressed over the threat from the Communists and Chinese secret societies, particularly Andrew Yipp. I wondered if he'd have stressed over Chen Guan Xi if he'd known the businessman was still in the country. Probably.

Coates's successor, Phil Norris, was a similar age, with similar edginess, although he was slim and I saw no evidence of the alcohol and tobacco addiction that blighted Coates.

"You worked for us last year," Norris said after introductions.

"Mostly investigating Chinese secret societies. Looking for evidence of an internal threat."

"Do you believe the societies exist?"

I hesitated, wondering if he was testing me, before saying, "Undoubtedly."

He nodded. "I could do with a good man."

"My time working for the government is at an end," I said. "However, if I come across relevant information, I'll share it with you. In return, all I ask is for access to the records."

Norris pondered this, playing with his moustache as he regarded me. "All right," he finally agreed. "You're unofficial, which means not on the payroll, which suits me. Come by the office tomorrow and we'll have an ID made up for you—just in case you need it. Unofficial until necessary." He winked before shaking my hand again.

The ID came in more use than I anticipated, because it got me into the police station and Customs without questions.

Partly, my objective was to gain access to their records but I also knew that word would get back to Chen. I wanted him to know that I was actively investigating for him, whether I found anything or not.

From the police documents, I focused on serious crimes, particularly murders and drug dealing. Nothing pointed to organized crime and there was no mention of anyone working for Chen or Yipp's businesses.

A Customs officer told me that the new strategy of stamping *Duty Paid* on cigarette packets and alcohol entering the country legally was helping identify the ones where the shipments were allegedly in transit but were actually bound for internal consumption. When I'd met with Chen, he'd randomly told me his cigarette was legal. It was a clear reference to the new law and I figured it hadn't been stamped. Or, more likely, he had illegal goods stamped.

I didn't bother explaining the likely loophole to the Customs man. His other story was that they had uncovered a gang impersonating dockworkers, using forged medallions as ID.

Was there evidence of big businesses being involved? He said not.

My final port of call was Gillman Barracks, the home of 200 Provost company.

The CO, Lieutenant Colonel Ambrose, showed genuine delight at my appearance. He was one of those men who, because of their presence, look larger than they really are. He was probably five ten or eleven with wide shoulders and strong arms. He had creases around his eyes that I figured came from the tragic loss of his wife through cancer, but he smiled and had a firm handshake.

After offering my support, I asked him whether the army was sourcing morphine from Yipp. He asked me to leave it with him. He'd find out.

Ambrose didn't get a message to me for two days. In that time I travelled around the city, visiting contacts, factories and hospitals asking questions. I found nothing incriminating against Yipp. I didn't expect to. He was a clever man with an organization that had more legs than an octopus. If one illegal activity became jeopardized I was sure that he'd simply cut off the limb and grow another.

Ambrose reported that there had been an increasing shortage of morphine due to the Korean War.

"All supplies come from the MOD," he explained. "There's a long paper trail, so unofficial boxes couldn't get into the system."

His mention of boxes made me think back to an operation over six months ago. The police had followed a Chinese gang suspected of trafficking drugs. In a botched raid at Singorah airfield—north of the island—an airplane managed to get away. The police found no drugs but did wonder why British Army crates were marked with "Medical Supplies". Had these crates originally contained the drugs? It seemed possible.

We had suspected that the gang was working for Yipp but, after a shootout, only one gang member survived, and he denied it. I had no doubt that the Singapore police had been very persuasive. Their relaxed attitude towards torture was more than a rumour. However, the connection between Yipp and drug trafficking remained unproven.

I said, "Could the crates be official?"

"What do you mean?"

"The contents get switched? They get used army crates and use them for smuggling." Even as I asked, I decided it didn't make sense. Why would someone switch morphine for morphine?

He said, "You could investigate. I could spare a man for support."

And so I did, accompanied by a bright-eyed young private called Whitehead. We worked for four days. I obtained documentation of medical supplies arriving into Singapore and leaving. I phoned barracks where the crates had been delivered and confirmed consignment numbers and volume.

Whitehead drove me to local barracks and hospitals where crates had been delivered and we audited their records and counted bottles and ampules. Everything matched.

My next move would have been further afield, possibly Kuala Lumpur, but it was Tuesday June 2nd. National holidays were being declared all over the British Empire because it was coronation day.

Singapore celebrated. Union flags festooned every building and Elizabeth's image appeared on posters in windows and on posts.

The time difference meant that the official celebration would be on Wednesday. There would be a huge parade with every armed force represented, marching bands and fifty floats supported by local businesses. It would be like a New Year's celebration without the Chinese razzmatazz of dancers, dragons and fireworks.

I joined the officers at Gillman, gathered around a radio from 6pm, listening to the BBC broadcast from Westminster. It started just after eleven in the morning back home with Elizabeth and her husband, the Duke of Edinburgh, driven from Buckingham Palace to

Westminster Abbey in the Gold State Coach. Three hours later we were still there to hear the cheers of the public as the thousands welcomed their new queen outside the abbey.

It would be another day before the theatres throughout the city showed the film of the ceremony, and thousands flocked to watch it for free in multiple sittings.

Watching the parade on Wednesday, I was struck by the degree of enthusiasm for the new queen and everything British. Was it genuine? It seemed to be. All the concerns about the future of the island and yet the patriotism appeared as strong as at home.

Of course, I only saw the people celebrating, and there could have been equal numbers who were anti. However, they weren't in evidence and there was no rumour of a terrorist threat.

I watched from the *Padang* and noticed a float sponsored by one of Chen's biggest businesses, Ho Ho Biscuits, when I realized someone was standing close behind me. I smelled her perfume and guessed who it was before she spoke.

"Don't turn around," Su Ling said softly. I saw her arm wave a Union Flag as soldiers marched by. "Are you all right?"

"I'm fine."

"You're back in the apartment."

"I'd had enough of slinking around. I'm grateful for the room... and your midnight visit. I might have stayed longer if it'd become a regular feature."

"What are you talking about?"

"That first night."

She said nothing, and I suddenly questioned whether it had been Su Ling in my bed that night. On the other hand, maybe she didn't want to admit it.

More floats went past.

Finally, she said, "Have you resolved your issue with your *enemy*?"

I hadn't told her about the Palestinians, but the way she stressed the word made me wonder if she knew something.

"I have," I said.

"Good. You've been... prominent."

"Prominent?"

"People have noticed your activities."

"I've been training hard, working out at the boxing club."

She laughed. "You know what I mean. Is that something to do with the enemy?"

"I'm just keeping busy," I said.

When she didn't say anything for a while, I glanced over my shoulder. She was gone. I looked up and down the crowded pavement but couldn't spot her anywhere.

After the last float and final marching band, some of the crowd disbursed, but many enjoyed the last of the sun.

I sat on the sea wall for a while and watched the sun set over the island. Boats crowded the harbour as usual but the activity of bumboats and larger tongkangs was coming to a close.

In the warm star-speckled evening, I took a stroll to the river. The streets still maintained a party atmosphere and fireworks crackled every few minutes. I followed a flow of people and crossed Cavenagh Bridge and then looped back over Elgin. Back around the *Padang,* I continued towards my apartment. Most of the crowd leaving the esplanade turned left up Stamford Road, heading for Happy World, I figured. It was one of three entertainment parks, normally out of bounds for soldiers

142

after 7pm, but that restriction had been lifted and I suspected the MPs would be busy later tonight.

For a second I thought I smelled Su Ling's perfume and that she was by my side. I was right. But she didn't stop or look at me.

She slipped something into my jacket pocket and then she was gone with the rest of the crowd.

I stood on the corner of North Bridge Road and Stamford and watched her disappear in the throng. Desperate to find out what she'd given me, I hurried home. No way would I risk looking at it out in the open. She'd been secretive for a reason.

Once behind a closed door I felt in my pocket and pulled out a piece of paper. Unfolding it, I saw a diagram and, in disguised handwriting, the words "Monkey King" scribbled underneath.

TWENTY-SIX

The diagram was a series of pencil lines that looked like a hoe, the stave running top left to bottom right. Then there was a line or bar followed by a sort of blade part: a segment with a short line in the middle at the bottom. But I didn't think "hoe", I thought "map". Su Ling had drawn me a map. Although I couldn't make sense of it.

Monkey King was relevant.

The Monkey King was her favourite myth, and there was a place west of the city where all the stories were told with statues and scenes amid the landscaped gardens: Haw Par Villa.

Su Ling might have meant me to meet her there, but then why the diagram? No. I was sure I was meant to find a clue at the Monkey King scene.

I caught a taxi and ten minutes later told him to stop and wait around the corner from the ornate gardens.

The gates were locked for the night and the lights off, although, in the moonlight, I could see the central pagoda. Checking there was no one around, I scaled the gates. Then, with my torch, I located the monkey statue, which was as big as an average man. He was looking at a mirror while his magic staff pointed over a bridge to a cave. I remember Su Ling telling me that he was searching for the source of the river and persuaded the other monkeys to jump into the water and cave and then declare him the handsome king. At least I think that was the bizarre story. He also appeared to have been made from a stone egg and had magical powers—as you'd expect for a god.

Shining my light around, I wondered if I'd been mistaken. Why tell me about this place? She meant for me to come inside otherwise she'd have simply mentioned the location.

I was about to give up when it struck me. I'd been a fool. She didn't intend me to come here. She was telling me about the mirror. The lake was a mirror. She was telling me to look at the diagram in a mirror.

I clambered over the rocks and squatted beside the mirror on the ground. Shining the torch at the paper, I looked at its reflection. Now the hoe was the other way up, and looked more like a kite. The string ran bottom left to top right. Then a bar and then the kite head with a short line up the middle. And as I looked closely, I realized there was a cross at the top of the line. The drawing was indeed a map. A street map. And I knew the spot.

The cross represented a village north-east of the city, called Kallang Dua. I jumped the gates, ran back to the taxi driver and asked him to take me to Gillman Barracks.

Once there, I persuaded the motor pool sergeant to lend me a jeep, and five minutes of paperwork later, I was racing back the way I'd come from my apartment. However, rather than get onto Beach Road, I cut past the Cathay Building and got onto Selegie Road.

This was the start of the kite string, and I was soon out of the city with jungle on my left and swampland to my right. Less than a mile and a half later, I crossed the

Kallang River and came to the junction. This was the bar at the base of the segment. The road split along the segment lines but I continued straight, taking a lane through heavy woodland.

The whole time, I cursed my stupidity. I'd wasted almost an hour going to Haw Par Villa when I just needed to hold the paper up to a mirror.

I prayed that this wasn't time critical and that I wasn't too late.

The village lay ahead and I knew the lane terminated after less than half a mile. If I drove through the village, I'd need to turn around at the end and come straight back. Not great for covert surveillance—which is what I anticipated. With this in mind, when I saw a place to hide the Land Rover, I drove into the undergrowth and continued on foot.

I'd driven around here when working with the police and knew that there were no factories out here, and no warehouses. However, in addition to the usual kampong attap huts, I remembered a scrapyard. It was the first thing I came to on the outskirts of the village, an ugly scar after the natural jungle.

I stood in the long grass and peered through the metal fence. Cicadas buzzed all around me and I saw a dim light from a shed at the back of the yard. It was maybe eighty yards distant and I figured I could get closer by circling the area. However, two things made me hesitate. There was a sign warning of a guard dog, for one. The second issue was the ground. By the lane, moonlight made the undergrowth visible. Within a few paces I would be moving into the dark and the unknown. No way could I use a torch, so I decided to check out the other side.

I crossed over the lane and snuck past the yard's entrance and then back again to the fence. It was darker here, probably even harder to get around the side. I stood under a tree and watched the hut for a while. I figured it was about fifteen paces wide, an office probably, and had at least one man inside. I saw him pass in front of a window as he walked around.

Then someone opened the door, left it ajar and took a piss into the dirt. Another man complained about the open door and it was closed briefly before the first one went back inside.

Only two men, I decided, probably nightwatchmen, probably of little interest.

I was in the process of deciding that I'd check out the village first and come back if I had to when I heard a vehicle. Something heavy coming along the lane.

It had no lights on and travelled up the lane towards the village. Hard to see in the dark, but I guessed it to be a Bedford RL truck maybe. They were sometimes used as a larger troop carrier, sometimes as a load bed for goods.

As it rumbled past, I hoped to see the contents, but the back was covered with tarpaulin. However, if there had been anything under the covers, it couldn't have been very big. Nothing protruded above the sides.

I followed the truck, keeping to the long grass and moving slowly, cautious because of uneven ground and wary in case there was a sentry waiting by the road.

I met no one, and a hundred yards later I came to the first dwelling places. It was after ten o'clock and I saw a few torches burning in the night. However, I couldn't see any villagers. It was possible they were all in bed, but unlikely.

There were twelve huts, all empty, but that wasn't what surprised me the most. There was no sign of the truck that had passed. As far as I was aware, the lane ended at the village.

I got to the far end and found the turning circle I expected. However, I also found another track—not a formal lane but a route through the trees, rutted by vehicles.

I followed the curving track and within twenty paces saw lights. Not the flames of torches, but a harsh electric light, blue-white between the dark trees. I cut away from the track, walking even more carefully over branches and unseen stones until I was close enough to see better.

Ahead was a building, an ugly concrete block, unfinished and quickly constructed. The lights were spots, illuminating the truck and open double doors. A sentry squad stood out front, rifles slung over their shoulders. But these guys were more interested in the other people there than any intruders.

The villagers young and old were inside the building. I could see them through the small glass-less windows and the wide-open doors. They were lined up like on a conveyor belt—factory workers hammering and gluing and painting. Constructing wooden boxes.

After my standard training exercises, I took a morning run along the coast. There was no breeze, and I watched the sun come up, golden and glorious. Then, after a shower, I drove over to Gillman and returned the Land Rover. I walked up the hill to the office block where the Union Flag stood out proudly, wired so that it couldn't droop.

"Sir," the desk clerk said as I entered, "you had a phone call last night, sir." He handed me a slip of blue paper, but before I could read it, Ambrose came in behind me and grumbled.

"I need good news," he said. "Please tell me you have good news." Today, his voice matched the wrinkles around his eyes and there was no jovial smile.

"I do," I said, following him into his office.

Ambrose was shaking his head as though he hadn't really expected that response, hadn't been listening. He said, "We should never have relaxed the rules—the out of bounds."

"Trouble?"

"Two dead locals, one dead soldier and two more with serious knife wounds." He shook his head. "Now, what were you saying?"

"I do have good news."

He perked up. "Yes?"

"About the morphine, I think. You know I followed the paper trail and found nothing. I still don't know what's going on, but I've discovered a factory making fake army crates." I wrote down the address.

He said something but I wasn't listening. As I had straightened up, I looked at the message on the blue slip of paper in my hand.

"Ash?" Ambrose said.

"Sorry, sir, I need to go to Penang."

I read the phone message again. It was from Colonel Dexter, and it simply said: I need you here ASAP.

TWENTY-SEVEN

It took me all day to drive through Malaya up to Perai, the town by the ferry terminal. Ambrose had let me borrow the jeep and even offered Private Whitehead as my driver.

Before I left, I went back to my apartment on Beach Road to grab a bag. There was a small parcel on my doorstep. It was addressed to Li Ping Gao and wrapped in brown paper. I figured this was the item Su Ling wanted me to take up to Penang for her aunt.

I let Whitehead drive the first stretch, up to Woodlands and the crossing into Malaya. He'd done that journey a few times and was comfortable.

While he drove, I thought about Su Ling. She'd not instructed me to go to the village in the jungle, she'd just left a diagram that I'd interpreted as a map. Me working it out, not her telling me. There was a big difference. I knew how she operated, how she was expected to operate. It wouldn't have been seemly to point the finger at her boss, but she had provided covert assistance.

Making fake army boxes made it a military matter and Ambrose would deal with it. If he informed police, it would be after the event. When I worked for Secretary Coates, the politician hoped that I could improve liaison between the forces, but some things never change.

150

Ambrose would deal with this himself and he'd send armed MPs to investigate tonight.

As we journeyed north, Whitehead became increasingly agitated. Each time I took the wheel, he carried his rifle like he was riding shotgun. It was his first time out of Singapore and he knew the stories of bandit attacks. But nothing happened except for his constant wittering, a two-hour downpour north of Kuala Lumpur and an overheated engine in Kampar, a town I knew well.

After the radiator cooled and was topped up, we were on our way again and I'd already decided I'd had enough of Whitehead's dull company. Short journeys around Singapore were one thing, but a day in the jeep with him had left me craving silence. So at Perai I asked him to jump out and catch the train home. He was grateful.

I suspected that Ambrose wouldn't be too keen on me keeping the Land Rover, but then he was too far away to do anything about it and I'd return it in a few days. I figured Colonel Dexter's problem couldn't take long. Maybe he needed me to deal with Hannah Quinn, the reporter, again.

I queued for the last ferry across the strait and it was totally dark by the time I pulled up the hill and into Minden Barracks.

When I reported in, the duty clerk said that Dexter was waiting for me in his office.

"You were right," he said after I knocked and entered.

"About what?" I'd called the colonel from Gillman but he said he didn't want to explain over the phone. He just needed my help. Now he was ready to explain.

"Tanner's death was suspicious," he said with a resigned look on his face.

"What's happened, Jim?"

"Another death," he said. "I didn't want to say over the phone. You know, operators talk and all that."

I did know. Telephone calls weren't secure, and I realized Dexter was concerned he had more than another accident on his hands. It wouldn't look good.

He said, "Talk me through Corporal Tanner's death. How it happened in your eyes."

I took a breath, looked out into the dark night and saw my own reflection and imagined myself in uniform, maybe a red cap under my arm. "It's Wednesday May 13th, Tanner's birthday. At approximately ten to seven in the evening, Tanner and three others scheduled for night patrol pick up their weapons from the armoury. Tanner gets rifle 66, which amuses the QM, Sergeant Cooper, because of an extra six making it the Number of the Beast. Tanner is superstitious and nervous. He and Private Reeder patrol the perimeter separately." I shook my head. "It would be usual to patrol in pairs, but maybe because of Tanner's nervousness they go in opposite directions, meeting occasionally as they passed."

Dexter nodded, watching me closely.

"Tanner stops in the woods to the west of the camp. He's seen there by Reeder and also the head of the engineering unit, Sergeant Cox. Reeder again says that Tanner is scared and reports that the man had his gun set to fire."

"Against regs," Dexter said.

"And common practice in the jungle, although not on patrol in quiet Penang."

Dexter nodded for me to continue.

"Cox reports that Tanner wanted a smoke," I said, "and that he wasn't wearing shoes. Neither Cox nor Reeder are close when they hear a gunshot, and both assume it's Tanner shooting at something imagined.

152

Reeder goes to investigate on the off-chance there's a security issue and finds Tanner dead, presumably having shot himself by accident. You assured me—"

"Forget what I said before."

"I find it highly unlikely that the gun went off having struck something hard on the ground. I saw nothing that looked hard enough, although I accept it could have been moved. Sergeant Cox suggested that Tanner could have deliberately shot himself. He couldn't have achieved this by holding the rifle under his chin and pulling the trigger because his arms weren't long enough. It's possible that he pulled the trigger with a toe."

"Why?"

"Why kill himself?" Again I looked at my reflection. "People commit suicide for all sorts of reasons, although a cry for help is the most common I believe. They attempt it in the hope that they are saved. However, that is highly unlikely in this case, as is depression. It was his birthday and he was reportedly happy until being spooked by the 666."

"So why?" Dexter prompted.

"Under the influence of drugs or alcohol could be another reason. However, Major Dawson dismissed anything like that."

"Under the influence of an evil spirit?"

I said, "I don't believe in ghosts."

"What does your gut say?"

"Murder," I said. "I know you want that even less than a suicide, but I think you've come to the same conclusion."

"Any pointers to it?"

"The only one I can think of is this supposed ghost. Reeder and Cox described it as a shadow. Obviously it was dark, but there was a moon, and a man flitting between the trees could have looked like a shadow."

He nodded thoughtfully.

I waited a beat before saying, "Tell me about the recent death."

"Private Roy Reeder," Dexter said.

"Shit!"

"He was found dead yesterday morning. Last seen in the mess hall for dinner at six thirty. He told his mates that he was going to meet someone in town."

"Do we know who?"

"No, nor do we know whether he made it or where he went because he walked. He wasn't missed later because nearly everyone was listing to the coronation on the wireless."

I nodded.

Dexter continued: "He was reported missing in the morning at six and was found at nine twenty, face down in the mud. He died of suffocation, mud in his mouth and nose."

"Where?" I asked.

Dexter took a breath. "The edge of the jungle," he said. "Just by the assault course."

TWENTY-EIGHT

I checked into the Palisades hotel and was pleased with my room. Although smaller than the officers' quarters, I had a window that opened out on a partial view of the strait. However, I was content with the breeze that cooled the room more than the view itself.

The following morning, I met Dexter for breakfast and we reviewed the incident before he showed me where Reeder had been found. Then he set me up in an office and I started interviewing people.

I met the soldier who had found Reeder at the assault course. I spoke to the men from Reeder's squad who confirmed that the kid hadn't stayed with them to listen to the coronation and that he'd left at around 6pm. No one had seen him return. No one knew who he'd gone to meet or where. I learned that Roy Reeder wasn't popular. One of the privates called him arrogant and a loner.

I asked each man about the assault course and they all confirmed their hate for it. However two of the six men I interviewed mentioned Reeder being picked on.

"What do you mean?" I asked.

"You know, there's always some poor sod who gets picked on—gets treated badly."

"Because?"

"Because the instructors are all bastards—if you'll excuse the language?" The kid squirmed. "Give some poor sod a hard time and the rest all think, thank God it's not me! It's being shown the punishment, rather than getting it, if you know what I mean?"

I did, but didn't learn anything else. No one could give me a reason for Reeder being the whipping boy.

After the squaddies, it was the turn of the assault course crew. I went through two juniors before getting to Sergeant Brookes. He was the first of my interviewees who didn't look nervous. In fact he seemed supremely comfortable.

I may not have been an official MP but I was clearly here under the auspices of the CO and yet he was as relaxed as a dog in the noonday sun.

"It wasn't me," he said, his eyes and voice calm.

"Tell me what happened."

"The kid was found dead in the pool. The one by the final rope swing."

I shook my head. "No, Sergeant. Tell me what happened to him."

"How should I know?"

"It's your assault course."

He bit his lip and said nothing.

"Reeder was found two days ago. Tell me what happened on the day before. Tell me about Tuesday."

"The queen's coronation—God bless her."

I glared at him.

He shrugged. "Was a typical day."

"All right, then how many squads did you have at the assault course?"

"Two."

"And Reeder was in the second." I already knew this from Dexter.

"Apparently. I don't really pay attention to who's who. My job is to make sure those kids are prepared for the worst."

"By being worse."

He shrugged.

"You relish being called a bastard. When we first met you even called yourself Bastard Brookes."

He smiled. "Yes, I do. The men hate me and that's a good thing."

"Did you punish Reeder?"

"Not that I recall." For the first time, I detected uncertainty in his eyes. He must have known I'd already interviewed his two junior instructors although they said very little. My guess was that they'd already conferred and decided what to say.

I said, "I've had a report that Reeder was singled out."

Surprise flickered briefly on his face. Neither of the subordinates had disclosed this, so it was just a punt by me. However, I couldn't tell whether the surprise was that they'd talk or that he really didn't know.

When he didn't comment, I said, "Let me paint a scenario for you. Let's say you singled him out as an example to the other men. Let's say he failed to successfully complete the course on Tuesday."

"I didn't kill him if that's what you're going to suggest."

I said, "Let's say he was embarrassed at his failure. Might he have returned on Tuesday night and practised? Might he have tried to swing across the pool in the dark and fallen? Maybe he banged his head and lost consciousness in the water?"

Brookes studied my eyes for a moment, assessing before he spoke. "Maybe."

"But there was no evidence of a bang to the head," I said.

He shrugged.

I said, "The reporter thought you were guilty of beasting the men."

"Like I told you before, I don't go in for that."

"Tell me about the other soldier who died."

"Private Tanner?"

"Has there been more than two?" I challenged him.

He shrugged.

"And I'm sure you know he was a corporal."

He shrugged facially. "What about him?"

"You gave him a hard time just two days before he died."

"So you said. I don't recall the names."

I said nothing and let him think about it. He seemed to study the paint on the wall before focusing back on me.

He said, "His death was nothing to do with me." Pause. "And neither was Reeder's. Anyway, Tanner's death was an accident."

"You believe that?"

He shrugged.

I said, "Reeder was on patrol the night Tanner died."

He said nothing and looked at the paint again.

"A coincidence, don't you think?"

"Maybe."

I said, "Here's a theory. It's connected to the suggestion of beasting." I waited and he looked back at me before I continued. "When Tanner collected his gun on the night he died, it had the Number of the Beast on it. What if it was a message? What if he wasn't afraid of a ghost but thought he was about to be punished. What if 666 symbolizes beasting?"

"It's an interesting theory," he said.

"Reeder saw something in the woods. He said it was a ghost, but what if it was a man? What if he saw the person who killed Tanner?"

Brookes shook his head.

"What if he thought it was you? Confronted you? You'd have motive then, wouldn't you, Brookes?"

He gave me a cold-eye stare. "I have a different theory."

"You do?"

"First off, let's say I've got nothing to do with this," he said. "Let's say Tanner's death wasn't an accident and what if Reeder wasn't actually practising on the assault course. And his wasn't an accident either."

"All right."

"Tanner died in the woods not far from the assault course." He paused and watched my eyes closely.

The distance was about half a mile, but directionally I could see the link. I nodded, encouraging him. "Are you saying the assault course is relevant?"

He smiled in a sad way. "Work it out, Captain Carter."

"You'll have to tell me."

"If I killed those boys, do you think I'd do it at the assault course?"

I said nothing.

"No." He shook his head. "If they were killed, then someone wanted to implicate me." He cocked an eyebrow and nodded at the same time, like he was saying *get it?*

I had thought of the possibility but wanted to put pressure on the sergeant. I'd hoped he'd give something away. Instead, he remained unconcerned.

"Who?" I said. "Who would do that, Sergeant?"

He smiled. "That, my dear chap, is the big question."

"There's another possibility," I said. "It could be a double bluff."

"What do you mean?" Suddenly all of his confidence evaporated.

"Provide the excuse that it couldn't be you because of the location." I paused and watched his mind whirring. Then I said, "Perhaps you should think about who would want to implicate you—assuming it's not a double bluff."

"It's not," he said. "Seriously, it's not." Brookes was no longer a dog lazing in the sun. Now he looked like a dog expecting to be beaten, tail between his legs, eyes imploring.

I ended the meeting and told him to think about his enemies. Who hated him enough to kill someone and make him a suspect?

On a whim, I called for Sergeant Lee Cooper. The QM didn't keep me waiting long.

"What's it about?" he said, sitting down and looking keen.

"Private Reeder's death."

"Yes, I heard." He gave a little awkward laugh. "Of course, everyone's heard. An accident at the assault course."

I said nothing and tried to read him.

"How can I help?" he asked.

"Is it connected with Corporal Tanner's death?"

He frowned. "In what way?"

I said nothing.

He smiled. "The ghosts?"

I said, "Did the Number of the Beast have anything to do with Reeder's death, Sergeant?"

Cooper took a breath. "Like the 666 you mean?" he shook his head and raised both hands. "I didn't give him the 666 rifle if that's what you're asking."

160

"Ever?"

"Not as far as I can remember. No, I'm pretty sure he never had it."

"Tell me about Sergeant Tony Brookes."

Cooper frowned and thought. "What do you want to know? He's in charge of the assault course."

"What do you think of him?"

"He does his job, like I do mine." He shrugged and smiled. "People don't like him, but he's good at what he does, I guess."

"Could he have anything to do with Reeder's death?"

"You mean, apart from him dying at the assault course? You mean deliberate? No."

I said, "You like jokes, right?"

"As much as the next man."

"Did you play a joke on Private Reeder on Tuesday night?"

Cooper fixed me with narrowed eyes. "Who's been saying stuff?"

I didn't comment and watched his mind whirring.

He said, "Has Brookes implicated me?"

"Why would he?"

"Because he doesn't like me."

"I thought you respected him."

"Doesn't mean we like one another." Cooper took a long breath. "Look, Captain, I promise I had nothing to do with Reeder's death—or Tanner's for that matter. Strange things happen around here, whether they are because of ghosts or something else, I don't know, but I promise you it's nothing to do with me."

"Do you believe in ghosts, sergeant?"

"No, sir."

"But you like to scare the men."

"No harm in that."

"Unless it ends in them dead."

"Nothing to do with me."

"Then give me a name. If it's not you and it's not Brookes, then who is it?"

He looked concerned. "I don't know. I really don't know."

"Give me a name."

"Sergeant Walsh."

TWENTY-NINE

I waited for Sergeant Cooper to elaborate. When he didn't I asked, "Why name Walsh?"

"Because he likes all this ghost nonsense. Relishes in it."

Cooper didn't have anything else for me so I dismissed him and sent for Sergeant Walsh.

I called him into my borrowed office and he said, "What?" as he entered.

He didn't sit. Instead, he chose to lean against the back of the visitor's chair.

"Was Reeder's death connected to Tanner's?"

Walsh rubbed a cloth on his thick neck. I could see he was sweating, but it was hot and humid and he worked in a garage. I was sure he'd be constantly sweating.

I found his placid face unreadable as he said, "They both did guard duty the night Corporal Tanner died in the woods."

Stating the obvious. I waited for more.

He added: "The woods are haunted. They were both scared. Maybe it's something to do with the ghosts. My theory is that Reeder went into the woods looking for it—looking for the ghost."

"Based on what, Sergeant?"

"Why I think he went looking for a ghost? I don't know. He had a scare when Tanner blew his head off, didn't he? OK he was found at the assault course but it's right there by the haunted woods."

"And you really believe this stuff?"

Now he smiled. "It's not a matter of what I believe it's what the men believe. You get that, right?"

"What do the men believe about the assault course?"

"I don't know. Motor pool guys don't go through the paces there."

"But you must know about Sergeant Brookes."

He grinned. "Old Bastard Brookes. Of course I know his reputation. He loves it."

"Do you think he had anything to do with Reeder's death?"

"I wouldn't know. But he's a man not a ghost."

I said, "I'm looking for a man. I don't believe in ghosts."

Walsh grinned. "Well, Captain Carter, maybe you should." He straightened. "Remember I saw one in the garage."

I said nothing, studying his face. The grin had gone, the emotionless face was back.

After a moment, he said, "If you haven't any more questions, I have work to do."

I let him go and then popped into Dexter's office and debriefed him.

"What next?" Dexter asked, as frustrated as me.

"I suppose I could talk to Colour Sergeant Harper."

Dexter shook his head. "Harper is as baffled as the rest of us. He was the first person I asked. Even he doesn't know what's going on."

"Maybe nothing is going on," I said unconvincingly.

"They might just be accidents after all, and we have nothing to worry about."

Although I doubted it, I agreed.

"Which I prefer." He nodded. "As soon as we make this a formal investigation, I lose control. So, what do you do next?"

"I'm staying at the Palisades hotel and think I'll be more approachable there. Anyone wanting to tell me something without others knowing, it'll be better off barracks. And I continue to ask questions and poke the hornets' nest."

He nodded. "I'll give you a week. After that, it becomes official."

Returning to my hotel, I collected a parcel from my case and drove north along the coast road, passing plantations on the left and beaches on my right.

I went through the town of Batu Feringgi and followed the road as it rose into foothills. At Li Ping Gao's grand house, I parked the jeep and walked up to the front door.

There was a long delay after I'd pulled on the doorbell. I was about to try again when I heard a noise on the other side of the door. When Mrs Gao appeared I thought she looked different, perhaps older, although it could have been my memory playing tricks.

"Yes?" she said, and I realized she didn't recognize me.

"Mrs Gao, I'm Ash Carter, your niece's friend."

"Oh yes, oh yes," she said, still looking uncertain.

"May I come in?"

She bowed her head and walked backwards into the hall. I closed the door behind me and followed her into the same room as before, the one with the bay window and amazing view.

Mrs Gao guided me to a chair and offered tea, like she had before.

I said, "It's just a brief visit, Mrs Gao. Su Ling asked me to give you this." I handed her the small parcel and she eased away the brown wrapping paper. I noticed a shake in her fingers and related it to her age.

There was a mahogany box inside, and she stared at it for a long time before lifting the lid. A ballerina popped up. She had white skin, long legs and a pink tutu. Music played. I recognized it from a ballet called *Giselle*, although the sound was distorted either by the age or limitation of the instrument.

Tears brimmed in Mrs Gao's eyes and then burst over the edges and ran down her cheeks.

We sat in silence for a long time until the music slowed and died.

When she spoke, Mrs Gao didn't look at me. She said, "Su Ling wanted to be a ballerina. I bought her this for her sixth birthday." After a sigh, she said, "Such a beautiful child, full of wonder and hope."

I said, "She meant a lot to you."

"Yes." And then she looked at me with narrow thoughtful eyes. "She gave this to you?"

"To bring here. I think she would have come herself if she could."

Mrs Gao nodded, her eyes still on mine. "And she's giving me this to remind me of the good times."

"To say she loves you," I said. "That's how I'd interpret it."

"Let's have that tea," she said.

She disappeared for fifteen minutes and I paced the room looking at the pictures and photographs like I had before. When she returned, I felt she seemed more confident, perhaps happy with the gift from her niece and the memories.

After pouring weak green tea into a bone china cup, she sat back and studied me with those narrowed eyes again.

"Tell me you aren't working for Andrew Yipp," she said.

"I'm not."

"You were asking about my sister because Su Ling wanted you to find me?" After I nodded, she asked, "Why?"

I figured she wasn't questioning why a daughter would want to locate her mother so I explained, "Because I was an investigator—still am, I suppose."

"You find people."

"That was part of my job."

She sipped her tea and I noticed the cup shake.

She said, "I didn't tell you everything last time."

I leaned forward.

She said, "I had a recent letter from my sister."

THIRTY

As I drove back to George Town, I considered the implications of a letter Mrs Gao had shown me. Su Ling's mother was alive and well and living in Kuala Lumpur.

The letter was in Chinese and Mrs Gao wouldn't let me take it, but I saw the postmark. It was stamped with the mark of the General Post Office in Kuala Lumpur and dated five days ago.

Mrs Gao said that her sister was employed but didn't know what she did. She'd always been a personal assistant, so that was her best guess. That didn't give me much to go on, but worse was to come. Apparently she had changed her name and Mrs Gao didn't know it.

She wrote that she often thought about Su Ling and wanted them to be together but was afraid of Andrew Yipp and his henchmen. If he found her, he'd kill her.

"So you must be very careful," Mrs Gao implored me. "Perhaps it would be better for you to explain to Su Ling rather than locate her mother."

I was still wondering what the right course of action was when I jogged up the steps of the hotel. And then I almost missed a step, because standing just inside the revolving doors was the reporter, Hannah Quinn.

"You're back," she said, holding out her hand.

"You're still here."

"You've not forgiven me," she said, sensing the coolness in my handshake.

"Should I?"

"I apologize. Sincerely, I mean."

I nodded.

"Can we talk?" She pointed to a couple of chairs and implored me with her eyes.

As we both sat, I said, "I'm not discussing the previous situation."

"The ghost stories or the potential beasting?"

I started to rise but she held my arm.

She said, "I'm not interested in that anymore. I've found another story."

"You have? Not involving the army?"

"Don't worry. It's nothing to do with Minden Barracks. This is different. This is on the mainland."

I waited for her to elaborate.

Eventually she said, "I'll trade you. Spend the afternoon with me and I'll show you what I'm investigating."

"And the trade?" I asked.

"I'll tell you what I discovered about the bomoh."

"Why?"

"Because you'll want to know about the witch doctor."

"No. I meant why me? Why do you want me to go with you?"

"Two reasons," she said with a twinkle in her eye. "One, I like you, and two, I need protection. Malaya's not safe and you carry a gun."

We caught the ferry, and after Perai, we took Route One, following the rail line south. As I drove, I said, "So tell me about the bomoh."

"Not before you tell me something personal about yourself."

"Really?" I said with disbelief.

"OK," she said with a laugh in her voice. "What's your favourite book?"

"I don't read much."

"As a kid?"

"*The Three Musketeers.*"

"Ah, very you: camaraderie and sticking to your principles in the face of adversity."

"And *The Count of Monte Cristo.*"

"Another Dumas story. A classic with many themes: revenge, justice, forgiveness, faith and death."

I laughed. A journalist, a literary expert. "Just ripping yarns," I said. "Good adventure stories like *Treasure Island.*"

"Which is a story of self-discovery," she said seriously. "And the character of Long John Silver challenges conventional views of morality. Is he bad or is he good?"

"I just read it as a story about pirates, treasure maps and tropical islands. I'm glad I didn't know you back then, you'd have killed my naïve enthusiasm."

She laughed. "All right, they're just good adventure stories."

"Thanks."

"I have another story for you. One about fear and control."

We turned left off the main road and then left again. The roads became rutted as dark jungle passed on either side, broken only by the occasional clearing and small kampongs.

"I'm listening," I prompted.

"I found the bomoh. I didn't speak to him, but he has a man who arranges appointments—an agent, would you believe? I spoke to him. The witch doctor's name is Putih Mati."

"White Death?" I knew the Malay word for dead from one of the islands close to Singapore: Pulau Blakang Mati, which was interpreted by many locals to mean Back Island of Death. Legends told of warrior spirits there, but it was also said that the original settlers were found dead in mass graves on the small island.

"It can mean death or dead," Hannah said. "I got a meeting with the agent on the basis of a blessing for my marriage—which they do as well. Apparently it's about making sure your spirit ancestors are happy, otherwise they can cause problems later."

"You're getting married?"

She laughed again. "No! It was just my story to get a meeting, and once he saw the colour of my money he didn't mind my questions."

I looked over at her. She sat, relaxed, one arm resting on the passenger door. "What were your questions?"

"I asked him about the exorcisms at the barracks. I asked him about the ghosts around the motor pool and in the Royal Engineers' huts."

"OK?"

"It took a lot of persuasion but eventually he said Putih Mati wasn't impressed. He said that there weren't any ghosts."

"But he performed the exorcism anyway?"

"Because of the money. He said the sergeant wanted to convince the men of an evil presence. He said the sergeant told him what to do. And afterwards he gave each man a talisman to ward off the evil—only the sergeant had provided them. They had no special powers."

As she spoke I was thinking motor pool sergeant or Royal Engineer sergeant: Walsh or Cox?

"Which one?" I asked.

"He didn't know."

"Interesting," I said as we drove, and I continued thinking.

"We're here," Hannah said as we drove into a village. "The temple. Stop outside the temple."

We got out and she pointed at the building. Hindu, I guessed, but less elaborate than many. There was colourful material dangled outside rather than carvings of gods and animals. I looked around and saw a handful of shophouses along the road and a smattering of huts.

"Where's the story?"

"The temple," she said. "Let's go inside."

We removed our shoes and stepped into a large white room. I saw a screen at the far end and there were wooden statues. Two men approached us, hands together in prayer, and bowed.

Hannah greeted them in Malay and they responded. She spoke to them for a moment before turning to me.

"The temple has been burgled," she said. "Anything precious has been taken—anything of value: a little gold and silver but also ivory and alabaster icons."

"Who by?" I asked.

"They don't know, but I've heard this is going on all over the region, and this will be my story."

THIRTY-ONE

Hannah interviewed both the men, who she explained were religious elders. Afterwards, we were taken to a hut close by and met a woman who had first discovered the burglary.

Hannah spoke to her for almost half an hour and I figured she was getting background details and personal information for the human interest. When she was done she told me there were three other temples within an hour's drive and they had been burgled as well.

"What did you learn?" I asked as we drove through the jungle, a syncopation of light and dark as bright patches of sunlight broke through the trees.

"It happened three nights ago during darkness," she said, shielding her eyes from sudden brilliance. "No one saw anything, although the woman thinks she heard a truck but thought nothing of it. It's not unusual for vehicles go through there at night, although she said it sounded heavy. Possibly a diesel."

The next temple also looked Hindu, with a more typical conical roof with sculptures all around. There was no one inside, and after a quick glance around, we drove another half mile to the next village. Here we heard the same story. A vehicle at night, probably a truck, and the theft of anything valuable and some things

173

that weren't. Two of the external statues had been chiselled off and one man told us of urine found against a statue of Lord Shiva.

"Same night," Hannah said.

"They were bolder here," I said in the jeep as we discussed the case. "They weren't afraid to make a noise and they wanted to make a statement. Pissing is an animalistic instinct, a marking of territory."

"They aren't Hindus," Hannah said.

"No," I agreed, "they aren't. Doesn't say what they are though. This could be about desecration more than theft. The limited damage could mean they're religious. Of course, Muslims and Hindus have history."

We drove again and put the roof up as the clouds opened. The jeep slid on the muddy track that was rapidly turning into a stream.

"Is this a ten-minute downpour, Mr Weatherman?" she asked.

"I hope so."

Because of the poor vision, I missed a fork in the road and the wheels spun and skidded as I turned. I bumped into ruts, deep and long.

"What is it?" Hannah asked as I opened the door to look out. Then I stepped out into the rain and took a few paces before getting back in.

"Tyre marks," I said, slamming the door shut and shaking water from my head. "A fairly heavy vehicle came this way and did the same as me: missed the turn."

We got back on the track and journeyed another five miles to the fourth temple, again Hindu. It appeared to be a pattern, although Hannah told me most temples around here were Hindu.

The rain stopped and we got out. People were sheltering in the temple and a shed beside it, although when I could see beyond the people, I saw a cow and newborn calf being treated with reverence. The temple was similar to the second, with a frieze of gods and animals outside, but also bright-coloured streamers. These also festooned the cowshed.

We were greeted and given bread. Hannah asked questions and quickly nodded to me. "Another one. Same night."

Moving from villager to villager, she asked questions and took notes. I watched steam rise all around as the sun rapidly warmed the earth. It swirled above the temple roof, giving the effect of smoke from a fire.

Removing my shoes, I went inside and received polite bows and thoughtful faces. As I circled the prayer room I again noticed damage to statues and missing statues, and I was beside by a decapitated one when I realized a man was standing at my shoulder.

"You are army?" the man said. Dressed in a wraparound sheet, he could have been a priest. His dark skin was wrinkled with a hundred years of thought and maybe pain.

"No," I said.

The man nodded like he didn't believe me. A large white man out here, miles away from a city? I didn't look like a worker or a plantation owner. So what was I?

I said, "I used to be in the army."

He smiled. "I see."

"What do you see?"

"The army did this," he said. "This damage. This theft."

"You have evidence?"

"I saw them. It was dark, but I saw them. One man had a rifle. The others left army boot marks in the earth."

"An army, but only one man had a gun?"

175

Watery eyes looked at me as though my question was unreasonable.

I said, "Could they have been Chinese terrorists? Bandits?"

"They were big," he said. "Like you. I saw silhouettes, so I know they were big. Chinese soldiers are small."

I nodded. "And have you seen any British soldiers during the day?" I asked.

"Out here?"

I nodded again.

"Not for a long time. I saw the army pass through a few years ago. Lots of trucks and Land Rovers like yours outside." He studied me again. "Are you police?"

"No," I said.

"Shame," he said. "Police have not investigated. Army have not investigated."

And then he moved faster than appeared reasonable for his age. He took hold of my arm with a vice-like grip. "Please," he implored with moist eyes, "find out who did this and stop them."

THIRTY-TWO

Hannah interviewed more villagers before we set off again.

As we drove the lanes through the jungle she said, "It seems ridiculous."

"What does?"

"These are poor people and yet there is wealth in their places of worship—or at least would be if it hadn't been stolen. These people go without so that a statue can have a golden rod or a silver skull cap."

"Same the world over," I said. "Always has been. The more you give relative to your earnings, the more worthy you are. Same in England."

"I guess," she said. "But it's not as extreme. There's real poverty here. It's what makes the thefts so much more painful."

"For them."

"Me as well."

We were lost in our thoughts and back on the main drag west before she spoke again.

"Who's doing it?" she asked.

I said nothing and focused on the road.

She said, "It can't be someone religious."

"Of course it can. Religious wars are as old as mankind—and it doesn't matter how similar the beliefs are. Sometimes it's about the way you worship."

She said, "Temples throughout the region have been raided irrespective of denomination. We've seen Hindu temples here but I've heard it's also Muslim and Buddhist."

We joined Route One and met more traffic. Diesel lorries carrying coal or ore or timber rumbled past.

"A lorry at night," she said. "Does that make sense?"

"The dark makes sense."

"I mean the lorry. Wouldn't it be better to be in and out stealthily? A lorry doesn't make sense."

"Unless that's all you have," I said.

I felt her eyes bore into me. "D'you have a theory?"

I did. Ever since I'd missed the turn in the rain and seen the tyre marks in the mud. A vehicle, reasonably long, like a lorry. Most of the trucks we saw coming the other way could have fit that description but most were also too heavy and difficult to turn, like we had been. And then there were the tyre marks. Not distinct, but clear enough despite being a few days old—because nothing else had driven over that mud until I did.

"No," I said. "But you have your story, right? It's about the thefts and the people rather than the lorry."

She said nothing for a moment. I heard her breathe out, more of a huff than a normal breath. Then she said what was on her mind.

"I can't believe it."

"What?"

"I thought you were better. I thought you were an investigator. I thought you'd want to know the truth."

I didn't respond until we'd bumped onto the ferry at Perai and parked. I said, "I have a job to do."

"What's that?"

She didn't know about the second death, didn't know I was investigating that, and Dexter wanted it to stay that way. Hannah was a reporter, and two suspicious deaths at the base were more interesting than some stolen icons. At least that was what I thought.

"More babysitting work for the CO," I said, trying to sound bored.

"Like I said,"—she climbed out and slammed the door—"I thought you were better than that. I respected you the first time we met."

I stayed in the jeep and watched her march away. Apart from a handful of crew, I was the only one below decks. The on-ramp clanged shut and chains rattled and the giant engines strained as we pulled away. The air thickened and the steel hull set into a regular vibration. I closed my eyes and let the cogs in my mind turn in time to the strange rhythm.

Hannah didn't return when we docked in George Town and I think I saw her in the crowd leaving the terminal.

Call me a coward, but I drove the other way, along the harbour and the warehouses. I passed Souter and Hancock Shipping Company's office, where I'd met Dr Suleiman, and I must have passed another twenty before I saw something that caught my attention. It was the name on the board across the front of an old warehouse. Or rather, it was the faded name that had been painted over. Gao Carpets. The business that Su Ling's aunt's husband had owned.

I don't know why, but I stopped outside. Call it an investigator's instinct or curiosity. I went inside and saw a busy operation. Not carpets, but bamboo furniture.

I nodded to a few men in blue overalls. They showed no real interest but then one called out in Chinese and a Chinese man appeared from an office. The boss. He had long grey hair and wore a threadbare Western-looking suit, probably second-hand. Or maybe he only owned one suit and had been wearing it for the last thirty years.

"Help you?" he said in clear English. "Are you buying?"

"Just browsing," I said, and he frowned.

"Browsing and then buying?"

I said, "This used to be Gao Carpets?"

"Yes," he said, suddenly suspicious.

I said, "I'm not police or Customs. I'm just interested."

"Ah," he said, and I saw that my guess had been correct. He had something to hide, but then I figured most of such businesses did. Chip away at the veneer enough and you'd find some illegality, probably dodging tax somehow or maybe employing people illegally. Did the wharves here have the same union rules that we had in Singapore? Were they effectively run by secret societies? I didn't know.

I continued: "I'm just interested in the old business."

"Yes," he said expectantly, like people do when they have information rather than just understanding.

"Were you here then?" I asked.

"I worked here," he said. "Much younger then and my suit much newer."

"What happened?"

"It has been cleaned too many times," he said with a knowing grin. "But you don't mean my suit, do you?"

"No. What happened to the business?"

"It was never good," he said. "I learned how not to run a business from Mr Gao. And then there was the trouble."

"The trouble?"

"I don't know the detail, but one night Mr Gao found someone here and the man attacked him. And he died."

"Mr Gao?"

"No... well yes, but not straight away. Mr Gao managed to beat the other man in a knife fight. The other man died straight away. Mr Gao died a week or so later from his injuries. He had been stabbed in the gut and got infected."

"Nasty way to die," I said. "Who was the other man?"

"I don't know. A stranger."

"Why did they fight?"

The long-haired guy shrugged, and thin, shiny patches on his shoulders caught the lights. "Perhaps he was here to steal some carpets. Or perhaps he was owed money. I don't know, I'm afraid. Why did you say you are interested?"

"I know the family."

"Ah," he said.

"So this was when?"

"December 1945."

"Did Mrs Gao not take over the business?"

"A woman?" He scoffed and then saw that I'd been serious. "It was a bad business and she had no interest."

I remembered that Dr Suleiman had said something about Mr Gao being a bad businessman and this guy had confirmed the carpets business was bad.

I said, "So you took over."

"I sold the wares." He looked at me at first suspiciously and then with a glint in his eye. I figured this was the dodgy part of his transaction and he was proud of it although still suspicious of me. He continued: "But I don't owe Mrs Gao anything. And even if I did, then it was too long ago. I hope you aren't here to cause trouble."

At this point I realized there were four men in blue overalls closing in, listening, waiting in case their boss needed help.

I forced a laugh. "No trouble. Just interested." The four men relaxed. "One final thing," I said. "How did Gao make his money? What business was he in before carpets?"

"He never said." The guy shrugged. "Made it before he set up here. Now, before you go, let me tell you about the future of affordable furniture…"

THIRTY-THREE

The story of Su Ling's family was a sad one. She'd never known her father and it was possible he'd been killed in the war. Her mother had run away, leaving her when she was eleven. Mr Gao, her uncle, had been killed in Penang by a stranger and her grandfather had been executed as an informer by the Japanese. And her grandmother had died shortly afterwards. At least Su Ling's aunt and mother were still alive, although Miao Wei Yong was on the run after stealing from Andrew Yipp, who now had Su Ling. He was both her guardian and captor it seemed to me.

But this wasn't my primary concern at the moment. I needed to confirm my suspicions about the temple thefts and then talk to Jim Dexter. I had bad news.

I went over to the motor pool and looked for Sergeant Walsh. "Not available," I was told by a corporal.

"Well, he'd better make himself available," I said tersely.

"Sorry, sir, but I mean he's not here."

"Right then, you'll have to do. I want to see the records."

"The records?" The corporal looked uncomfortable.

"All vehicle movements over the past week."

"Why?"

"Because I want to see them," I snapped. He hesitated, and I could almost hear his mind processing the pros and cons, maybe wondering what his boss would want, maybe questioning whether my authority stretched this far. "Now!" I added, to help him make the right decision.

"Of course," he said without conviction, and he led me into the office, where he pulled a file. It had all the vehicles signed out and back in. Names, departments and destinations. The corporal stood to one side but watched closely.

"Perfect," I said as I flipped the folder closed.

"What were you looking for?"

I said, "Where's the sergeant?"

"I think he's in town."

"How did he get there?"

"Land Rover."

I pointed to the register. "He hasn't signed anything out."

The corporal shrugged, looked confused. "Well, he's the boss, isn't he?"

"Walsh doesn't sign his transport in and out?"

"No, sir. He doesn't—"

If he was going to say anything further, I didn't hear it. I walked out of the office and out of the motor pool compound.

Jim Dexter was in the corridor outside his office as I approached. He suggested we catch up in the officers' mess, but I told him we needed to talk in private.

"You've learned something about Private Reeder's death?" he asked.

"Not yet. Let's sit down, Jim."

"Why?" he said, but took one of his armchairs. I sat close and leaned in.

184

"I think you have a problem." I took a breath. "I've been over on the mainland driving around with the reporter."

"What the hell? Miss Quinn's still here? Don't tell me she knows about the second death."

I raised a placatory hand. "Not so far as I'm aware."

"Then what—?"

"She's now writing a piece on the thefts from temples."

He nodded, but there was still uncertainty in his voice. "I've heard about them."

"We followed a route between temples and I missed a turn. I saw tyre tracks."

"And?"

"People reported a diesel engine and possibly a lorry. The tyre tracks looked army to me."

"They could be any—"

"Right, they could be anything, but I'd lay a bet on them being from a Bedford. More than a tonne, less than two. I paced out the front and rear wheel tracks. Smaller than a Bedford RL."

He smiled but there was no humour in it. "Bedford Fifteen hundred." The small army troop carrier.

"Right," I said. "I went over to the motor pool and checked the records. There were four Bedfords out at the time although none of them were anywhere near."

"So not one of ours."

"But it doesn't mean they didn't divert. There's no tracking. There's nothing to say they didn't go to those villages at night. But there's a bigger issue."

He leaned forward and waited.

I said, "The motor pool sergeant takes vehicles out and no one keeps a record. He's off the books."

"Shit," he said.

"It could be him," I said. "Probably a few mates with him. At least three of them I figure. A driver and two of them to remove the items."

Dexter shook his head, maybe struggling to process the idea. "So they're driving to temples, stealing stuff and then... what?"

"I don't know."

"And how is it connected to the deaths of Reeder and Tanner?"

"I don't know," I repeated.

"But you have an idea. I know you, Ash."

"I have a feeling, that's all. Something's going on. Two men are dead and the motor pool sergeant behaves suspiciously."

"I could raid the garage and their bunkhouse."

"You won't find anything," I said, shaking my head. "If I'm right then they wouldn't be so foolish. They'll be doing something with the stuff they steal."

Dexter tapped two fingers on his lips as he thought, before saying, "You're right, we have nothing, just your suspicion and circumstantial evidence. Keep the pressure up. Work on the suspicious deaths and find out about those thefts."

THIRTY-FOUR

That's what I intended. I just wanted to let Dexter know what I suspected so that there would be no surprises.

I didn't see the reporter that evening at the hotel, nor at breakfast in the morning.

On the way to the barracks I went into the motor pool and was told that Sergeant Walsh was out again.

I could have waited there or played the covert surveillance game: sat and watched the motor pool from somewhere comfortable. Instead, I got a folding chair and propped it in the shade by the back of the hospital. From there I had sight of the western end of the base—the QM's office and armoury to my right, the bunkhouses straight ahead, rubber trees and then woods. To my right was the hedge and the main road beyond. I was close to the path that cut through to the main road and the entrance to the motor pool.

I had a good view. More importantly, people could see me.

I liked the idea of Sergeant Cooper looking out of his window and seeing me across the way. I didn't like the whole Number of the Beast and beastings thing. I liked it that people in the motor pool could see me too. I didn't know if any of it fit in or how, but just in case, I sat there and hoped someone felt uncomfortable.

The CO's man brought me sandwiches and drinks to keep me going. Then, just before two in the afternoon, a jeep came up the road from George Town and turned through the motor pool gates. Sergeant Walsh got out. The corporal I'd spoken to earlier—at least it looked like him from the distance—ran over as Walsh jumped out. Then they both looked in my direction. Yes, I was sure it was the corporal informing his boss of my interest.

I waited ten minutes, giving Walsh the opportunity to approach me. When he didn't reappear from the motor pool's office, I levered myself out of the chair and marched down the track, crossed the road and went into the compound.

Walsh was sitting at his desk and I was sure he was waiting for me. He had papers in front of him, but he didn't appear to be reading.

I shut the door heavily and he raised his head like he was surprised to see me.

I said, "Where were you four nights ago, Walsh?"

"Sleeping," he said, showing no interest as to why I'd ask.

"Before you were sleeping?"

"I don't know. Usual day, I suppose. Why four nights ago?"

"Did you take a Bedford out?"

His eyes narrowed a touch. "No."

"Do you have proof?"

"Why should I need proof?"

"You don't keep records of when you take vehicles out."

"Because I don't need to," he said. I saw a muscle in his jaw twitch and figured he was suppressing annoyance.

I said, "I want to know your movements of Monday June 1st."

"Four days ago?" He responded. Delaying with a question I thought.

"You need an alibi."

"For what?"

"That you were here and not out in a fifteen hundred weight."

He sighed and wiped his sweaty thick neck. "Fine I'll talk to the men and get a few statements, but tell me why first."

"It's possible that a Bedford truck has been involved in a crime."

"One of mine?" He looked alarmed. "I'll do what I can to help, but I assure you that it's nothing to do with me!"

"Fine," I said. "I may take you up on that offer. In the meantime you give me names and I get their statements."

"How many names?"

I thought about what I'd said to Dexter. At least three men. That meant Walsh and two others. But it could be many more. The whole damn motor pool could be in on it. "Three," I said. "At least two of them need to be from another unit."

"Fine," he said, and scribbled three names on a piece of paper before pushing it across the desk at me. Two corporals and a sergeant. I recognized the latter: Sergeant Cox, from the Royal Engineers.

"What's your connection with Cox?" I asked.

"We're both in the army." He chuckled. "Sorry, I couldn't resist. We drink together." He laughed again. "Bugger, is there a law against fraternizing with a sapper now?"

"And the other two?"

"I wasn't drinking with them. You've got Corporal Mackenzie—the soldier you spoke to earlier—and Corporal Rizzolo."

"Is Rizzolo one of yours too?"

He raised his eyebrows and smiled. "No. He's infantry. One of the last men who saw me that night when I came back with Sergeant Cox. Thought I'd give you another one from outside my bunch so you believe me."

I nodded, counted to ten, then said, "Tell me about Tanner and Reeder," like I knew something.

"You asked me about them yesterday. Both infantry. Both dead," he said. "Nothing changed there."

"Tell me about their connection to you?" I continued with my false confidence.

"None." He squinted at me, thinking. "Is this about them? Monday was after Tanner died and before Reeder was found dead on Wednesday. But you're asking about Monday night..."

I didn't comment. This guy could be cocky and I liked that he couldn't second guess me.

He looked at me for a long time with neither of us saying anything.

"Don't leave this office," I said eventually. "I'm going to have a chat with your alibis and I don't want you moving until I'm done. Understood?"

"Don't take too long over it."

I winked. "It'll take as long as it takes."

The motor pool corporal was lurking around outside and took just a few minutes to confirm Walsh's story. No surprise there. Although he said that Walsh didn't drive the Bedfords. When he took a vehicle out it was always a jeep.

Of course, there was no proof backing up that statement, although I took a mental note in case I could check it later.

Leaving the motor pool, I trekked over to the Royal Engineer's hut and found Sergeant Stewart Cox inside. In fact, all his men were inside. I'd have expected them to be lounging, chatting, playing cards, but they were standing, and everyone's head turned to look at me.

"Officer on deck," he said in his north-east accent. The other men suppressed chuckles, although I sensed discomfort in some of their eyes. I was used to that. They undoubtedly knew I was an ex-MP, and MPs weren't to be trusted by the rank and file.

I nodded to the door. "Let's talk outside, Sarge."

"What's it about?"

I turned and left the room. Behind me I heard his chair scrape against the wooden boards as he pushed away.

"What?" he said when he joined me.

"Last Monday," I said. "Where were you?"

"Monday? What time?"

"Start where you like."

"We'd been mending a section of road—"

"Where?" I interrupted.

"East of Bandar Baharu."

I blinked. "Where exactly."

"I don't know the name, but I can show you on a map."

"Near Serdang?"

"Before Serdang... No wait, sorry, that was Sunday not Monday."

Damn! The temples had been in that area but burgled on the following night.

"Where were you on Monday 1st then?"

"Back here. Had a day off." He nodded. "We have detailed work schedules if you want the evidence."

"I'd like to see those."

"I'll get them to you in the morning if that's OK?"

"So tell me about Monday."

"Took it easy all day. Stayed on the island. In the evening I ate in the mess with the guys and then headed into town."

"On your own?"

"No, just me and Shunter."

"Shunter?"

"Sergeant Walsh," he said. "Sorry, it's his nickname. Anyway, we went for a drink as I recall."

"Where?"

"Penny Black. It's a pub in George Town."

"And?" I prompted.

"And then we came back."

"What time?"

He shrugged. "I don't know. Maybe eleven. Maybe later. He was as pissed as a newt. Can't hold his liquor, you know. Wait... Monday? No we picked up a couple of girls"—he laughed—"Now I remember. He was too pissed to... you know what. Wasted his money, but I bet he can't remember or is too embarrassed to tell you. He didn't tell you about that, did he?" Cox was grinning now, enjoying the conversation.

I said, "What were the girls' names?"

He laughed again. "You're joking, right? I didn't ask mine and I'm pretty sure Shunter can't remember his."

I had Corporal Rizzolo meet me in the mess hall. He was a twitchy young kid, but then again many of the men were.

He said, "Yeah, I saw Sergeant Walsh on Monday night. He was pissed as a newt."

I looked at him hard. "Do you always remember everyone you see each day?"

For a second I thought he was going to crack but then he smiled. "No," he said. "I was on duty that night and he tried to bum a ciggy off me. That's why I remember—a sarge asking me for a ciggy. Know what I mean?"

I thanked him and hung around the mess hall for a while, drinking tea and catching men's eyes, hoping someone would approach me and tell me something useful. No one did. While I was there, I saw the Royal Engineers pass the window, heading for the main gate I guessed. That's why they'd all been standing. They were getting ready to go out. When I decided Sergeant Shunter Walsh had waited long enough, I trekked back to the motor pool.

Walsh had his feet up on the desk, arms behind his head when I opened his office door.

"OK?" I said.

"Of course." He grinned.

"For now." I paused, hoping to see his relaxed veneer change. It didn't. I said, "I'm still not convinced you aren't connected."

"To what?" he said, lifting his legs and rocking back to a seated position.

I didn't answer, raised an eyebrow like I knew something.

"You know nothing," he finally said.

"Like what?"

"You're all over the place. You're asking about two deaths that might have been and probably were just accidents and now you're also asking about my movements and the trucks."

I said, "Tell me about the talisman."

"What talisman?"

"For protection from the ghosts. I was told the witch doctor gave the men a talisman each."

"Oh yes. I've seen some of the men wearing something to ward off the ghouls and ghosties." He laughed. "I know I played along with it for that cute reporter—and you, yesterday—but I don't really believe in ghosts."

I said, "You *played along*? This is serious. Two men are dead!"

His demeanour changed like he was taking in the seriousness and potential consequences.

I said, "Why did you get a witch doctor to perform an exorcism?"

"For everyone else's sake." He shrugged. "But also for fun. OK, I admit it, I enjoy the fact the kids are scared of ghosts."

I fixed him with a glare. "I'll ask you one more time, Sergeant. Did you have anything to do with Tanner or Reeder's deaths?"

"No! I didn't witness either and I didn't have anything to do with them."

"Do you think their deaths had anything to do with the curse?"

"That's what people say."

"But what do you think?"

He looked at me and I could almost see his mind working behind his blue eyes. He sniffed and rubbed his nose and I figured he'd come to a conclusion.

"Yes?" I prompted.

He breathed out. "Maybe I shouldn't tell you this, but I suspect this whole thing isn't about spooks; it's about drugs. Bad drugs. Speak to Major Dawson. Ask Dawson about the morphine."

THIRTY-FIVE

Major Dawson lived in married quarters off base and he'd gone home for the evening. Just because Walsh directed me to the major, it didn't mean that I was going to disturb his private time.

I walked back to the hotel, breathing in warm air that smelled of grass and half listening to the hum of the cicadas. I was thinking, trying to piece it all together: bad spirit and morphine; two infantrymen dead; a motor pool sergeant who didn't keep track of his use of vehicles; thefts from temples, and beasting. Were they connected, and how was I going to make progress?

Hannah was sitting in the foyer as I entered the hotel. She stood and stepped towards me.

"Sorry," she said. "I expected more from you."

"Is that an apology?" I said. "It sounds like half of one."

"It's supposed to be a full apology." She held out her hand and it felt small and cool in mine. "If you change your mind about helping me, let me know. Have you eaten dinner?"

Her switch of subject took me by surprise.

Because of my hesitation, she added: "I'm buying."

"I've eaten," I lied. "And I have something I need to do."

I bade her good evening and headed back outside. Whether she realized I'd just come in and gone straight out again, I don't know. I didn't really have anything urgent on my mind but I had an idea for killing an hour or so. It would also be a good distraction from what was going on at the barracks.

I walked through the town to the main police station on Jalang Penang, a long white building, white stone and lots of glass windows. The entrance was midway along the hundred-yard stretch and, as I entered, I realized this was a police barracks and headquarters. I asked for the duty officer and met a captain who looked cautiously at me until I flashed my Singapore ID.

"How can I help you, Captain Carter?" he asked.

"I'm interested in what happened to Mr Gao?"

"Mr Gao?"

I told him the story that I'd been told by the Chinese guy with the long grey hair at the bamboo furniture warehouse. "December 1945," I added.

"After the occupation." The captain nodded and showed me to a room, left me with a glass of tepid water and promised to dig out the details. He returned sooner than I anticipated but with a downcast expression.

"There's a file but the documents must have been archived," he said. "They're not here."

"Can you get it? I can come back another day."

Now he smiled. "Actually I can probably do better. Detective Inspector Noble would like to meet you. He's retired now, but it was his case and he's on his way. He'll be here in about twenty minutes."

The captain went on to explain that Noble had left a note in the empty file asking to be contacted should anyone enquire about the case.

I was intrigued. Why would a retired detective be so keen to talk to me?

Rather than wait in the stuffy room, I killed the time by finding a street vendor and buying a plate of noodles. I was unsure what I was getting but it tasted like chicken and made me realize just how hungry I'd been. After a second portion and a happy vendor, I went back into the police station.

Inspector Noble was waiting in the room for me. He stood up, a ramrod back and strong chin. His white hair needed a trim as did the bushy eyebrows that shaded his eyes.

"You're thinking I'm too old to have been a detective in 1945," he said.

I shook his offered hand. It was strong, belying his age that I guessed to be between seventy and eighty.

"I was the inspector here before the occupation. Thirty years, man and boy," he said. "I retired just before the Japanese came, but I returned as soon as I could. Love it here, you see?"

I nodded.

He looked like he was expecting me to comment, but then continued. "We needed someone to take charge, so I stepped in for a while. My swansong, just four more years."

"And the Gao case?"

"Has always bothered me. You know how it is? A case that you can't quite understand. It didn't make sense. That's why I put a note in the file—in case anything came up that would put an old man's mind at rest."

"Tell me about it," I said.

"It was December 15th. We got a call about a fight at Gao's warehouse and four officers were deployed. Only they didn't find a fight when they arrived. It was all over. A man was dead, and the owner, Mr Gao, was injured.

Mortally as it turned out. He had been stabbed in the stomach and it got infected. He died a week later."

I said, "What couldn't you understand?"

He peered at me through his eyebrows, like an admonishment for the interruption. "Mr Gao said that he was working late in his office when a stranger appeared. The man had a knife and attacked Mr Gao. He said he struck the other man with a bamboo pole, which knocked him to the ground. The man jumped up, lunged and stabbed Mr Gao. Almost immediately Gao managed to strike the stranger again, which caused him to fall off the balcony outside the office. The coroner said the impact killed the man immediately, fractured his skull."

"It sounds reasonable," I said.

"It bothers me that I couldn't identify the stranger," Noble said. "What was his motivation for attacking Gao? Gao said it was random, said there was no demand for money. Then why?"

"It happens," I said. "Had the stranger been drinking?"

"No evidence of it." Noble sighed. "But that's not what bothered me the most. You see, I think Mr Gao was lying. I think more went on than he admitted."

"Like what?"

"Firstly, I established that Gao rarely worked late, and when he did, there was usually someone else there. However, that night he'd insisted on working alone and sent his staff away."

"So you think he may have known the other man was coming?"

"Possibly, but it's more than that. You see, Gao had other injuries, cuts on his body and marks on his wrists like he'd been tied up."

"Tortured?" I asked.

"Tortured," he said, nodding sagely. "But Gao flat refused to discuss it. He stuck to his story with no explanation of the other cuts."

"You suspect the other man tortured him first and somehow Gao managed to escape, managed to push the stranger off the balcony."

"Yes," Noble said. "And I'd like to know why. Just an old man's curiosity. I'd like to know what happened that night and why Gao didn't tell the truth. Can you help me?"

"Not yet," I said, but I was thinking of Andrew Yipp. Torture wasn't beyond him and he had a motive. Su Ling's mother had stolen from him and it was likely that Yipp suspected that the sister and Gao had information, knew where she'd gone.

After a pause I asked, "What can you tell me about the other man?"

"Chinese, about five eight, in his fifties we thought. He had a welt on his face, and at first I thought it was from Gao's bamboo stick, but I was told the mark was old like a scar. And of course he had no papers. That was also suspicious, since straight after the war, everyone still carried ID."

"A tramp?"

"He was wearing a suit. Although it was dirty, he didn't strike me as a hobo."

We talked some more but I gained no new information. Noble's face showed disappointment at learning nothing new but I promised to let him know if I discovered anything. I, on the other hand, had learned of Yipp's reach. I got further confirmation of this in the morning.

* * *

199

I came into the hotel from an early morning run, before the heat and humidity of the day kicked in. The sky had streaks of pink and orange beneath heavy clouds.

The bellboy raised his hand.

"Mr Carter. Telegram and a letter, sir."

He handed me both. The letter was actually an envelope with the Royal Engineers' worksheets. I tucked it under my arm and looked at the telegram.

It was from Li Ping Gao and said, **Please stop or Su Ling will die.**

THIRTY-SIX

Being reasonably well off, Mrs Gao would have a telephone in her home, I figured. I was right. The operator found her number and connected me.

"I received your telegram," I said.

There was a hesitation, and when she spoke, her voice trembled. "Two men visited me last night. They beat me. They threatened my niece. They wanted to know where Miao Wei is hiding." She took a shuddering breath. "I told them nothing. They hurt me but I told them nothing."

"Have you reported it to the police?"

"No police." There was strength in her voice now. "No police. Those men will come back and hurt me more."

"Your message said that Su Ling would die, Mrs Gao. How is that?"

"They said they would kill Su Ling if I didn't tell them where my sister was. I told them I didn't know."

"Why would they—?"

"It was probably just a threat and it will work the other way," she explained. "I know criminals like that. They are thinking they will kill someone so they pretend they will do it if you don't help them. If I had given them what they wanted they would have killed me. Then they would find my sister and kill her and probably kill Su Ling too."

"But you don't know where your sister is exactly."

"No more than I told you. If you find her, she will be killed. Maybe you will be killed too." She paused, possibly thinking. "You should be careful. Perhaps they already know you are asking questions. Perhaps that is why they also came to me. You mustn't tell them anything, Mr Carter. Her life is in danger. Your life is probably in danger too."

I told her to call the police if the men came back. Next time they would be more desperate. The first time could be fishing. If they came back it would be more serious. She wasn't happy but agreed. Again she insisted that I stop asking questions, and I finally agreed—for a while at least.

THIRTY-SEVEN

"How many times must I say I'm sorry?" Hannah asked as she approached me in the lobby.

I said, "I have a job to do. I'm not your chauffeur."

"No, you're not. Will you have breakfast with me?"

I agreed, and after we'd been served, she said, "You think there's a connection, don't you?"

I deliberately took a forkful of food so that I couldn't respond.

She filled the silence. "You're worried that the army is involved in the thefts."

"Why do you say that?"

"The tyre tracks."

I said nothing.

"Can you tell me why you've come back to Penang?"

"No."

"Could it be linked to the thefts?"

I said nothing and felt her eyes boring into me as though she could read my mind.

"I promise I won't use whatever it is."

"Like you promised not to mention beasting?"

She grimaced and nodded. "I apologize for that too."

"You already have, but I can't trust you."

She reached over and touched my arm. "You can," she said, and I was almost convinced.

"I'll tell you what," I said, "give me a list of all the dates and locations of the thefts and—if there's a connection—then I'll share with you. But on one condition."

She nodded eagerly, and for the first time I saw a childlike quality to her.

"You don't use anything about the army without Colonel Dexter's express permission."

Major Dawson was working at the hospital and wouldn't be available until ten o'clock. I took up my seat against the hospital wall and watched the motor pool. Men came and went. I saw a jeep drive away and didn't recognize the passenger or driver.

Hannah had compiled a list of eighteen locations and the date of the thefts. Most were approximate, and she explained that the older ones were harder to confirm. The recent ones, like the night of 1st June, were marked as confirmed.

As I waited, I flicked through the Royal Engineers' worksheets and looked at their activity. I already knew they'd been near the site of the thefts on Sunday 31st.

What I now recognized was a bit of a pattern. Admittedly the Engineers were all over northern Malaya, but all of the thefts occurred in places near where they had worked, although the dates didn't match.

I played back what I knew: Tanner had blown his head off on his birthday, allegedly after being afraid of ghosts in the woods. He'd either dropped the loaded rifle or had shot himself using his toe. Reeder had been the first on the scene and also died in strange circumstances. Reeder had been found at the assault course, implicating Sergeant Brookes, a man who was probably a bully and may have punished both of the deceased on the day before they died.

204

Sergeant Cox of the Royal Engineers had seen Tanner smoking just before he died. However, Tanner's pockets didn't contain a packet of cigarettes. Of course, it was possible that he'd had loose ones. Player's cigarettes also came in large tins, although Tanner had no loose ones on him and there had been no evidence of stubs on the ground where he'd died.

Sergeant Walsh. Where did he fit in, if at all? He was Cox's friend and was his alibi for Monday 1st when the temple near Serdang had been burgled. So they were each other's alibi.

I watched as a squad marched across the parade ground and on into the enclosure. They got into a Bedford lorry and drove out of the base. I got up and headed for the motor pool. Walsh wasn't there but Corporal Mackenzie was. I asked to see who had signed out the lorry and their destination. It was on the island, going out for an exercise in the south.

I also went through the motor pool's records of vehicles and destinations. I checked against a map and saw that some journeys went close to thefts, but there was less of a pattern than for the Engineers.

I hung around for a bit and figuratively kicked a few tyres before returning to my chair.

The clouds had continued to gather since early morning, and by half past nine I figured it would soon rain. I saw men come and go from every hut except the Royal Engineers. I watched squads square-bashing on the parade ground and I saw three more jeeps leave the motor pool.

The rain started and quickly went from a smattering to a torrent. I ran inside and found the common room. There was a solitary soldier hunched over, reading at a desk. His intensity suggested he was studying. He briefly glanced up and I recognized him: Colour Sergeant Harper. We exchanged nods.

On the walls were photographs of the squads. Over the top was a board that read: 1st Manchester Company A. Beneath that was their coat of arms and then six photographs labelled Platoon 1 to 6. Each had twenty to thirty men sitting in rows for their formal group photograph. They were on the parade ground, the main building square on behind them.

I found Corporals Reeder and Tanner. Reeder was in 2 Platoon, Tanner in 4. I found myself staring at Tanner. Despite being so small, I could swear he had something around his neck just poking up above his collar. Definitely not acceptable and gone unnoticed.

"How's it going, Captain?" The colour sergeant came up behind me. "Something interesting?"

"I don't know."

"Don't know how it's going or whether it's something interesting?" He chuckled.

"Probably both."

"You've been asking questions about Tony Brookes."

"I have."

"He's a good guy."

I said nothing.

"You questioned him about beasting. I can't believe he'd do that. He can be a bit tough sometimes, but that's all part of the image, isn't it? You get that, right?"

"Has anyone complained to you?"

He looked away, said nothing.

"Colour Sergeant?"

"Sir?"

"Have soldiers complained about Brookes in the past?"

"Yes, but they never pursued it. Nothing serious." He looked concerned at my dubious expression. "Honestly, if there was a pattern or someone complained twice I would have acted, but that's never happened."

I shook my head. It wasn't easy to complain. Maybe it was something for me to raise with Dexter. For now I filed the information away, along with concern that Brookes might be a bully.

I turned back to the photograph and tapped it. "What do you reckon that is?"

Sergeant Harper squinted hard at Tanner's picture for a few beats. "Don't know."

I checked my watch. Almost ten. "Will you still be here in half an hour, Colour?"

"Yes, sir."

"Great. I'll see you then."

I flung a coat over my head and splashed my way across the base to the hospital. Once under cover again, I shook the rain off like a dog and hung the coat by the door. Then I set off to find Dawson.

He looked tired. More than tired. His eyes said exhausted and his bald pate had lost its shine.

"Yes?" he said, although it was less like a question than an acceptance. We were in the basement, cool, where the bodies were kept.

"Tell me about the morphine."

"I've done nothing wrong," he said, although his voice lacked any defiance.

"Tell me."

"You know there's a shortage. The Korean War has been a nightmare for non-combat hospitals, but we still need the medicines, especially morphine."

"And?"

"So I get it through unofficial channels."

"And it's not the same quality," I stated. "It's bad, isn't it? It's this bad spirit people refer to."

"No," he said, and now the defiance was there. "I won't accept that. I wouldn't use a low-grade drug."

"No matter how desperate you were?"

"Why would I?" he asked, and I got the point. He said, "I admit to getting the morphine from unofficial channels but I'll be damned if I admit to negligence— and that's what it would be, Captain. Negligence to administer a poor-quality painkiller."

I let the echo of his raised voice die into silence. Then I spoke softly. "I want to know the source. How are you getting it, where's it coming from?"

"Singapore," he said. "I don't know how it gets on Royal Navy ships, but I get notification that a shipment is coming in and it gets dropped off. Everything looks kosher, like they're official."

"Army medical crates?" I said.

"Yes, but not army, I swear. We aren't getting this stuff in priority over combat zones."

"We?"

"As far as I'm aware, all the bases along the west coast get them. It's been going on for years. There's no problem with the quality, I swear. We'd know if there was."

"I want details and I want samples," I said.

"You'll tell Dexter?"

"Of course I'll tell Dexter, but I think it would be better coming from you first."

"Thank you."

He nodded and I turned to go.

"Captain?"

I turned back.

"I found something in Corporal Reeder's stomach. Undigested and indigestible. Looked like a lump of grass, small and matted, about an inch long, and kind of looks like a figure."

"A figure?"

"You know, like a doll."

I looked into his eyes, processing the information. He waited.

"You've still got Corporal Tanner's belongings?"

"Yes."

"Let's go through them."

He looked unsure. "Why?"

"Let's look."

Dawson took me into a storeroom containing metal shelves and wooden boxes. He reached up and I saw Tanner's name in chalk on the front of one he pulled out.

"These were the clothes he was wearing when he shot himself," Dawson said, tipping the contents onto a bench.

It was his uniform, shirt, shorts, boots, socks and belt plus personal things: a handkerchief, a Timex watch, a wallet and a packet. Not a packet of cigarettes, a well-used pack of playing cards.

"Where are the cigarettes?" I asked.

"None here."

I handled the cards before setting them aside, then I picked up the shorts and put my hands in the pockets. Empty. No surprise, since the cards and other items will have been in his pockets.

I picked up the shirt and felt the breast pockets. The left one had a lump. I fished inside and pulled out a small item on a string.

A necklace.

It had an inch-long figure made of grass. This was what I'd seen in the platoon photographs.

Dawson reached for it. "Damn, the same thing as I found in Reeder's stomach." He sniffed it and handed it back to me to smell.

"Grass," he said. "Only this grass isn't ordinary grass. It's weed. Latin name *cannabis sativa forma indica*, more commonly known as marijuana."

THIRTY-EIGHT

There was a connection between Tanner and Reeder. They both had figures made of marijuana. How did this help me? Was this relevant? Was marijuana widely available at Minden Barracks and the cause of the problems? Perhaps people saw ghosts when under the influence. Perhaps Tanner had been smoking marijuana when he shot himself. Perhaps Reeder had drowned in the pool because of the drug. I'd never smoked the stuff but heard it affected people in different ways.

I grabbed the raincoat and ran back to the main building and common room. I was late but the colour sergeant was still there, studying.

I said, "Are you aware of a marijuana problem on the base, Colour?"

He stood up. "No, sir."

I looked at him hard. "I want the truth now."

"No, sir!" he said. "I'd know about it if the men were smoking reefers."

I said, "Both Tanner and Reeder were in possession of it."

I waited for the sergeant to speak, and he finally said, "I can't explain that."

We both stood there. I was hoping he'd say more but he simply looked expectant, waiting for me.

He broke the silence. "Anything else, sir?"

"Nothing," I started to say, but then a thought struck me. "You assign all the duties, don't you?"

"Of course."

"You decide who does the assault course training and who does patrols, for example."

"Yes."

"You selected Tanner and Reeder for the patrol on the night Tanner died."

"Yes. But the selection is fairly random unless I get requests for certain tasks."

"Like what?" I said, intrigued.

"Like support for other units. Once they learn the ropes and fit in, it's easier than having someone green assigned. Like force protection."

Force protection was an armed support that accompanied an unarmed unit. Like the Royal Engineers, I thought.

"Did either Tanner or Reeder act as force protection for the sappers?"

"Yes," he said. "Both of them. There're just a handful of men that Cox is happy with so I usually assign the same men for him."

Something pinged in the back of my brain.

"Shit," I said.

"What?"

"I saw the Royal Engineers unit leave the base yesterday. Where were they going?"

"Mainland. A bridge repair."

"But they left without transport."

"Really?" He looked surprised, and then realization dawned on him. "They have their own compound, you know? Their equipment and vehicles are off base."

THIRTY-NINE

The Royal Engineers had a secure compound off the main road, half a mile away. The metal fences were locked and I rattled them hard until a dishevelled young soldier came out of a hut to open them.

I looked around at the piles of metal, pipes, wires, sections for Bailey bridges, all the spares I should have expected for a Royal Engineering unit—all the equipment I hadn't seen in the motor pool. I kicked myself for not spotting it before.

There were four vehicles in the yard: an Austin Gantry, the little truck with the beam and pulley sticking out over the cab; a Bedford RL; and a Land Rover.

"Where's Sergeant Cox?" I demanded.

"Out. The whole unit's out."

I pointed at the four vehicles. "What else do you have?"

"In total we've got two Austin Gantries, a Scammell, the Land Rover the Bedford RL and two Fifteen hundreds."

"So they've taken the Scammell truck, an Austin Gantry and the Fifteen hundreds?"

"Yes, but just one of the Fifteen hundreds."

I pulled his arm towards the hut and he scuttled along beside me. I said, "Show me on a map where they've gone."

Inside, the kid pointed to a map on the wall. "Here," he said. It was north, close to the border with Thailand, between fifty and sixty miles away. "Middle of nowhere. Repairing a bridge."

I tore the map from the wall and ran back to the barracks where my own jeep was parked. Hannah approached and looked like she'd been in the main building.

"What is it?" she asked, clearly aware of my excitement. "It's about the temples isn't it?"

I hesitated, then I saw Colonel Dexter shutting a door behind him. He waved me over.

"I've got to go," I said, running up to him.

"What have you found out?"

"The Royal Engineers might be linked to the thefts from the temples—"

He opened his mouth, presumably about to ask me what the link was, but then nodded for me to continue.

I said, "Locations of the temples match some of their journeys. And both Tanner and Reeder regularly acted as protection for them."

"Where does Walsh fit in? I thought you were suspicious…?"

"I don't know. Maybe not at all." I glanced back at the jeep, keen to get away.

"Sorry, I'm holding you up," Dexter said. "Go, but take Miss Quinn with you."

I glanced again and she was now climbing into the jeep. Dexter shook his head at me, like he was saying: *Don't ask.*

★ ★ ★

Forty minutes later I was pulling off the ferry and heading for Route One. Instead of going south, I turned left on the road to Thailand.

"So where are we going?" she asked.

I pointed to the map in the footwell between us and she opened it up. I'd marked the route while on the ferry and she now traced it with her finger.

"You can give me directions," I said.

"You compared my list of the thefts with something, didn't you?"

"Royal Engineers' jobs. Not exact, but similar dates and locations. Enough to be suspicious." I didn't mention the protection force or the connection to the two deaths. This was still on a need-to-know basis as far as I was concerned.

As we passed RAF Butterworth, I asked, "How did you persuade the colonel?"

"I promised him what I promised you. Nothing goes to print without his express permission."

"I'm amazed."

She smiled sweetly. "The power of persuasion."

We continued up along Route One, with rice fields all around and the sea to our left.

"Sungai Petani," I said, as we came to a major town and she located it on the map. I continued to drive fast and hard and we met jungle on either side of the road.

She called out the right turn and the wheels met laterite, sending little stones clattering under the wheel arches. Now the jungle was thick and dark, the descending sun warm on my neck.

After five miles I turned left in a valley and the road became a track. I'd spent a few months in Kinta Valley, and following a river through wetlands took me back to that time. Only this lumpy ground with thinly scattered trees and long grass didn't have the scars of industry that I'd seen in Kinta Valley.

I passed kampongs of attap huts where children ran out and waved and dogs gave half-hearted chase. And within ten miles of my destination we came upon a crowd. They were standing outside a temple of yellow ochre and red.

"Oh no!" Hannah said.

I stopped and jumped out, but it was soon clear that these people weren't mourning the theft from their temple. They were gathered around a low flat building to the right of the temple.

We moved through the crowd and I saw that the building was a concrete stable with some kind of ceremony going on inside.

Hannah wasn't by my side and then she caught up. A broad smile lit her face.

"What?"

"The sacred cow," she said, pointing. "This is a Hindu temple and they have a cow. I don't think it's supposed to happen but it's just given birth."

Now I could see the cow and a newborn calf in the stable with it.

"So, no theft."

"Not here," she said. "Not yet."

We continued through foothills. The ground steamed, the hot air was thick and I reached mangroves. A putrid smell like rotten eggs rose up from decaying vegetation in the swamps. Then, as quickly as they had come, the mangroves ended and I was driving beside a river, scrubland either side and then jungle.

"They should be around here," I said.

Then we saw two vehicles heading towards us. A Scammell and an Austin Gantry. The Royal Engineers.

I pulled over. The Scammell went by with three sappers inside. No, wait, two of them were infantry—the protection force guys. I recognized Rizzolo peering at us through the windscreen. Then the Austin Gantry stopped alongside us. It had a single occupant.

"Where's Sergeant Cox?"

"Gone on, sir," the driver said.

"Gone on where?"

"Further upriver—a problem."

"How far?"

He shrugged. "Won't be too far."

"Without protection?" I said thinking of the infantry men in the Scammell.

The driver raised his fingers in a kind of shrug. "His choice."

I thanked the guy and let the heavy truck pull away. The light was fading fast now, partly because of the low sun, partly due to lowering clouds. And I thought I could hear thunder in the mountains. I pulled the roof up and clipped it on then set off north, following the river.

We passed a bridge that I figured had just been repaired, but saw no sign of the Bedford truck or Cox.

Crossing the bridge we continued north, with lakes on both sides and then jungle. The track got thinner and thinner and I wondered where Cox and his team were heading. Then we came to a crossroads and I got out.

Tracks ran every which way. My gut said straight on but the freshest tyre tracks went right.

I went right.

A big mistake.

FORTY

As soon as the road started climbing, I should have turned around. First, rain started pelting the windscreen and roof. Then, as I turned through a bend, Hannah called out.

"Up there!" She pointed ahead where the trees thinned and the higher ground had rocky outcrops with darker patches. There were caves north of Kuala Lumpur that looked similar.

A narrow track cut away towards them and I took it. After a hundred yards it became more of a path and I could drive no further. I looked back and figured we were well hidden from the road. I'm not a great botanist but recognized rhododendron bushes all around.

"What are you thinking?" Hannah asked as I got out into the rain and studied the ground.

"That Cox would need somewhere to hide the stuff. A cave would be ideal and this spot is hidden. There are tyre tracks…"

"But?"

"Hard to tell. Lots of tracks, but I don't think they're army tyres."

I reversed back to the road and continued around the bend. We took two more curves and then Hannah called out again.

"Stop!" she said, and pointed at a hump beside the road. A body.

The stench of decaying flesh hit me. However, it wasn't human.

"Black bear," I said, taking a closer look through the window. Its body had been mutilated, sliced open, and its paws cut off.

"Chinese," she said quietly.

"Chinese?"

"Bear parts, even their bile, is highly prized."

That's when I heard the thunder again, although this time I realized it wasn't natural. An explosion boomed and growled through the hills.

I took out my revolver. "We may have more to deal with here than Cox's men."

I looked up the road. Turn round or keep going?

Ahead was jungle and more jungle. The sun must have set now with the light fading.

I glanced at Hannah, trying to decide. On my own I'd have continued, hoping to find Cox and his crew. But I had Hannah to consider and I didn't know for sure that Cox had come this way.

"Keep going," she said, reading my mind. "I'll drive, you ride shotgun."

Without waiting for an answer, she used the steering wheel to lever herself over me. "Move then!" she said, laughter in her voice.

I squirmed out, over the gearstick and into the passenger seat.

"There are easier ways to switch places."

"But nowhere near the fun," she said. "And it's pissing down."

With a pump of the clutch she jammed the jeep into gear and we were off again.

"Chinese," she said. "What's Sergeant Cox up to? Could he be involved with the bandits as well?"

Surely not, I thought. I knew of people collaborating with the enemy, but Royal Engineers?

We kept on going through the foothills, and I switched on the headlights.

"We should go back," I said. We were a few miles from the river. The driver of the Austin Gantry had said *not far.*

"Just like that?" she said, dismayed without slowing. "I thought you were brave."

I said, "Hannah, there are bandits around here. I may want to trace Cox, but—"

"But discretion is the better part of valour."

"Henry the Fourth part one," I said. "Falstaff."

"Very good—especially for someone who doesn't read much."

"A bit of Shakespeare at—"

Just then our headlights swept over a man coming out of the trees. Despite the poor light, I saw a khaki uniform and a cloth hat. MNLA. Chinese terrorist.

"Hannah!" I yelled. "Spin us around."

I needn't have said anything. She was already reacting, and faster than the bandit, who looked surprised. But Hannah didn't turn in the road. She slammed the jeep into reverse with a whirring crunch that would have made any driving instructor pass out.

The next second we were going backwards, then accelerating. The whole time my eyes were on the Chinese guy—just thirty or so yards away. He was raising his rifle, aiming at us.

I had the window down and my gun out. As I pulled the trigger, my world went into a crazy spin. Hannah had spun the wheel, jerked the handbrake and slammed the gearstick into first.

We stalled.

A bullet pinged off the back of the jeep.

Now facing the wrong way and with the wrong hand, I scooted around on the seat and fired back at the bandit.

Hannah frantically turned the key. It didn't catch.

She tried again and again. More shots ricocheted off metal. I saw more men coming out of the forest.

"Hannah!" I shouted unhelpfully.

On her fourth attempt, the engine spluttered and then roared as she pressed her foot to the floor. The wheels spun in the mud and she fought the steering, first one way and then the other, until she had it under control.

I fired a couple more shots and swivelled back into the seat.

"Bloody shit!" she said.

I was about to say something similar when a loud explosion buffeted my ears. Then I saw the flash up ahead then another further to our right.

"Shit," she said again, and started to slow. "The bridge?"

"Closer," I said, breathless with adrenaline. "Maybe the crossroads."

"We're trapped."

"The caves!" I said. "Lights off and find that turning on the left."

I watched the road behind and in front expecting to see bandits at any moment. Hannah rolled us forward at maybe fifteen miles an hour, not too loud and slow enough to spot the track.

"After this bend," I said, spotting where we'd turned after rejoining the road. Then I saw it. "There!"

Hannah bumped onto the track and eased us as far as we'd been before then stopped, rhododendron bushes pressed in on both sides, the path ahead half the width of the jeep.

I pulled a mac over my head, took a torch from the door well and got out into the rain. With my hand restricting the beam, I walked away and along the path.

Within twenty paces I'd found what I'd prayed for: a spur and dip. Probably more of an animal track than a path, but good enough. Jogging back to Hannah I told her to follow me and drive through the undergrowth. Then at the spur I flashed my light down it and she pushed right, thumping against and over big rocks until she could go no further.

I was already pulling and pushing bushes back into place and trying to disguise the tyre tracks.

Was it good enough? Anyone looking closely, anyone looking for the jeep, would surely find it. But maybe they weren't looking. And if they did…? Well, we'd better not be here.

I helped Hannah out and across the undergrowth. She clutched her little bag like it was precious. Branches and thorns tore at our trousers but we pressed on, out of the spur and along the path. Then we were out in the open. Sharing the rain mac over our heads, we ran up the hill towards where we'd seen the caves. Only we couldn't see them anymore.

"How far?" she whispered, breathing hard.

"Not far," I said, out of hope more than anything. Then the ground changed from grass to rock and we knew we were near the top and the caves.

The first one we saw, I pulled her away from.

"Higher," I said, and we pressed on. I also verged south and finally settled on the fourth opening we found.

"Happy now?" she said as we got out of the rain. Her tone was mocking, and I was glad she'd relaxed from our close encounter with the enemy.

"Never," I said. I hunkered down in the mouth and watched the hillside. The rain stopped and the clouds must have lifted because it became lighter. The moon was forcing its way through somewhere up there. I could just about make out the snaking road we'd left and the track. Which meant I could judge where the jeep was.

Hannah sat beside me.

"The cave goes way back."

I nodded. "No bears?"

She gave a little laugh. "Why not the first cave we came to?"

I was about to say that it was a simple precaution. Anyone coming up the same route would find the first cave. But the words stuck in my throat. Lights appeared at the foot of the hill. Torches.

Then voices. Whispered Chinese voices carrying on the night air.

And then we saw soldiers walking up towards us.

FORTY-ONE

We shrank away from the entrance. No one would see us in the darkness but it was natural instinct. I lay down, edged forward until I could see the slope, and counted twenty-eight men all coming our way.

"What do we do now?" Hannah whispered close beside me. I felt her body tremble.

I edged back and pulled her to her feet, held her for a moment. "We'll be OK."

She nodded, although I'm sure she recognized a platitude when she heard it.

We moved away from the entrance and the cave narrowed. I thought it petered out, but Hannah told me to keep going. It was a squeeze but after a pinch point the cave widened again, although now I was hunched over. We went back a bit further and I stopped.

"We'll be OK," I repeated. "If they come in here they'll have to get through the gap... one at a time. They'll be easy targets."

I could see that she wasn't convinced. The bandits could just shoot through and not come this far, but if she thought that, she didn't say anything.

I sat and waited, my gun ready, her breathing loud beside me.

At least an hour went by and nothing happened. No one came in and we heard no sound. I signalled for Hannah to stay put and squeezed back through the gap. Once on the other side I lay down again and crawled to the entrance.

The bandits had made camp below us in the first two caves. My subconscious had wondered whether Cox and his men could be involved with the bandits somehow. But there was no sign of them.

I saw men patrolling. Sentry duty, not searching. When we'd first seen them park I worried they'd been after us. Now I felt sure they weren't looking for two people and a jeep. This was just a place to spend the night.

I went back to Hannah but she wasn't there.

"Hannah?" I whispered.

Her voice hissed from deeper in the cave.

I scrabbled on hands and knees, also touching the roof of the tunnel so that I didn't bang my head. Then I felt the ceiling rise and I could stand up. The stone was cold and wet here.

"There's a trickle of water back there," she said in the darkness. "I hope it's OK, because I drank some."

She gripped my hand and I sensed that she was calmer now. Then she guided me to wet rocks and I caught a small handful. It had a slight metallic tang, but it was fresh, and after the initial test, I lapped it up and got more.

"They've made camp for the night," I said, my thirst quenched.

She breathed out, relieved.

"It may be safer, but it's too dank here. We'll be OK back there."

She let me lead her all the way to the entrance and lay by my side, peering out into the night, watching for danger. For the first time, I saw a knife in her hand. Protection. Smart.

The bandits hadn't built a fire. They sat in huddles and were probably chatting quietly, although their voices couldn't be heard above the cicadas and distant jungle sounds. I guessed they were eating picked fruit.

Every now and then I saw a guard patrolling an established perimeter.

Through the broken clouds a wan moon rose and cast a weak glow over the slope. The light made it easier for me to watch and I saw that there were three sentries at any one time. They didn't patrol in an organized way, but each had a sector they covered. The one nearest to our cave occasionally came within ten yards. He looked up the slope and along it. As yet, he hadn't looked our way.

Around midnight the guard changed. One headed straight for us. We shrank back to the pinch point.

The guard stood, silhouetted in the cave entrance, but rather than enter, he lit a cigarette. After a long drag he blew out a stream of smoke, repeated the procedure then stubbed out the light.

He moved away.

We both breathed out, waited a minute and then slid back to the opening.

The guard was well away from us now. I realized Hannah was lying on her side, looking at me.

"We could die here," she whispered.

"Where did you learn to drive like that?" I asked, avoiding the discussion.

"Like what?"

"The handbrake turn."

"I failed."

"The jeep's fault, not yours."

"Misspent youth," she said. "My brother taught me."

"Glad he did."

In the faint light I saw her smile.

"Thanks," she said. "You know, you aren't too bad."

That surprised me.

She continued, "I thought you were formal—hard work, since you don't share anything personal—but you have a caring side."

"I thought the same about you," I said, and she laughed quietly then stopped.

"You changed the subject when I said we could die here."

"There's no point in worrying about it."

"But we could."

"Yes, we could."

The silence grew and then I heard her praying softly.

When she stopped, she said, "Do you believe in God? In everlasting life?"

"I believe in something more than this, although I'm not sure what it is or that I could describe it. I figure you only find out afterwards."

"You're very logical, aren't you?"

"Science teaches you to be rational. Einstein, despite being a Jew, doesn't believe in God. However, have you heard of Pascal's Wager?"

"No." She seemed genuinely interested.

"He was a French philosopher and mathematician who posited that it was better to believe in God than not. The probability works in your favour if you believe. Because if you don't and there is a God then you lose. If you believe and there isn't then you'd have lost anyway."

"Better to be a mathematician than a scientist then," she said.

I didn't bother explaining that Pascal was also a physicist. Instead I glanced at the knife—a decent folding pocket knife, brown handle and four-inch blade—now lying on the ground by her hand.

"I knew you had a camera in your bag, but not a knife."

"It was part of the deal," she said. "My mother wouldn't let me come to Malaya unless I promised to always carry the knife."

"A flick knife."

"It was my brother's."

I said, "I've resisted so far, but based on current circumstances…"

"What?"

"There's a connection between you and the colonel, isn't there?"

"Why do you say that?"

"Because you got access to the barracks to cover the ghost stories despite it being a sensitive time. And he chose me as a chaperone rather than staff. He wanted to help you but keep it unofficial."

I could see I was right but she didn't respond.

"And then he wanted you to accompany me today— after you'd upset him with the questions about beasting."

She said, "I promised…"

"I know Jim doesn't have any children, so I figure you must be related. Why else feel obligated? A niece perhaps?"

"Margret Dexter, his wife, is my godmother. No one's supposed to know. I promised I wouldn't say."

I nodded. That made sense. Not just obligated to Hannah but pressure from his wife.

"I won't mention it," I said. "Not unless the colonel brings it up first."

"Thanks."

228

We talked about other things, random little thoughts that came and went and filled the time. Then I said, "In my spare time I box."

"As in pugilism?"

"Yes, and I'm OK at it."

"Is this supposed to be something personal about yourself? Your hobby is boxing?"

"What would you like to know?"

"About the real Ash Carter."

I whistled softly. "I'm not a psychologist."

"Tell me about your father."

I looked out of the cave for a long moment. Still no one anywhere near. Still safe.

"There's an issue between you and your father."

I sighed. "We don't see eye to eye."

She asked probing questions and eventually I gave in. I told her about the great RAF pilot who had then worked for the MOD and Home Office. A hero to everyone but me. I told her stories of how he'd punish me by locking me in a cupboard for hours, and a typical story of his rage, like when I broke a dinner plate by accident. I learned to read his eyes. I could tell when he was going to hit me.

"I became quite good at dodging and riding punches and I'm certain that's why I'm a pretty good b—"

I stopped abruptly because the guard halted, seemed to be listening and then switched our way.

Had he heard us talking?

I held out my revolver and we carefully got into a crouch ready to move if we had to.

Something flashed by. Then more flickers, silhouettes against the moonlight.

Hannah held my gun arm and I knew she'd seen them too. "Bats!" she said.

After a few minutes of frenetic aerial activity, it stopped. The bats were suddenly gone. The sentry resumed his casual patrol.

We lay down again and watched. She moved close and I put my right arm around her, keeping the Beretta on the floor by my left hand.

After an hour or so, Hannah snuggled closer and placed her head on my chest.

Sometime during the night she fell asleep.

I lay awake and thought.

It was dark and I was in a cave. I'd talked about my childhood and realized it had been prompted by our situation. Besides being locked in a cupboard I also used to get away and hide in a confined attic space. The dark hadn't scared me then and I'd used the time to develop my mind. Thinking through mathematical calculations and solving problems. Psychologists called it dissociation, the way I could disconnect from reality and focus on something else.

My attention had been on Cox and the Royal Engineers. The two dead men had both been working protection for them. They'd requested it, which was suspicious.

Tanner had been seen by Reeder and Cox—but they weren't necessarily reliable witnesses. Had Reeder seen something that then got him killed? The assault course and Sergeant Brookes was a red herring. He was an easy patsy. The men hated him. He appeared to be a bully and both Reeder and Tanner had been subject to his wrath. Too obvious.

But then again was Cox too obvious? What if he was like Reeder? What if he was then implicated by witnessing Tanner's death? What if part of what he'd said was true?

Tanner had been smoking but with no sign of a packet or cigarette butt.

Cannabis sativa forma indica, more commonly known as marijuana. That was what was in Tanner's pocket: the talisman. What if marijuana wasn't just for protection? What if Tanner had been smoking it?

Cox would have known. He'd have smelled it. So he removed the evidence. Which means he was involved. He knew the men had access to grass. His sappers had access to grass.

From what I knew of the drug, it made men happy, but it also made them paranoid. Afraid of ghosts perhaps?

Which led me to thinking about the witch doctor and exorcism. Hannah herself had told me: it was about fear and control. Cox and Walsh. Buddies. Where did Walsh fit in? I went round and round with my thinking but a crucial piece seemed elusive.

I visualized sitting against the hospital wall, watching. I saw men and vehicles come and go from the motor pool. I saw an ambulance, a small team of four marching out, men going into the mess hall, men square-bashing on the parade ground. All normal activity.

I thought about Rizzolo and the other protection guy in the Scammell truck. Why hadn't they been with Cox and his crew?

Maybe we should get back to Minden Barracks and wait for Cox and his Bedford truck to return and confront him. Maybe even find out if the temple we'd passed last night had been burgled. Maybe even find the evidence.

But of course nothing is ever that easy. And as the predawn light leached across the valley, I realized we had a problem.

A big problem.

The bandits were up and a whole squad was heading our way.

FORTY-TWO

I nudged Hannah and she jolted awake, looked at me with wide eyes and then looked outside.

"Get back," I said, pointing at the pinch point. "Hide and I'll draw them away."

Before she could argue, I slipped out of the entrance and scrambled to the nearest rock. I held my gun ready, focused on the next rock, crouched low and ran.

No gunshots. No shouting. I dived for the cover of the rock. Should I stand and fight here? Was I too close? I swung the revolver towards the Chinese. Six of them were running my way, but then they dived for cover too—only they faced the same way as me.

What's going on?

Something caught my eye at the bottom of the hill. The trees seemed to shimmer. At first I wondered if it was a visual trick in the poor light. Then I saw movement again and was sure it was a line of men walking at the edge of the jungle, mostly hidden.

I counted the movements and figured it was a platoon of sixteen. Moving into position.

The six bandits were only thirty yards from where I crouched. I saw other MNLA soldiers moving into positions. They'd clearly spotted the soldiers below and were preparing. They had the advantage of higher ground but could be trapped in the caves, and the hillside offered little protection except the odd boulder.

I watched and waited.

The movement below stopped and I figured they were in position. Did they realize the Chinese knew they were there?

Only one thing for it.

I killed four of the bandits hiding in front of me before the others started shooting back. Then the platoon below opened fire and I ducked down as bullets rattled all around.

All six men nearby were now dead and the focus of the gunfight was away to my right. I ran full tilt back to the cave.

"What's going on?" Hannah called from the darkness.

"Our men, fighting it out with the bandits."

I lay in the opening and watched as men in jungle fatigues finally appeared and began advancing up the hill.

Chinese shouts filled the air and there was an intense clatter of returned fire. But then I saw MNLA soldiers break away from their hiding places and run. And then it became a rout as the British soldiers swept up the hill firing.

I saw a handful of bandits go down as soon as the British started firing volleys. One Chinese soldier ran my way and I took him out. Two more who were following switched direction and then all the remaining bandits were running for the far trees.

The British moved from cover to cover and let the Chinese run into the jungle. They didn't give chase and stopped firing when the last bandit had disappeared.

I stood up and called Hannah. She rushed out of the darkness and threw her arms around me.

"Thank God," she panted. I held her trembling body and then told her to follow me.

"British officer and a lady," I shouted, and emerged from the cave. Hannah was pressed close to my back.

A few British soldiers glanced our way, nodded and continued what they were doing. They checked the enemy for survivors and dragged the bodies into a pile.

"Oh Jesus," Hannah said, and I thought it was because of the gunshot. A soldier had just killed a wounded man. But it wasn't. She stopped walking and stared.

A semi-naked native man was with the platoon. He bent over the Chinese bodies and removed something from each one.

Just as I realized what he was doing, Hannah said, "That man's scalping them!"

"Who the hell's in charge here?" I shouted.

"Captain Thorpe," a well-spoken officer said as he stepped up the slope towards us. He offered a hand and I introduced myself.

He said, "22nd SAS. Looks like we got here in the nick of time." He looked at Hannah, who had the camera in her hands. "Reporter?"

"I am." I could see the disgust on her face despite the fact that she'd taken out her camera.

Thorpe put a hand in front of it. "No photographs."

She pouted but complied, returning the camera to her bag.

"Sorry you had to see that," Thorpe said. "He's an Iban from North Borneo. The jungle patrols use them as trackers. Better than a bloodhound they are, but they come with a price tag. You see, Ibans are headhunters. This is a sort of rite of passage for their warriors. They've been coming over to Malaya for years. All we're doing is letting them work for us while they do it."

"It's horrible," Hannah said.

"We have managed to stop them taking the whole head, mind you. But we sort of turn a blind eye to the scalpings." He shrugged. "The ugly side of war, I'm afraid. I will need your assurance that you don't report what you have seen. It's not something the public need to know about. These Iban trackers are amazing. We've been following these bandits for three days. Crossed the Perak River three times and of course heard them blow the bridge again. Our tracker picked up on a cigarette this morning and it led us straight to them. Bloody idiots, smoking out here!"

"But you let them go," I said.

"Just a few. If we were to go after them we'd run the risk of being ambushed. Much better to let them go and catch them later unawares," Thorpe said. "We don't take any unnecessary risks. So far I've lost only one man and we must have captured and killed a couple of score. The strategy of patience."

"And brutality," Hannah said.

Thorpe gave a wry smile and looked at me. "What were you doing up here?"

"We had been looking for a team of sappers."

"Headed by a sergeant called Cox?"

I nodded.

"Met him last night—told him they'd blow the bridge again—told him to get out of here."

"Wish we'd done the same," I said. "Which way did he go?"

Thorpe called a man over and showed us on a map. Cox had been sent left at the crossroads where we'd gone right.

I shook Thorpe's hand and thanked him for rescuing us. "Look me up in Singapore sometime. I owe you a beer."

"You owe my whole platoon a beer!" Thorpe said with a nod.

I took Hannah's hand and led her away, jogging down to where the Land Rover was hidden.

As we left, Thorpe called out, "Don't forget to tell everyone that the SAS saved the day!"

"Barbaric," Hannah said, and then, "What's the hurry?"

"We need to get back and confront Cox," I said.

FORTY-THREE

There were four bullet holes in the back of the jeep and one in a side panel. I saw her look at them hard, maybe realizing how lucky we'd been yesterday evening, but she didn't say a word.

I reversed out of the dip to the track and then back to the road.

We went west, through the crossroads and then circled around. I wanted to go back to the town with the temple and newborn calf.

"You're expecting it to have been burgled, aren't you?" Hannah said.

"The exact opposite."

"Because we were following the Engineers?"

"No. Because I did a lot of thinking last night. Now I'm not so sure they're guilty."

"Why?"

"Because, like you said, this is about control."

She waited for me to say more but I didn't.

She said, "Why don't you want to tell me?"

"In case I'm wrong."

"I won't think any less of you."

I kept my focus on the bumpy road.

She said, "I'll use that personal information about you and your father if you don't tell me." I could tell she was joking from her tone.

"Not really newsworthy."

"Unless you've got a famous father."

I took a breath. I hadn't told her who he was and I'd taken a different surname but figured she'd work it out.

I said, "Three reasons. One, I don't think Cox really saw Tanner before he died. Which I think means he was covering for someone."

"Providing Private Reeder with a backup, corroborating his story?"

"Which would make Reeder guilty." But then someone killed Reeder. I didn't say this out loud because I was fairly sure Hannah didn't know about the second death. And if she didn't then I didn't want to be the one to break the news.

"The second reason?" she asked.

"We've seen that some thefts occur after the Royal Engineers have been places."

"But doesn't that mean...?"

"After, not during."

"OK," she said uncertainly.

"Three—and most importantly—the protection force. Tanner, Reeder and now Rizzolo have all been involved."

"Again, that implies the Royal Engineer unit."

"Rizzolo and the other protection guy didn't stay with them yesterday. They were in the Scammell. And it's a Bedford truck we're looking for."

We came back into the town along the road we'd used yesterday, only this time the streets weren't clogged with worshippers.

We stopped at the temple and checked inside. No problems. No sign of disturbance. Icons, statues and treasures intact as far as I could see.

"But if they didn't raid this temple last night then it's a circular argument," she said.

"Maybe," I said. "And that's why I'm holding onto my conclusion."

However my theory was about to be shattered.

FORTY-FOUR

A local man came up to us and bowed.

"Can I help you?"

Hannah said, "You've had no trouble here?"

"Trouble?"

"Theft or damage."

He looked from her to me. "You aren't police."

"I'm a reporter. I'm investigating thefts from temples. We just thought maybe…"

"That we'd been targeted?"

"Right."

He shook his head. "Perhaps we have been lucky. You have seen the temple at Wat Kalai already? They had trouble last night."

"Where?" I asked.

The man led us outside, pointed back the way we had come and gave other directions. "About five miles," he said.

We jumped back in the jeep and raced further west. After crossing a river we turned right through thick jungle. The river appeared again on our right and then a series of villages. A short distance further we entered a village with crowds of distressed people. The milled around outside a Buddhist temple looking dazed, like patients allowed to walk the corridors in hospital—in pain perhaps, their destiny in other people's hands, living in limbo.

We got out and a man said, "It's all been stolen." There was no anger in his voice, just resignation. "Everything."

He led us towards the temple and we took our shoes off before entering. We were in a large square room with pedestals all around, maybe twenty. "Missing statues?" I asked.

"All of them, including the golden Buddha."

"When did it happen?"

"Overnight," he said. "No one saw or heard anything."

"No diesel engine? No truck?"

He looked at me askance before responding. "Someone else asked that."

"You've informed the police?"

"We have, but they won't be much help. There's nothing to go on. Not here or the other temples."

Now it was my turn to be surprised. "Other temples?"

He said, "Yes, there were three Buddhist temples raided last night. All within ten miles of here, although Wat Kalai had more riches. And now we have nothing. Who would do this?"

I said nothing.

He said, "Apparently the Padang Lembu temple had gold taken from its dome."

I said, "I'm sorry."

He looked at me with piercing eyes. "Why are you sorry?"

I didn't want to explain who I was and what my suspicions were. Not without proof. "Did you see any army vehicles?" I asked.

"Last night? No. Yesterday I saw a big British truck."

I described a Scammell.

"Yes, but it just drove through."

After Wat Kalai we visited the other towns. Three temples within close proximity, and they'd all been attacked last night.

"You were wrong," Hannah said as we drove back down Route One. "You thought it was a Bedford truck but they were driving the Scammell."

"Maybe," I said, thinking. Three raids in one night. I didn't say anything but I recognized this behaviour. It was accelerating. Despite my presence, someone—whoever it was—had stepped up the operation.

When I returned to Minden Barracks, the first thing I did was head for the Royal Engineer's hut. I was alone, having insisted that Hannah wait for me at the hotel.

She didn't complain. The idea of a bath and fresh clothes was more appealing than confronting those who I'd said weren't guilty. If I'd been in her shoes, I wouldn't have believed me. Hell, I wasn't that sure myself, but the next few minutes would tell me one way or the other.

"Why didn't you go back with the Scammell?" I asked Cox once we were alone. He had a weary expression, like he hadn't slept well.

"I knew of another job—a damaged pipe a few miles north. No point in taking the big old truck up there. I wanted to check it out, evaluate what we'd need. We're going back tomorrow—fix the pipe and mend the bridge again. It was blown up again last night."

"I know. We both met a SAS unit tracking the bandits."

"We did, and they directed us away. We came straight back. Planned to catch the last ferry, but got the one before."

"Evidence?"

"That we were back? You could ask the rest of my team but I guess you won't believe them. How about Sergeant Walsh? I went out for a drink with him last night."

I shook my head. Each other's alibis as usual. "Someone else?"

"Our worksheets? Our yard?"

I shook my head again.

He laughed like he was playing along the whole time. "Ask at the CP. Dexter's got us checking in at the moment. He's got everyone checking in and out."

I didn't bother checking at the Command Post. Cox wouldn't have directed me there if the records would show he'd lied. Instead, I went over to the Royal Engineer's compound where they kept their vehicles.

The same dishevelled kid I'd met before was sitting at a desk in the hut. He joined me outside.

"Vehicles," I said. "Are they all here?"

"Yes, sir."

I could see two Bedfords, one of which was a Fifteen hundred, the other one larger. The Austin Gantry was also there along with the Scammell truck and a Land Rover."

"What time did they come back?"

He scooted inside and returned with a sheet. "We had the Fifteen hundred, Gantry and Scammell out yesterday. The Fifteen hundred was back at ten past eight last night. The Gantry and Scammell were at thirteen minutes past nine."

"Last night?"

He looked at the log, although I figured he didn't need to check. "Yes, sir."

"You're sure the Scammell didn't come back this morning, Private?"

"I was here, sir. I saw it."

"And Sergeant Cox?"

"Was in the Fifteen hundred."

"What about the protection force guys—the infantry men?"

"Don't know, sir. Dropped off before is what usually happens." He dropped his voice, like he was telling me a conspiracy. "We don't like them."

"What do you mean?"

I could see in his eyes that he wished he'd kept quiet. They darted left and right then back at me. A decision.

"They're different, that's all, sir. You know. They aren't Engineers. The men say we're more likely to get trouble than be protected."

I was looking at the vehicles again. The man in the temple had mentioned the Scammell passing through. No mention of the Austin Gantry. And both trucks had been back before the temple raid. There was also the issue that I'd seen tracks in the mud. The Scammell was definitely too heavy and too long. The Austin Gantry's wheelbase may have been all right, but still too heavy a vehicle. I was sure I was looking for a Bedford Fifteen hundred and yet the Bedford truck had also been back early.

And then it struck me: "You previously told me you have two Bedford Fifteen hundreds," I said. "So all your vehicles aren't here."

"No, sir. The other's in the garage."

Now I decided to visit the Command Post, the office closest to the barracks' entrance. Two clerks sat up smartly as I entered.

"Sergeant Cox," I said. "What time did he enter the barracks last night?"

I got my answer quickly: just after the Fifteen hundred had been returned.

"And his squad?"

"All except two. They came in just over an hour later."

I nodded. That fit.

"Corporal Rizzolo?"

The guy frowned then ran his finger down a page, tapped it and said. "We've got him going out with the sappers yesterday but not returned yet."

The other clerk said, "I have him down for special public service duty."

"Oh right!" the first clerk acknowledged.

"Special public service duty?" I prompted.

"Over on the mainland. I guess he didn't return last night because of the special duty."

"Yeah, that'll be right," the second clerk said. "The others left early evening."

"How many?"

"Two others. There's usually four of them."

"Who was the other soldier protecting the Royal Engineers yesterday?"

"With Rizzolo? That was..." He checked the list again. "Private White. And yes, he was on special duty too."

I took a breath, my mind whirring. "Who picks these guys?"

"I think they volunteer." The first clerk shrugged and the second nodded.

"Who to?"

"Colour Sergeant Harper."

I thanked them and jogged over to the common room but Harper wasn't there. I was directed to an office on the second floor but he wasn't there either.

I went back to the Command Post.

"Stupid question," I said. "Colour Sergeant Harper on base?"

They both nodded.

"Who else would know about the special duties? I need to find Corporal Rizzolo."

They both shrugged.

Damn, I'd have to wait until I located Harper.

Back to the problem of the Fifteen hundred—and the motor pool.

FORTY-FIVE

Sergeant Walsh wasn't around, but Mackenzie, his number two, was. He was bent over, studying an engine in the garage.

"Which of your Fifteen hundreds was out last night?" I barked as I bore down on him.

He raised his head, looked at me, blinked. "What?"

"The Bedford MW, commonly referred to as a Fifteen hundred," I said unnecessarily and annoyed. "Which ones were out last night?"

Again he blinked, as though trying to process the question. Finally he wiped his hands on his overalls and shook his head. "None of them."

"Show me."

I nodded to the office and he ambled over through the door and picked up the ledger. He flipped it around and pointed to the column with yesterday's date.

"None of them," he said again.

I went down the list, picking out each of the Bedfords, checking it had been returned and hadn't been taken out.

"What about Walsh? Did he take one out that's not been recorded?"

"No, sir."

I looked at the list again. "Which of these is the sappers' truck?"

"They have their own yard."

I clenched my teeth. "That wasn't the question. I know they have their own compound but they have a Fifteen hundred in here."

He did the blink thing again, processing my statement. Then: "No they don't."

"The kid in their office said it was in the garage. You're telling me he was lying?"

"Garage? Oh, he didn't mean the motor pool. He meant their lock-up."

"Their lock-up?"

"Sure, they have a lock-up on the mainland."

Now it was my turn to blink.

Mackenzie carried on: "They keep some equipment over there in case of emergency. I guess they also keep a Fifteen hundred in there."

"Where is it?"

"End of a bank of sheds beyond the train station. There's a sign. It's clearly marked."

"Where's Sergeant Walsh—right this minute?"

"I have no idea. He took a jeep out—"

Before he finished, I was heading out of the door and then running across the road and along to the barracks' entrance.

Someone was sitting outside Tucker's café-bar. Hannah. She stood up as I passed.

"What's going on, Ash?"

I slowed but continued towards the driveway. "I've got a lead."

"Were you going to tell me?" she said, falling in beside me.

"Yes... No... Maybe."

"You weren't! I suspected as much."

I started to jog again. "All right you can come. On one condition. Any sign of danger and that's it. You go no further."

She shook her head.

I stopped and faced her. "I'm serious, Hannah. Last night I almost got you killed. I'm not taking that risk again. You promise or you aren't coming."

She promised but did her chin-raise thing.

"I'm serious."

"All right," she said. "I promise."

Seconds later I was stamping on the accelerator and we were heading for George Town and the ferry.

I filled her in as we queued for the boat.

"So Sergeant Walsh can come and go without showing up on the records."

"Right."

"And has access to the Engineer's truck?"

"He's best mates with Sergeant Cox."

She thought for a second. "So instead of Cox covering for Reeder, he was probably covering for Walsh?"

I said, "Maybe Reeder and Walsh regarding Tanner's death."

"And the temple thefts... It's not the Royal Engineers doing the jobs but someone using their truck."

"Right."

We trundled on, parked on the lower deck and headed up for fresh air.

When we were at the railings, looking at the mainland, she said, "Who's doing it?"

"The protection guys. I think they act as scouts, which is why temples get raided after the Engineers have been close by. Not the same day as the Engineers are there and on days when the Engineers are in barracks.

250

They're volunteering for other work to be on the mainland. I didn't manage to speak to Colour Sergeant Harper. He'd have told me where they were doing special duty work. Only, I'd guarantee they aren't there."

"Where does Sergeant Walsh fit in?"

"The Bedford."

"Isn't Cox more likely?"

I was about to say, "He's on base when it happens," then remembered his alibis were dubious.

"Damn," I said, "the barracks aren't walled. I've cut through to the motor pool myself. Anyone could do it, could be seen coming back and then slip out again."

"Maybe I should be a detective rather than a reporter." She smiled and it lifted my spirits.

Perai got closer, as did the answer to our puzzle.

FORTY-SIX

The shed was certainly big enough to hold a truck. There were no windows and a big padlock held twin doors shut. But a lock is only as good as the wood. It splintered easily when I kicked it, and I was in.

Inside was indeed like a small garage, with tools and cans and the smell of oil. But no truck.

Marks on the floor told me a large vehicle had been in here.

"So you've confirmed that there's a truck missing and could have been used."

I nodded.

"What now? We find out if anyone saw it leave?"

"No need," I said. "I know where they went."

"Where?"

"The temple with the cow and calf. They didn't do it last night so I—"

I stopped as a car pulled up outside. No, not a car, a Land Rover.

Colour Sergeant Harper got out. "Found you!" he said almost breathless. He looked from me to Hannah and back again. "We need to talk... in private."

We walked towards the station and well beyond where Hannah could hear. I glanced back and saw her frowning at me.

"Reporter," Harper said. "This is much too sensitive for her ears." He paused and seemed to be struggling with the words.

"Just say it," I said.

"It's where I start." He raised his eyebrows and prepared himself. "OK, I think men from the barracks are stealing from the temples. Actually, it's more than think. I've had my suspicions and been following them."

"Who?"

"The young men who volunteer. When that kid Reeder died, I started to put two and two together, realized they were using the sapper's Fifteen hundred."

I nodded.

"You worked it out too?"

"The only thing I'm not sure about is who's in charge. These kids aren't doing it on their own."

Now he nodded and glanced at Hannah. "What does she know?"

"Quite a bit," I said.

He blew out air. "It could be damaging. It's Cox and Walsh. Together. I think Walsh coordinates and Cox goes along with it. Lets Walsh and the soldiers use the truck."

I nodded. "What now?"

"I know where they stash the goods."

"Where?"

He nodded towards his jeep and we started walking back towards the garage. "It's not far—a couple of miles. I'll show you and we can decide how to handle it... and without the reporter."

"I'll deal with her," I said. "She can go back and tell Dexter."

He stopped me with a hand. "Let's wait. If we can limit the damage... better for him."

I wasn't sure.

He said, "Ash, I retire soon. Just six more days. Let me fix this so it doesn't look so bad for Colonel Dexter or me. I don't want the records showing this happened on my watch."

He held my gaze for a long time, his eyes pleading.

"What can you do?"

"Let's talk about it on the way. I have a half-baked idea. I'm hoping you can help."

We started walking again and I veered off and spoke to Hannah.

"Go back?" she said defiantly.

"Or wait here. Your choice, but this is dangerous and you aren't coming."

She pouted her lips but didn't move as I ran over to Harper's jeep. I jumped in beside him, he U-turned around my jeep and Hannah, and I raised my hand. She didn't wave back, just continued to pout, her hands on her hips.

Harper drove fast out of Perai and then south on Route One.

"Where do the drugs fit in?" I asked.

"You know about the marijuana." A statement not a question. "I suspected it from the strange behaviour."

"The motor pool guys and the Engineers." Now it was my turn to make a statement.

"Yes. I suspect that's why they see ghosts. I suspect it's why Corporal Tanner was so jumpy the night he shot himself."

"You're sure he shot himself?"

Harper glanced at me, concern on his face. "Please don't tell me it wasn't an accident."

"What about Reeder?"

"Didn't he just over-train at the assault course—fall in the pool in the dark and drown?"

"That's what it looks like," I said, "but I don't believe in coincidences. Both men were involved in this operation."

"God!" he said. "Maybe I can't limit the damage after all. I was going to make the guys take the stuff back— every last stolen item."

He turned off the road and headed for a small series of hillocks on their own before the real foothills started.

I said, "They'll be going to the temple near the blown bridge tonight."

"Yes. I'll show you their stash and then we'll go to the village and wait for them."

That had been my plan, so I was happy with the idea, although something still bothered me. "It's accelerating," I said.

"Is it?"

"They did three jobs last night and they're continuing despite my investigations."

"Overconfident," he said. "They don't expect to be caught."

I nodded and thought about how cocky Walsh was. He definitely thought he was a law unto himself.

We turned off and bumped down a muddy track. "Almost there," Harper said.

It was a good location: in the trees on the side of a hill facing away from any habitation, from any prying eyes.

We parked and Harper took me up a track that wound up the hill between the trees.

He said quietly, "I think it's a disused open mine, although it looks like someone started and gave up. The ground is too loose." As we went on he lowered into more of a crouch. Probably in case any of the soldiers were about. I copied him.

I heard nothing except the call of birds and monkeys.

255

We rounded the slope and I saw another track, one that looked wide enough for a vehicle.

"That's the way they come up," Harper whispered.

"When did you see them?"

"Last night."

We crept forward and I saw no sign of the vehicle or soldiers. "They're armed of course. I could have confronted them last night, but... well, I thought I'd ask for your advice first."

He looked around and then we dropped down to the wider track. Ahead was an opening—a tunnel that was almost circular, about six feet tall. I could see why the mine had been abandoned. The ground looked unstable.

A pile of cut branches on the floor suggested camouflage. Were we too late? Had they been and gone?

And then I saw movement. A man came out of the mine. Rizzolo.

Harper whispered, "Do you have a gun?"

I reached for my ankle, but before I touched my Berretta, I heard Harper say something else.

By the time the words registered, it was already too late.

"Sorry."

I felt a sharp explosion of pain in the back of my head and darkness rushed in.

FORTY-SEVEN

I breathed in dirt, my nose pressed to the ground. In absolute darkness, I sat up and felt the back of my head. A lump the size of a billiard ball was coming up, painful but not wet. No blood.

My forehead hurt like hell too. But apart from a headache, I figured I was fine.

There was no light. Total darkness. I blinked a few times, worried about my eyesight. I could smell earth and dry air. Was I inside the cave? If so, then why no light?

Standing, still woozy from the head injury, I felt around and touched cold stone. I also listened but had already figured I was alone.

Harper wasn't here.

Harper had hit me.

I made my way along the wall and felt the cave getting narrower so I turned back and felt the other way. And then my fears were confirmed.

The entrance was blocked.

Harper hadn't just knocked me out and moved me into the cave, he'd totally blocked it. Somehow he'd triggered a landslide. I felt the wall where I figure the entrance had once been: rocks and earth.

I pushed at it and felt no give. It could be yards deep.

I tried to picture how far in I could be, how far the roof had collapsed. I had no sense of depth. Ten feet? Maybe more.

Harper hadn't killed me. He didn't need to. I'd die in here and, should anyone find my body, it would look like an accident.

Damned if I was going to let that happen!

I made my way to the back and felt around. No stolen items, although I didn't expect any. If they had been here they'd been taken now.

I searched for something to lever the rocks away. Nothing. They'd taken everything and probably made sure I wouldn't find a tool.

I began pulling stones out of the wall and scooping handfuls of dirt. I made progress but every now and again more stones and earth would come down and fill where I'd dug.

After an hour of labour, I rested. Sweat soaked my shirt and I blinked it from my blind eyes. My hands ached and all my nails felt broken.

And then I heard something: the crack of stone on stone. More rocks falling on the blockage, trapping me even more.

"No!" I raged at the wall and begun digging again. "You will not beat me!"

Despite my exhaustion, I could hear Sammy, my old boxing coach, screaming at me. He used to say that you discovered who you were when you thought there was nothing left. It showed your true mettle. Never give up. Keep on fighting. In the darkness I could feel his presence demanding every last ounce of energy.

Another painful ten minutes or so and I paused. The falling stone sound was louder, scraping, thudding. And something else maybe? Yes! Voices. I could hear people out there.

Despite the aches and my thudding heart, I redoubled my efforts. I shouted too, shouted until my throat hurt.

For a moment, I thought the voices had been my imagination. They stopped but then started again, people calling over the increased clatter of stones.

When light broke through at the top, I pushed my fingers towards it and pulled at the nearest rocks. When they came away a hole appeared and then hands scrabbling in and out, widening the gap until a face appeared. It was a man. Someone local perhaps. Our eyes held before he moved away and another face appeared.

Hannah Quinn.

"Almost there, Ash! Hold on."

Stones tumbled through on my side and I backed up. Hands pushed, dislodging stones until the top of the blockage collapsed, sliding down around my feet. Dust billowed around me.

Even before everything settled, I was climbing on hands and legs up through the hole and into the daylight.

Hands helped me over the edge. Hannah had stepped back while three men grabbed my hands and arms and guided me down the far side to the ground. Only then did Hannah rush forward and throw her arms around me.

My body sagged under her grip, my muscles spent, my blood flushed with adrenaline. It was like I'd been in a boxing ring and fought until every ounce of strength had gone. And like in a ring, I was handed water. Hannah moved away as I drank hungrily, the liquid better than anything I had ever tasted.

"You look a state," she said, stepping back in and raising a hand towards my head.

"You should see the other guy."

"Really?"

259

"No," I said. "I never saw it coming. Harper fooled me."

I looked around, focusing on the other men for the first time. They were all of Indian descent, all watching me with concern etched on their faces.

"Who—?" I started.

"Just people who agreed to help..."

One of the men stepped forward, put his palms together and inclined his head. I nodded back, thanked him and then thanked the others. They all bowed.

I saw my jeep down the slope and some bicycles.

I turned my attention back to Hannah. "We need to go."

"You're in no state to drive," she said, running behind me as I strode towards the jeep. But instead of getting in the driver's seat, I scooted around the other side.

"Get us back to Penang," I said.

FORTY-EIGHT

I leaned back in the seat and felt my strength returning.

"Why Penang? Why not the temple, like we originally planned?"

"Because Harper mentioned it. Too obvious. That's where he wants us to go."

She nodded and drove on. I said Penang but I didn't think they'd risk taking the goods there. Too many eyes on the ferry. Which meant they'd need a port. Most likely Perai.

I asked, "Why were you there? How—?"

"I followed you," she said. "I know I promised... but... anyway, it was a good job I did. I waited until you were well ahead but then an army truck came out of the road behind the warehouses in Perai."

"The Fifteen hundred," I said.

"Yes, but I wasn't sure at first. I thought about overtaking and finding Sergeant Harper's Land Rover but when it turned off and headed for the hills, I was sure I was right. Then I passed the Land Rover at the foot of the hill. I hid yours and scouted around until I spotted the army guys. Ash, they were loading statues and other objects—the ones stolen from the temples."

I nodded.

"Of course, you know. They were in the cave when you arrived."

"I didn't see anything, but I guessed."

She continued as she drove hard and fast: "When they left, they reversed the truck into the entrance again and again until half the hill came away, sliding down, covering it. I wondered what the hell was going on, and then I spotted Sergeant Harper and it suddenly made sense. He'd lured you here and you might be dead."

"And the other men?"

"Villagers. As soon as the soldiers drove off, I checked on the rockslide and decided I needed help. First man I asked agreed to help and he got two friends." She exhaled. "I thought you were dead."

"No, I'm alive."

"I don't understand. Why didn't they kill you?"

"It was supposed to look like another accident. I went in the cave and maybe banged my head then got trapped. I figure that's why I was hit on the front as well as the back of the head."

She said nothing for a minute, before asking: "So it'd *look* like another accident?"

I hesitated. As far as she knew, Tanner's death was an accident. She also didn't know about Reeder. Or maybe Dexter had told her.

"Ash?" she prompted. "Come on, I just saved your life for Christ's sake! I deserve to know what's going on."

I'd done a lot of thinking in the time I'd been trapped.

Control. I should have guessed it was all about control. Not the drugs and ghosts, or at least not just that. They were linked. Who had control over the men apart from the CO and other officers? Who had the *real* control? The sergeant who decides what soldiers do. Who does which tasks. Who does assault course training. Who goes to the mainland.

262

The colour sergeant. Harper.

So obvious in hindsight.

What the hell? I thought. I figured Hannah was right. I owed her.

"Sergeant Harper's been coordinating it all and using a select group of soldiers as his team. Maybe Walsh and Cox knew. Probably, but I think Harper bought their silence with drugs."

"Drugs?"

"Marijuana. It was like a secret club, a society. The men got marijuana—even a talisman made from the stuff—and in return they kept quiet."

We hit the main road and she drove faster. I could smell the sea.

"Christ!"

"I think Tanner was one of Harper's team. I think he stepped out of line and the colour sergeant killed him."

"Really?"

"Or maybe it was an accident. I think Tanner had been smoking the weed and Harper didn't know the gun was loaded. I figure they tussled and the gun went off."

"But the witnesses?"

"Reeder was also in on it. And maybe Cox wasn't even there or covered for Harper. Maybe he was also high on the marijuana." I watched the flat landscape and the rice fields, but I wasn't really looking. I was visualizing Tanner's gun going off under his chin. I bet Harper was the ghostly black shape Cox had mentioned.

I said, "And then we turned up, asking awkward questions."

"OK," she said.

"Maybe Tanner was killed to silence Reeder. Maybe both of them were just supposed to be scared off. But it didn't work. Seems that my questioning worried Reeder

263

more. He was going to confess—or at least Harper thought he was—so he killed him too."

"Christ! Roy Reeder was killed too?"

So she didn't know and in talking through the case, I'd told her. However I decided this was the least of Jim Dexter's problems now I knew of Harper's activities.

"What are you going to do?" she asked.

"Stop them," I said. "They've got the goods, probably been keeping the whole load in that cave until now. "This is the endgame."

"They're taking the items back to the barracks?"

I didn't comment.

"Ash!"

"It's best you don't know. I don't want you involved."

"But I am involved."

"They have guns, we don't," I lied. I'd checked my ankle holster and they'd left the gun. That confirmed my theory that my death was to look like an accident. It would look suspicious if I was found without my gun.

She was still complaining as we reached Perai. I asked her to get out and catch the next ferry.

"Where are you going?" she asked, refusing to budge from her seat.

"Hannah, I don't have time!"

"Tell me."

I gritted my teeth then nodded. "Dr Suleiman has warehouses on both sides of the strait. I remember seeing them."

"Sullyman was Suleiman? How's he connected?"

"Just thinking out loud. His warehouse is called Souter and Hancock Shipping Company. Look out for the jeep but my gut says there."

"OK," she said uncertainly.

I pointed to the harbour police building and said, "Use their phone. Call Colonel Dexter and tell him what's going on."

"But you need backup! I'll tell the police too."

"No, it's his decision and he'll have men over here." I paused as the realization struck me: she was worried. "You'll be fine," I said.

"It's not me I'm worried about," she said, getting out. "You should see your face!"

"Take a look at yourself." I laughed. She was grubby from digging me out of the cave. Not as bad as me, I was sure, but still in need of a good wash.

"Good luck." She grinned and waved as I slid over into the driver's seat. Spinning the jeep around, I stamped my foot down and headed for the wharf.

FORTY-NINE

I'd seen the Souter and Hancock Shipping name on the front of a building about a hundred yards along the wharf. Suleiman traded in many things, including medicines. He was concerned about bad morphine. Was he part of the morphine supply chain? Unlikely since he'd drawn my attention to it. However, I suspected he supplied the marijuana to men at the barracks. I'd look for the Bedford truck, but I'd check out Suleiman's place for sure.

The flow of goods to the waiting tongkangs meant that driving there would have been slower than walking. So I stayed on the road that ran along the backs of the warehouses. When Hannah had told me she'd seen the Bedford come from there, I figured that's where they'd go. With stolen goods, they needed access to shipping, which meant wharves.

I drove slowly, checking each building. Many had open doors at the rear but I saw no truck. After ninety yards I thought I recognized the Souter and Hancock building.

There were factory offices to one side with dark and dusty windows. I slid to a halt and drew my gun as I ran down the alleyway between a warehouse and the office building.

Bursting onto the wharf, I saw I'd been right; the warehouse was Suleiman's. Huge lime-green doors were wide open and a stream of workers carried boxes down to the quay and awaiting boats.

Men looked at me with surprise but no alarm and otherwise ignored me. I ran inside. It smelled of wood and dust. There were crates everywhere and a truck in the middle of the floor, but it was an American truck, not one I was looking for.

Sticking my gun in my pocket, I backed out of the building wondering how I could have been so wrong. Surely they were moving the stolen items ready for disposal. Maybe I'd been wrong about the Suleiman connection. Maybe he wasn't the marijuana supplier. Then who? No way could Harper handle disposal of these items without help.

I looked back along the wharf towards the ferry. It had docked and vehicles were starting to board.

None of the other properties along the wharf felt right. They all seemed far too active for a secret operation, for the team of soldiers and truck to hide in.

There were more warehouses in the other direction but also offices. I started walking north and passed operations that looked just like Suleiman's, like legitimate shipping and distribution firms.

Then there was a space, like a building had disappeared. The next one looked wider, maybe a factory rather than a warehouse. There were no workers outside the long wooden-slatted frontage. I looked through a dirty window at a large deserted room. One of my fingers pushed through the white painted frame— rotten. The surrounding wood had been white many years previously. About half of the paint had peeled away to reveal a lime-green undercoat. Suleiman's colour. An old property of his perhaps? The condition of the building suggested it was abandoned, but then I noticed a tall chimney on the far side. Grey smoke drew a line towards the heavens.

Ten paces further I came across sliding doors that were large enough to take the Bedford truck with room to spare. Rusted rail tracks ran under the doors. There were small windows high up and I stood on tiptoe to peek in.

Despite poor illumination, I could see a cavernous room with a great deal of equipment, scaffolding and hanging chains. Large metal stanchions supported the roof and could have come from a Victorian railway station. There were train carts to one side and rails that ran through double doors. My first impression was that there was no one around, but the smoke suggested otherwise.

Wide, double doors had a small door, a Judas gate, that creaked as I cracked it open and slipped through. Warm acrid air burned in my nostrils and I could hear a low rumble.

Standing against the door frame, I waited, gun in hand. The rumbling sound continued but I heard nothing else. No one appeared.

Now that I was inside I could see another set of doors. This first room was a loading bay area and the sound and smoke came through the doors ahead. I walked quietly over and looked through a gap between them.

In front of me was the Bedford truck. Beyond it was an arched furnace casting red and orange light over the rest of the factory. Smoke leeched out of the furnace doors and filled the upper levels of the room with an oppressive dark layer.

The rumble I'd heard was in fact the sound of the furnace and men taking. I slipped inside and stood behind a stanchion. By the furnace I could see two white men labouring in the heat, their shirts off, their bodies dirty and shining with sweat. One man was tapping the molten liquid, pouring it into moulds. The other was cooling it and knocking it out. A third man was sorting, packing and loading into the truck.

This was part of the four-man team—on special duty. One soldier short: Rizzolo. And no sign of Harper.

Where were they?

I left the upright and slunk around the back of the room looking for the other men. At the far side I came to another door that led back into the loading area. It was open, and beyond that I could see a series of doors on the right before a staircase to a second-floor balcony. I went through and listened at the first door before easing it open.

As I did so, Rizzolo came out of the farthest with his rifle slung over his shoulder.

Three men working. One man on sentry duty.

I ducked into the doorway and raised my gun, ready. But Rizzolo didn't come my way. I bobbed my head out and back, taking a quick look. The kid was walking towards the entrance, taking up his guard post.

I followed, hugging the wall, pretty sure the sounds from the other room were covering my footfall.

Rizzolo stopped beside the doors and seemed to be considering the Judas gate. Had I left it slightly open?

The kid eased the rifle off his shoulder and started to turn. Fortunately, he was rotating away from me and I closed the gap between us quickly.

I had my gun out, just in case, but switched it to my right hand at the last moment. By the time he heard me and reacted, I was already upon him. He moved into my left hook, his eyes startled like a deer in lights.

He collapsed, dazed but not unconscious. I caught him and clamped my hand over his mouth. At the same

269

time, I wrapped my other arm around his neck and put pressure on his carotid artery. There was fight in him but not enough, as I squeezed until his body went limp.

He would be out for a while, maybe an hour. I stood and listened, making sure no one was coming to investigate the sounds. Then I carried Rizzolo to the room he'd appeared from: a grimy toilet room that stank of piss.

After dumping him on the floor, I took his rifle and walked back into the loading area. As I passed the next door I glanced in at a workers' small kitchen. The next door had a key. It turned and revealed a storage space for packing materials. Satisfied, I went into the furnace room.

Two shots into the air got their attention.

"Stop! Line up by the truck, hands on your heads. Now!" I said it with the voice I'd been trained to use, a tone they'd been trained to obey.

Within a minute, I had all three lined up in front of me.

"Where's Sergeant Harper?" I shouted.

Two just stared at me, defiant. The third glanced over at the door, maybe expecting their colleague.

I said, "Rizzolo's been dealt with. Now I'll ask one more time." I glared at the two defiant ones. "Where's Harper?"

"Gone back to base," one of them said. The others nodded.

"Right." I waved the rifle towards the double doors. "Single file through there, keeping your hands on your heads."

I went ahead and pushed the doors wide and watched them skulk through. Then I directed them right and pointed to the storage room.

"Keep going. Into the room."

I locked them in and took the key. It fitted the key hole to the toilet so I locked Rizzolo in too. Then I jogged to the entrance, stepped out into the bright sunshine and looked down the wharf. Where was the cavalry? And where was Hannah?

FIFTY

Colour Sergeant John Harper sat inside an upstairs office in Souter and Hancock Shipping in Perai. He looked out of the window, half watching the activity on the quay and thinking.

A few days to go and retire a rich man. He'd meant to scare Jack Tanner and ended up shooting the poor kid. It wasn't his fault that the stupid idiot had locked and loaded his rifle. How could he have expected it to go off when he jammed it under the kid's chin? At first he thought it might look like suicide but realized Tanner's arms weren't long enough. That's when he took off the kid's boots. Years ago he'd heard of a soldier shooting himself like that. He was proud of his quick thinking under the circumstances but it turned out to be unnecessary because Tanner's death had been ruled an accident. Not suicide. Not murder.

But then that ex-MP had shown up and Cox panicked. The damned engineer thought he was being clever suggesting suicide but he should have kept quiet.

Cox had always been a risk, but getting him to say he was a witness had been a master stroke. If it all went south, Cox would be implicated—especially since it was his unit's truck that Harper used each time.

Sergeant Stewart Cox thought he was smart, had a college degree or something, but his accent made him sound dumb. And he was dumb. He was happy to take the marijuana and turn a blind eye to what Harper was doing with the truck.

And using the special team as the sappers' protection force was also genius. They protected the engineers but they also kept an eye on them.

Harper had started collecting items years ago—just the odd thing here and there. Nothing too valuable and not too often. And then he'd met Dr Suleiman and together they'd worked out a great retirement plan. With less than a year to go, Harper had realized that the Royal Engineers travelled the country in a truck with plenty of opportunity to make detours and relieve temples of the odd icon or precious metal. But using selected infantrymen and rewarding their loyalty was much better.

The sappers had been happy with the marijuana at the same time as being nervous of the ghosts. It was all a bit of fun, but Harper had noticed straight away how suspicious the men were and controllable through fear as well as drugs. In fact, the drugs seemed to enhance the fear.

The little unit had been happy with their drugs and rewards—the extra cash and the girls Harper paid for, but Tanner and Reeder had got cocky. They'd wanted more.

Punishing them on the assault course should have been enough, especially after Tanner's death. It was easy to get Brookes to give the two kids a hard time on the course. Brookes was a sadistic bastard and didn't need much encouragement.

After the ex-MP visited, Reeder had tried blackmail. The assault course treatment hadn't deterred him so

Harper didn't regret shoving the stupid spotty kid's face under the water. He deserved it—and it was easy to find two more willing members of the team.

And Brookes would look suspicious.

The last few weeks had been a big risk. They'd raided more temples in that period than they'd done in the month before. But time was running out. Suleiman needed the wares and Harper needed his pension.

He looked down the wharf. Where was Suleiman? They were supposed to be finalizing the deal before they went over to the old smelting factory. The ferry from Penang was just arriving. Maybe Suleiman had been delayed. Maybe he was on that ferry.

As he waited, Harper thought back over the day, seeing the ex-MP and the reporter drive off the ferry and head for the sappers' garage.

He smiled. Carter had totally bought the lie. Shooting him would have been easy but Harper had changed his mind. The cave-in was much better. That way, if Carter's body was found, they'd think it was another accident.

It was good that the reporter hadn't been there. Buried alive like that... well, the girl didn't deserve it. Harper thought of himself as a moral man. Tanner was an accident. Reeder deserved it. Carter? Well, he had signed his own death warrant by poking his nose in.

It had strengthened his position with the four soldiers. They feared him and he liked that. Knowing that he'd dealt with the ex-MP would also keep them quiet.

It took Harper's brain a couple of seconds to process what he just saw. A military police Land Rover approached the ferry terminal. It stopped, but not in the queue. Two people inside seemed to be talking and then the driver—a woman—got out. The damn reporter!

Then it took him another second to figure it out. The other person was Carter. Alive.

Now he cursed himself for not killing them both. She'd found the cave and somehow dug Carter out.

As Harper watched, the Land Rover turned and headed for the road behind the wharf.

Another second and Harper was up and running out of the office, his boots clanging down the metal stairs. Carter was looking for them. Bound to be. He'd dropped the girl off to fetch the police while he searched the wharf. He'd guess it was too risky to take the goods on the ferry. Too many eyes, too many questions.

Carter or the girl?

Carter was looking for the soldiers; the girl was fetching the police.

Carter would find the warehouse. No problem with that, but he'd also spot the factory. It looked deserted and the truck wasn't visible. Maybe he wouldn't go in, but if he did, Rizzolo was armed.

Right, Harper decided, the girl is the priority.

He came out onto the wharf, checked for Carter, and when he didn't spot him, started running towards the harbour police building.

A cargo boat had moored and there was a rush of activity as tongkangs were rapidly loaded, competing to reach the new arrival.

And then he saw the reporter. She was almost there. Harper tried to pick up the pace but the wharf was frenetic, workers, carts, everywhere.

She reached the office steps and he knew then that he'd be too late.

FIFTY-ONE

Hannah made her way steadily along the wharf. The excitement made her heart pound in her chest. Ash had raced off to find the crooks and she needed to get help. He was counting on her.

She had dodged carts laden with boxes of fruit and coolies staggering under the weight of giant sacks. All of a sudden the frenetic activity began as heavy goods were rushed to the quayside and loaded onto tongkangs.

She was held up for a couple of seconds and then weaved her way through. The ferry had just pulled in and the usual jostling to get on or off was causing mayhem on the terminal apron.

A stream of smelly old trucks rumbled past and she had to pull up. As she waited, she gripped her bag, the contact somehow providing security.

When a break in the traffic occurred, she walked forward. The offices were about thirty yards ahead but the apron was dense with people and vehicles slowing her progress. A water buffalo attached to a long fruit-laden cart bellowed, refusing to move. Hannah started to go around it just as the poor beast defecated steaming green slime. She placed a hand over her nose and mouth, stepped sideways to avoid being splashed, and hurried on.

Ahead, she could see harbour police in the queue for the ferry but she needed the phone. When she reached their office, she her breath came in gasps.

Three steps and she was inside.

"Can I help you, miss?"

A local man in uniform sat behind a desk staring at her.

"Phone," she said, realizing she sounded breathless. "Please can I use your phone? It's urgent."

She'd expected it to be straightforward; ask for the phone and be given it. But the officer just stared at her, waiting for an explanation. She could see a phone to the right of his desk.

"I need to call the CO of Minden Barracks." She took a step towards the phone, her eyes on it.

"Why?"

She halted, looked at him, and took a breath, trying not to sound exasperated. "I'm with a military policeman. There's an army team… they're criminals. Please. They're on the wharf here somewhere."

"I'll take it from here, Officer Mamat." A calm, commanding voice came from behind her.

She turned to see a smiling man, not a local, maybe Middle Eastern. He held out his hand. "Tell me what's going on."

She glanced back at the harbour policeman, who looked relieved, and then took the other man's hand. He led her outside as she quickly ran through the story about the sergeant from Minden and temple thefts.

"We think they're in one of these warehouses," she said, pointing down the quay.

He guided her in that direction, his hand on her arm, and she hesitated. "Sorry. Who are you?"

He smiled reassuringly. "The police wouldn't let you use their telephone, I'm afraid. No matter what—unless it was a harbour issue. I've an office telephone just up here. You can call from there."

They dodged people and goods but she was surprised as they passed the entrance to the first building.

"I thought—"

"The next one," he said, and led her onward, still holding her arm. After the first building was a gap, an alley. It was dark, but she caught a glimpse of movement in the shadows. Fast. Rushing towards her.

A hand grabbed her free arm.

"Hey!" She tried to pull away, looking at the Middle Eastern man for help. He just raised his eyebrows, smiled and released his hand.

She looked back at the other man still holding her arm. Harper. Suddenly, fear made her legs weak. He was hurting her as he pulled her further into the shadows.

"Walk," Harper said, dragging her along the alley and away from the harbour police office and the wharf.

Hannah shouted, "Help!" and tried to pull away from his grasp. But he was too strong and there was no one down here. His other hand clamped over her mouth and he pulled her backwards. Apart from the panic, her brain registered the oily smell of his thick hand under her nose.

When they reached the end of the alley they were at the road behind the warehouses. The main road and the queue for the ferry were to the right.

Pull away and run!

He must have guessed her intention because he slammed her into the wall, knocking the wind out of her.

He was speaking—a snarling angry tone—but the words didn't register. She was fumbling in her bag, one-handed, hoping to find her knife. Where was it? Her fingers wrapped around a pen. Could she stab him in the face?

But as she pulled her hand out, Harper batted her arm down. The pen and bag fell from her grasp. He punched her in the ribs and she doubled up.

"What's Carter's plan?" Harper snarled at her. His body pressed against her, his face an inch from her face.

Hannah heard blood thudding in her ears, took a breath and blocked the image of Harper pressing against her from her mind.

"The game's up, Harper," she said with false bravado. "Captain Carter's already arrested your men. He's also informed the authorities."

Suddenly her bravery vanished. Harper had picked up her knife, flicked it open next to her eyes, his other hand clamped around her throat.

"Rubbish," he said. "You were informing the authorities." He said *authorities* like it was a bad word. With the knife pressing against her, he removed his other hand and tipped her camera and notebook from her bag. Then he stuck the knife through the bag and poked it into her side. His other hand gripped her arm, fingers digging into the nerves near the armpit. Knife hidden, he hustled her out of the alley into the road behind the warehouses.

A couple of trucks and a car went past then a group of workers on bicycles.

He pulled her sharply away. "Make a sound and I'll stick you with the knife, you understand? I have nothing to lose now, so just do as I say."

She walked where Harper led, her head dizzy with the pain from her ribs and the pinch of his hand. More people, goods and buildings passed in a blur and then she spotted the Land Rover with its bullet holes.

There was a wider gap between buildings, like one had been demolished. The one on the right looked like a factory, maybe disused, maybe due for demolition.

Harper pulled and pushed her down the side of it. He was more anxious now, she could feel the tension in his close body, see him looking left and right.

"You won't get away with it," Hannah said.

"Shut up," he snapped, pressing the knife into her skin until she cried out, and then he pushed her harder.

They rounded the building cautiously, Harper looking along the wharf. Then, hugging the wall, he went right.

The pain in her side stopped and then the knife was at her throat, the bag gone.

Harper stopped her by big warehouse-like doors with a smaller one that was open. He glanced in before pushing her through and closing the door behind them.

"Rizzolo?" he hissed and waited for a moment, the knife still at her neck. Then he shouted, "Anyone?"

Banging and calls came from the left. She could see doors and a ladder leading to a balcony.

Harper hit a switch and lights came on. Now she could see they were in some sort of industrial loading area. The rails continued through double doors at the far end. There were metal girders and chains with hooks hanging down, and glass-fronted offices behind the balcony.

Harper pushed her hard and fast towards the banging sound. It was coming from the third door, men trapped inside a room. But before they reached it, the Judas gate crashed open and Harper spun around.

Ash Carter had his gun raised and pointed at them.

"Stop right there, Harper."

The colour sergeant jerked her and she yelped as the knife nicked her throat. But he didn't stop. He was forcing her up the metal staircase.

She glanced back to see Ash running towards them but then stopping before the bottom of the stairs.

"It's over, Harper," he called up as the sergeant pushed her to the balcony railings. The bars pressed into her thighs. This wasn't safe, she could go over.

And then she realized that Harper intended just that. She shrunk back, pressing against him but the knife cut deeper.

Ash shouted, "Give up, man. Come down and talk."

Harper laughed.

"Be reasonable," Ash continued. "What can you hope to achieve?"

"Plenty."

"Why? Because you have a hostage? How'd you think this is going to play out?"

"You could be a rich man," Harper said. "I could cut you in." Maybe it was the association with a knife, but the sharp end pricked Hannah's throat as he said *cut.*

She yelped.

"Don't hurt her!" Ash shouted.

"Drop your gun and come up here. There's more than enough to make us all rich men."

"What about Suleiman?"

Harper didn't immediately respond and she guessed he was thinking. Maybe he hadn't realized how much they knew about the operation.

Finally he said, "He'll agree. We've all come too far to lose it now. So put down the gun and let's talk."

"You won't hurt, Miss Quinn? You promise?"

"Promise."

Ash didn't comment or move.

"I need a decision, Captain."

"No deal," Ash said. "You're going to put down the knife and let Hannah go. Then you're going to come down the ladder and I'm going to arrest you."

Harper removed the knife from Hannah's neck. She relaxed. It was over. But then she felt a sharp sting in her leg. He hadn't dropped the knife, he'd slashed her. She stared in disbelief at the deep gash in her slacks and the blood gushing through the rent.

She didn't scream, but the shock made her legs give way and Harper gripped her to keep her upright, shielding his body.

"Drop the gun, Carter," he shouted.

Ash didn't move. Maybe he couldn't see what Carter had done.

Then Harper explained. "I've cut her femoral artery. Put down your gun or she'll die in minutes. If you want to save her, your only option is to put your gun down. Now!"

Hannah's vision blurred. Was Ash going to put his gun down? Was he considering it? She thought fast and spoke. At first her voice was weak and quaking, but she got it under control and hoped he could hear.

"Do what he says, Carter. I'm losing blood—fast. I'll die if this isn't over soon. Put the gun down. Please." She paused, glanced at the blood, and her vision swam in and out. Don't faint. Don't faint, she told herself.

She swallowed hard. "Sometimes it's all right to give up. Do you hear me? Even Dantès—the Count of Monte Christo—didn't escape. So don't shoot!" She paused and breathed. Summoned all the energy she could find. "Put the gun down—do it on the *count* of three. Right?"

As she spoke she looked sharply down and right. Could he see her clearly enough? Would he know?

Weakness crashed over her like a wave. She steeled herself to repeat her message, but her voice dried. She felt dizzy. Then she felt Harper relax slightly.

Ash had started to lower his gun.

"Put it down," she managed to say, although her voice seemed lost now. "One... two..."

On three she used her last ounce of energy to push away from Harper and dropped out of his grip. She felt the blade of the knife dig into her shoulder as he realized what she was doing.

Ash fired twice.

Harper lurched. He dropped the knife and tried to pull her up as a shield again. Before he could, Ash fired again and again.

Harper staggered and fell. He caught the handrail of the platform but his grip didn't hold. And then he was tumbling over the ladder and thudding onto the factory floor.

FIFTY-TWO

The evening rushed in but I could still see the coastline through Jim Dexter's office window. Harper was dead, Rizzolo and the other three were being held in separate cells, as was Sergeant Walsh from the motor pool and Sergeant Cox of the Royal Engineers.

Hannah's injuries had not been life-threatening. As soon as Harper had fallen, I had quickly mounted the stairs and tied a tourniquet on her leg. I'd carried her outside and flagged down a marine police patrol boat that took us swiftly quickly across the strait to George Town. She was now recovering in Minden Hospital. I'd ensured she got good treatment, said she was working on behalf of the CO, and stayed with her until she was comfortable.

"I still can't believe it." Dexter shook his head and looked at least ten years older than his forty-eight. "Murder?"

"Almost certainly," I said.

"Not suicide?" He knew the truth but struggled to accept it.

I said, "I think Sergeant Harper really intended to scare Tanner by jamming the rifle under his chin. But Tanner had it locked and loaded."

Sergeant Cox had admitted he'd been smoking marijuana with Tanner before Harper had turned up. He said that he'd been told to go away and he'd heard Harper angry with the kid before the gunshot.

Cox had been keen to talk. "Sergeant Harper told me what to say. He took Tanner's shoes off and I was to point to suicide if it wasn't ruled an accident."

He also claimed that he hadn't wanted to let Harper use the Bedford from the garage but didn't have any choice. He told me he didn't know what Harper was up to. That part, I didn't believe.

Dexter was shaking his head. "What an idiot loading his rifle!"

"Some of the kids do it despite the regs, despite the low risk," I said. "I think Tanner was really spooked. I think all of the men involved were afraid and the marijuana exacerbated it. Maybe if it hadn't been loaded, Tanner wouldn't have died."

"Reeder died because he knew the truth."

"In effect. He either lost his nerve when I got involved and would have confessed or he used the information, blackmailed them for a share of the operation. Either way, Harper killed him."

"Not an accident?"

"No, deliberate, and at the assault course, so I would suspect Sergeant Brookes. The second time I met Harper he tried to defend Brookes, but he was really confirming that Brookes was a bully. Clever. I'd bought it. I was even thinking of raising it with you."

He said, "Are you sure it wasn't Cox or Walsh? It's easy for them to point the finger at the guy who can't defend himself."

"I can't be a hundred per cent sure, but I'd bet on it. Walsh in particular liked the control thing. Cox was about drugs and the benefits. They told me that it started with the marijuana and they felt guilty. Harper controlled them that way. They may have agreed their story in advance, but I think they felt obliged to accept whatever Harper did, partly because of who he was and partly the marijuana. They also seem to believe the ghost mumbo jumbo, or certainly their men do. Fear of ghosts or Harper seems to have been their motivation rather than money. Most of that was for his retirement."

"Most? Who else was involved?"

"I can't be sure but I think it's Dr Suleiman. The old factory looks like it could be his. I think he was Harper's contact for disposing of the stolen goods. He trades in medicine and it makes sense that he'd be supplying Harper with the marijuana. From the start, Suleiman was also taking an unnatural interest in me and what I was doing. He claimed he traded information but I guessed there was more to it."

"You've notified the police about him?"

I looked towards the window, which now mostly reflected the room rather than showing the spectacular view across fields and the coast.

"Not yet," I said, eventually. Hannah had told me about the incident at the harbour police office and the Middle Eastern man who took her to the alleyway and Harper. That was Suleiman, I was sure. I continued: "I can't get anyone to admit his connection. Maybe the others really don't know where Harper got the drugs. Or maybe they'll change their tune when SIB gets here."

"Well done."

"Not really. I should have realized Harper was dodgy when he turned up at the garage in Perai. He said he'd been looking for me, but I'd just left the ferry. He would have been on the same ferry. And I was lucky that the reporter—"

"—Hannah."

Our eyes locked for a moment. The way he said her name. He knew that I knew about Hannah.

I continued: "Hannah saw the Bedford Fifteen hundred and followed. I wouldn't be here now if she hadn't got those men to dig me out of the mine."

Dexter nodded and then shook his head, still struggling to process it all. Finally he said, "How is she? Hannah?"

"She's fine. Cuts, bruises and stitches. They tell me they're only keeping her overnight as a precaution." I paused. "You should have told me."

"It was awkward. My wife's god-daughter," he said. "Difficult situation. I could have done without her being here, but... you know how it is."

I nodded. I knew nothing about god-daughters or pressure from wives, but I did know about favours. I was doing a favour to Dexter. I was also supposed to be helping Su Ling find her mother.

Looking for her in Kuala Lumpur was pointless. I knew nothing about her new life and had nowhere to start. Her sister, Li Ping Gao, had been beaten for not disclosing where her sister was now living, but it had been wasted loyalty. If I couldn't find her then others wouldn't either and I was certain Miao Wei Yong would have covered her tracks well. She might not even be in the city. She was afraid of being found so the smart thing would have been to travel before posting a letter.

Dexter offered me dinner but I said I was too tired. I promised to stay until the official investigator arrived in the morning before heading back to Singapore.

After I'd left Hannah in the hospital, I had about an hour before the Sergeants Cox and Walsh were picked up and put in Minden's jail. I'd cleaned up then but not had a bath. I wasn't one who enjoyed a soak normally, but with my own aches and pains, I decided I deserved one tonight.

However, I was hailed by the bellboy as I went through the foyer of the hotel. He handed me a brown envelope.

Inside was a brief note from the retired detective, Inspector Noble. It said: **Please tell me if you find out who the stranger was.**

And accompanying it were five photographs.

FIFTY-THREE

The SIB guy, Lieutenant Jenkins, was from Two Company. I'd been in SIB Three Company and never met him. Nor did he know about my past.

Although he'd travelled overnight, he still seemed fresh and focused. We ate breakfast together in the officers' mess and I told him everything I knew about the deaths and Harper's operation.

Like a good investigator, Jenkins immediately figured there must have been outside help and I told him about Suleiman providing marijuana and disposing of the stolen goods.

We discussed how to handle him and Jenkins agreed to leave it to me. I'd see Suleiman before I left Penang and would update Jenkins later.

In the SIB you never discuss a case with anyone not directly involved, however, he told me he'd been in the Genting Highlands when he'd got the message.

He shook his head. "Not the usual case."

"Not drugs or security or tracking someone down?"

"Tracking someone, that's for sure, but it's a bugger this one."

He looked at me, maybe wondering if I could help. Then he said, "You know I can't say, but I think I'm tracking a killer."

"Well, lucky you. You've got one here too."

He smiled, although it was half of a grimace. "Different," he said, but that was all.

I provided him with a written statement before shaking his hand and wishing him luck with his other case.

My next visit was to Major Dawson, in his office at the hospital. He got up from his desk and looked alarmed. He reached towards my head.

"You should get that looked at."

The lump on my forehead was still grossly large and livid purple. It hurt to touch but nothing more.

"I'll live," I said. "I'm here about the morphine."

He dropped his chin. "Right."

"I'd like two samples. One from the army medical supplies and one from your other source."

Dawson sighed and then took me to the locked storeroom where drugs were kept. The ampules looked similar but different enough for me to believe they were from the two sources. I put a black pen mark on one to distinguish them.

"You'll have them tested?" he asked.

"I'll let you know the results."

"Thanks," he said, "but I'm sure it's good quality."

He pumped my hand and I left him as I returned to Hannah's ward. They'd taken her off a drip and the nurse said she was allowed home.

I helped her to my jeep and drove her back to the hotel.

"Thank God you understood me," she said.

I turned and looked at her. She was smiling, but I shook my head.

"What?"

"When you shot at Harper on the balcony... you knew I wanted you to. You knew I would move right."

We pulled up to the hotel and I said nothing for a moment.

She said, "My Count of Monte Cristo reference."

"You said Dantès didn't escape and that he gave up, but he didn't."

"Yes, I meant the opposite. And I said 'right' so you'd know I would go right."

I hadn't been sure what Hannah had meant. Her voice had been weak and hard to understand. No way would I have put my gun down in a situation like that anyway.

"It was a good plan," I said and she smiled at my response.

"What now? Will you stay a while?" She touched my arm and looked at me in the way a woman can. She could say things with her eyes that she wouldn't vocalize.

I hesitated, tempted then shook the thoughts from my head. "I'm leaving," I said flatly. "Going back to Singapore. Things to do."

"Right," she said and the look was gone.

I kissed her on the cheek and wished her success with her career and left her on the steps of the Palisades.

But before I left the island I had two more house calls to make.

Mrs Gao's house on the outskirts of Batu Feringgi looked exactly as it had the last time I'd visited. Somehow I expected it to be different. Men had been here and threatened the old lady and yet the house looked the same, serene, the views just as spectacular.

I heard the bell ring inside and I waited. Curtains twitched upstairs but no one came. I rang it again and eventually I saw movement in the hallway. Mrs Gao opened the door looking frail and scared. She had a walking stick and around her head was a bandage.

"I didn't know who it was," she said.

"Did they do that?" I asked, indicating the bandage.

She nodded slightly as though a greater movement would cause her pain.

We stood facing one another, a little awkward for a moment before she asked if I wanted to come in.

"I won't keep you long," I said. In the front room with the window that overlooked the beach, I pulled out two of the five photographs.

The first was a nine- by seven-inch picture of the stranger lying on a mortuary slab, a head-to-toe shot with his clothes on. He appeared smart but not wealthy and I agreed with the detective's opinion that this wasn't a vagrant.

The second photograph was of his face after the blood had been cleaned up. His skull was concave on the left. His eyes were closed and out of line—presumably caused by the impact. There was a long old scar on the left that ran down his cheek.

I didn't show her the other three pictures. In them the clothes had been removed and they were close-ups. One showed old scars on his back like he'd been lashed but also fresh cuts and bruising. The next photo showed the cuts and welts on his front and also a scar on his left arm, high up, about four inches long. The final one showed more detail of the cranial damage.

Mrs Gao looked at both pictures and said nothing for what seemed like a long time. I heard a clock's heavy tick tock somewhere deep in the large house.

Her hands were shaking and she passed the photographs back to me. She began to cry then steeled herself for a moment before sitting on the sofa.

"Are you all right?"

"When you lose a loved one, it is the worst thing that can happen," she said, and I heard a tremble in her voice. "But over time we cope, we get on with life. Seeing that picture, the reality all comes back suddenly, like it was yesterday."

A tear ran down her cheek and I thought she'd start crying again but she wiped it away.

"I'm terribly sorry," I said. "I should have been more sensitive. It was wrong of me to show you your husband's attacker."

She took a long breath and blew out air.

"I don't recognize him," she said. "I wish I did, but I don't."

I shook her thin hand, which felt warmer than I expected, and said I was sorry again. On the way to the front door I said, "If those men come back, tell them everything you know. Tell them your sister is in KL, because they won't find her."

She looked startled. "They won't?"

"No, she's survived this long, Mrs Gao, so she'll be too hard to find."

I drove back to George Town, annoyed with myself for my insensitivity and angry with Andrew Yipp. Mrs Gao may not have recognized the stranger but I was sure he must be one of Yipp's men, just like I was certain that it had been his men who had attacked and threatened her.

My teeth were still clenched with anger as I parked outside Dr Suleiman's office.

I marched through the building, up the stairs and into his office. People scurried and flapped behind me and when I burst into his office, the man shooed them away.

Someone shut the door, leaving us alone.

"You aren't getting away with it," I said.

He smiled sadly. "Sit down, Mr Carter."

"I'm not staying long," I said.

"You're angry."

293

I scoffed. "You're party to criminal activity including theft and murder."

"Oh dear no," he said with a firm shake of the head. "You are mistaken. Those men were using my old factory illegally."

"I don't think so. I think you were their distributor. You'd sell the goods and then split the proceeds with them."

"Your evidence is circumstantial."

"You were the man who grabbed the reporter, weren't you?" I could have brought Hannah to identify Suleiman, but she'd been through enough and I didn't know how dangerous this man really was.

He just smiled at me.

"She will identify you," I said.

"I was helping," he said still smiling. "The police were too busy so I handed her over to a soldier." He gave a tiny shrug. "I'm not responsible if that soldier was crooked."

"You are, because you were part of the operation. Sergeant Cox will confirm it," I said, hoping the Engineer knew more than he claimed, hoping Suleiman didn't know either way.

Again Suleiman shook his head, but this time with a small smile. "No he won't."

I waited a beat. "How can you be so sure?"

"Because of who I am and who I represent. You don't think I'm alone, do you? I'm just part of a much bigger organization."

I shook my head. What was he telling me? "You'll kill him if he talks?"

"No, no, no!" he said firmly. "I wouldn't do anything of the sort. But who knows. Someone else might decide the sergeant needs to be made an example of. Or some of the other men."

"Who?"

He said nothing.

"Who do you work for, Suleiman?"

"Look," he said, "you can do one of two things. You can pursue this further and find yourself unsupported. You can be sure the police won't want to be involved."

"You own them?"

"One or two. The harbour police as well, but they know what's good for them. And then there's your better option."

"Which is?"

He smiled again. "To pursue that which is worth pursuing. I told you originally that I gather information. I also pass on information. I told you about the bad spirit—the morphine. Follow that lead."

"Tell me more about the morphine. How does the system work?"

He pursed his lips, maybe wondering whether to tell me. I saw a twinkle in his eye as he started to speak. "Your navy," he said. "They just come into port and drop it off, just like it was ordered. Only twice."

"Twice? What do you mean?"

"You work it out," he said. "You're going back to Singapore. It should be pretty easy to solve now you know how it's being shipped around."

I didn't like that he knew my intentions. Maybe it was just a lucky guess but I was pretty sure Suleiman was part of a secret society.

I said, "Do you work for Andrew Yipp?"

He laughed and then got serious. "Let's not dig too deeply, Mr Carter. Before you judge me, let me ask you about Sergeant Harper when you confronted him in my old factory. What did he do?"

"He dragged the reporter up to the balcony."

"Why?"

At the time I thought it odd. We could have negotiated on the ground. It looked more dramatic on the balcony and my initial thought was he'd threaten to throw Hannah off. But that would have been pointless. Killing your hostage was foolish unless you had an escape route.

I asked, "Was there another way off the balcony?" Even as I said it, I realized that Suleiman knew what had happened. He'd seen it.

"No, Colour Sergeant Harper was waiting for me," Suleiman said, confirming my suspicion. "He thought I would bring men to help but he was wrong. You see, he had already lost. It was over."

"Why?"

"Because of the bigger picture." He held out his hand and I found myself shaking it before I left.

FIFTY-FOUR

I was on my way to Kuala Lumpur with the morphine samples, but took a detour. In Perak, I came off Route One, drove through Ipoh and out again on the west side. The sun was directly overhead but now hidden by gathering dark clouds. The grunt and groan of gravel pumps filled the air and wetlands broke up the jungle.

The Kinta River flowed on my left and I knew there were giant dredgers further downriver. Before I reached them I took a side road that cut through the trees. It began raining. Hard.

Just outside a town called Batu Gajah, I pulled up a gravel track that led to a long timber shed that had once been a sawmill.

Outside was a sandy-camouflage-patterned Land Rover with Perak Protection stencilled on the side. I parked next to it and went inside the shed.

If he was surprised to see me, Scott "Slugger" Stevenson didn't show it. He glanced up and carried on pummelling the punchbag like it had called his mother something unmentionable. Sweat covered and flew off his broad torso and he didn't stop until he was totally spent.

"Carter," he wheezed, hands on his knees. "Want to show me what you've got?"

"Good to see you too, Slugger," I said, and bumped my fist against his glove.

"Are you back with the military police?" He'd obviously seen the markings on my Land Rover.

"Just borrowing it."

"Looking for a job?" he asked.

I laughed. "No thanks. I'm passing through. Thought I'd see if you were around for a bite of lunch."

Five minutes later we were sitting in his favourite café, the rain pounding the windows.

"Really just passing through?" he asked.

"Yes."

"Will you call in on the doctor?" He was referring to Heidi Allan, with whom I'd stayed for a few months before leaving for Penang.

"How is she?"

"Doing well. And we've put in a couple of standing pumps in villages. Yeah, she's happy, I'd say. More to do though."

I nodded. "Then it's better that I don't see her."

"Right," he said.

"How's it going with your girl?"

He grinned. "Going strong. To be honest it's what keeps me here even more than the pay. This bloody country. It's hot and it rains all the time. I got a tan working for the army. Now look at me!"

It was true, he looked pale, but his physique was good, better than before. Proper labour had given him definition, and I wondered if he'd beat me in the ring now.

He lit a cigarette, sucked deeply and then coughed. I recalled the wheezy breath after his workout and thought, *maybe not.*

"Cigarettes'll kill you," I said.

"Not according to the advertising. They're healthy."

"And that's why you're wheezing?"

"Well, if you're right then there are worse ways to go," he said, grinning.

We talked some more and finished our food. I told him about Penang and what Harper was up to.

"You should have called for me," he said.

"I dealt with it."

"By the look of your face, you didn't do it very well." He'd assiduously avoided looking at my injury up until now and I had to agree that Hannah had rescued me from the collapsed cave.

He laughed so hard that I thought he'd fall off his chair. It ended with a fit of coughing.

Then he said, "Saved by a woman. Good job I wasn't there." He grinned. "So is she attractive?"

"I thought you were happily married."

"For you, I meant."

"There was nothing going on between us."

He raised his eyebrows, grinning again. "But there could have been."

"It's good to see you, Slugger."

"You too, Carter. I'm glad it's over, but in the future if you need proper help, let me know. We're no longer just connected by phone to the police station. If you need me you can ask the operator for the PPF."

I thanked him.

"But only proper help, you hear," he said, pumping my hand. "I don't want to do a woman's job."

I left him asking for a second helping of dessert and drove back towards the trunk road in the rain. I passed the doctor's clinic and glanced that way in case she was looking and was then glad she wasn't. It really wouldn't have been fair to drop in and just say hello to someone I'd spent three months with. I wondered if she still occasionally went for a jog or whether that was just for me. I envisaged her lithe body in various yoga poses then shook the images from my mind.

I put my head down and drove, turned at the junction with Route One and pressed my foot to the floor.

The rain eased and then stopped after an hour and the road went from wet to steamy. Almost three hours later, the sun had broken through the clouds and I was on the outskirts of Kuala Lumpur.

Like I'd said, there was no point in looking for Su Ling's mother here or contacting the police. I was sure they wouldn't find her either. Instead, I drove to Kuala Lumpur Hospital, as big and ugly as a hospital can be.

The guard at the gate waved me through when he saw the military police markings and I parked close to the entrance.

Dr Shaheen Meah looked as tired and hassled as ever but greeted me with a smile and a rapid handshake. And then he looked uncertain.

"What have you got for me now, Captain Carter?"

"Morphine," I said. "Two samples that I'd like compared."

"How long have you got?"

He probably expected me to respond in days, but I said, "I'll wait."

He hesitated, gauged my seriousness and said, "What's your primary concern here?"

"The purity."

He rubbed under one eye. "You're concerned that one of these isn't what it's supposed to be? Morphine is most commonly extracted by the lime method, but the purity depends mostly on the filtration method and whether or not the morphine is an intermediate step in the process of heroin production. Full analysis of the purity will take hours, possibly more than a day with other priorities."

"What about a less than full analysis? I just want a view on the quality."

"I can look at the weight percentage of water, residual solvents and inorganic material."

"How long?"

"Is it important?" He rubbed his eye again before answering his own question. "Of course it is, otherwise you wouldn't ask. All right, I'll be as fast as I can."

It was the early hours of the morning when an orderly woke me with a cup of tea. I'd fallen asleep in a chair and my neck had stiffened.

The tea had sugar but I was grateful and drank it anyway. Dr Meah appeared fifteen minutes later, holding a piece of paper. He handed it to me.

"You owe me."

"I do," I agreed, looking at a page of numbers. "What does it mean?"

"Medicinal morphine of around 10 per cent is considered pure. Of the two samples, the one with the black mark is 9.5 per cent. The other is 10.7 per cent. So the one with the black mark isn't quite up to scratch but it's acceptable."

I thanked him profusely and set off, driving south through the night. I had my answer but it wasn't what I'd expected. The ampule with the black pen mark was from the official army source. The purer one was the illegal batch.

Outside, the warm night was filled with the soft song of insects. I took the hood off the Land Rover and headed south for over three hours.

For long stretches through the jungle I was alone on the road in total darkness. Time in hospitals can become distorted and the time of day meaningless. Out in the jungle with only the rumble of my tyres and wind in my

301

hair, time appeared to freeze. Endless trees and road lit by my headlights.

It was a relief when the monotony was punctuated by an odd light or fire from a village or an animal scurrying through my beams.

My mind kept going over what I knew about the morphine. Hospitals were getting much-needed, additional supplies. I'd followed the paperwork in Singapore. I'd checked the medical boxes shipped in. I'd checked them transported and I'd checked them delivered. How was he doing it?

By the time I reached the causeway connecting Malaya to Singapore, I'd worked it out. Simple. Obvious.

The crossing was closed for the night and wouldn't open for another two hours. I stopped by the water's edge and splashed my face before returning to the jeep and leaning back, staring up and the night sky.

When someone rapped on my bonnet, I bolted upright. I must have dropped off.

"Military police? You can go through, sir," a man with a torch said. A crossing guard, I realized. He'd seen me parked up and probably thought he was doing me a favour.

I shook the sleep from my brain and seconds later went under the barrier and traversed the thin strip of land to Singapore.

Slugger had said *I'm glad it's over*. It wasn't over, not yet. And I had the feeling that worse was yet to come.

FIFTY-FIVE

Sunrise was an hour away, so when I returned home, I splashed cold water in my face, changed into my training gear and drove the Land Rover back to Gillman Barracks.

The CO wasn't there, which suited me. I didn't feel ready to talk about the bullet holes, the temple thefts or morphine trade. So I ran down the hill out of the camp and went east.

With little cloud, the sky lightened rapidly. I ran along the perimeter fence of Keppel Harbour and noted that a liner was in Empire Dock. Coolies carried large bags and portmanteaux on their heads, bouncing along the gangplanks like casual high-wire artists.

I continued on over Fullerton Square, already crowded with parked cars and trishaws, and then across Cavenagh Bridge, the narrow, more attractive footbridge close to Anderson Bridge. The sun crested the horizon creating a pale orange sky, but the wharf along Boat Quay was still dark in the shadow of the godowns.

There was some activity along the quay, a few fishing boats returning from an early morning catch, a dozen merchants and staff preparing for the day, opening frontages and washing down their patches.

Instead of heading along the esplanade as I normally did, I turned and ran past Hill Street police station, with its tricorn front and one hundred shuttered windows.

I'd been attracted by a cluster of police twenty yards further along. As I neared, I could see why. A naked Chinese man had been hung from a lamppost like he'd been crucified. I arrived just in time to see the police pull him down.

I stopped and took a look at the man.

"Who is he?" I asked the closest officer.

Whether he recognized me or not, I don't know, but he responded immediately. "We don't know yet, sir. Naked, so clearly no identification papers."

"Gang?"

"An exhibition like this?" he said. "No doubt about it. Definitely a gang execution."

I walked away, back to Cavenagh Bridge, stood in the middle and just stared along the river. Unfocused. I thought of the harsh brutality that contradicted the beauty of this treasure island. Had the violence worsened or had it always been this way? The threat was insidious and endemic; Malaya struggled to control insurgents who saw Communism as a preferred alternative to British imperial rule. In Singapore the problem seemed to be that the gangs were part of society, that they were integrated, providing the illusion of normality.

I didn't have to wait long before I was picked up by a trishaw driver.

"Mr Chen would like to see you," the skinny cyclist said.

I insisted the man take me home first so that I could change. Once there, I took my time, dressed smartly and checked my Beretta before placing it in the ankle holster.

Then I was in the trishaw again and I knew the routine. I put the blindfold in place, leaned back in the seat and shut my eyes.

The journey was probably ten minutes. I would have been happy with longer, maybe I could have slept. But we stopped and I removed the mask. We were in a narrow alley, clothes strung on lines overhead between the buildings.

The cyclist pointed to one of the houses and I went inside. Two armed men then accompanied me upstairs where I found Chen Guan Xi. We were in a different building but the set-up was identical to previous times: gold and green, crimson dragon on the deep pile carpet, Chen at a desk in his business suit.

"Welcome home, Mr Carter. Did you have a successful trip to Penang again—so soon?" I stood three paces from his desk while he regarded me with his one good eye.

"Reasonable," I said.

He nodded and smiled. "You found your bad spirit—your bad morphine."

"The morphine is good quality. Better than the army medical supply."

"No matter," he said.

I said nothing.

"Quid pro quo," he said, unsmiling now.

I remained quiet.

He got up and moved round the desk to a chair close to me. After settling, he said, "We have dealt with your little Palestine problem, Mr Carter. In fact, we continue to keep an eye out"—he pointed to his good eye like it was a pun—"for trouble for you. You are safe with my protection."

"I'm grateful," I said.

305

"Good, so we have an understanding," Chen said. "Quid pro quo."

"What do you want me to do exactly?" I said, wanting him to spell it out so that I could consider my options.

"Take Andew Yipp out of the picture. Whatever. Have him arrested."

"Like I said, the morphine is good quality and needed. I'm not concerned about the production, it's the distribution—the military issue that should be addressed."

Chen shook his head. "Better to get the right man for the wrong crime."

"You're saying make the crime fit the man?"

He nodded.

"Two things," I said. "Dr Suleiman works for you, doesn't he?" I'd changed my mind as soon as I realized Chen wanted to use the morphine trade against Yipp.

"In a manner of speaking."

"What does that mean?"

Chen gave the slightest of shrugs, as though my question was meaningless, but then he said, "We have an arrangement. What you need to appreciate, Mr Carter, is that the outcome at the old foundry could have been very different. Dr Suleiman was told not to interfere."

"Because I'm more important than spoiling his little arrangement with Sergeant Harper?"

"That is correct."

"He thinks he's untouchable."

"Maybe he is. But I like to believe that no one is untouchable, not even Mr Yipp."

Dust motes spiralled over the elaborate carpet, which was incongruous in this shabby building where paint peeled off the walls. I let the silence of the room grow between us.

His eyes were still on mine.

Finally I said, "You must hate Andrew Yipp very much."

"It's business. Simply business," he said, explaining as though to a child or student.

I nodded. "He's number one and you want the position."

He said, "What was your other question?"

"I saw a murdered Chinese man outside the police station this morning—was that quid pro quo as well?"

"That man did not understand that debts need to be repaid, Mr Carter. You, on the other hand, are a smarter man."

I took a breath. I had no doubt that the same fate would be in store for me, should I not achieve what he wanted.

Chen stood and returned to his desk. "You have three days, Mr Carter. Work out how you will repay your debt."

FIFTY-SIX

The enemy of my enemy is my friend. Despite reciting this to myself, I didn't like the idea of being indebted to a man who was undoubtedly as bad as Andrew Yipp.

My instinct was to confront Yipp about his search for Su Ling's mother, about threatening Mrs Gao and killing her husband. But that wasn't the smart approach.

I spent an hour at the naval HQ outside Keppel Harbour looking through the records. Ships in and ships out. I was in luck. A shipment of medical supplies was due the following morning. Not only that, but HMAS *Condamine* was then scheduled to travel north, stopping at Port Swettenham, serving the Malayan capital before steaming on to Penang.

I turned up early and waited for the Australian vessel to dock. I watched goods being unloaded and others being loaded. As before, I checked the dockets and the crates and confirmed that the medical supplies were present and correct.

When I'd finished, I went on board the *Condamine* and introduced myself to the captain. He kindly gave me a tour of the ship before permitting me to repeat the exercise with the goods in his hold.

I had the information I needed but still no plan despite mulling it over for the good part of a day. Like

Pascal's Wager, there were four options. Only this wasn't about belief and reality. It was two cold hard realities. I could help or not. Favour Chen and I would still be beholden to him. If Yipp survived, or I was found out, then I'd also have his gang after me. Not a good outcome. I wondered if there was a way I could help Chen and Yipp somehow. I kept coming back to it but no scenario worked.

Favour Yipp over Chen and again I would continue to have trouble from Chen unless Yipp gave me protection. Under other circumstances this would have been a good option, but I felt responsible for Su Ling and she needed protection from Yipp.

Which left me with the only reasonable solution: Help neither but in a way that solved both problems. Strategically ideal, practically impossible.

Still without a plan, I kept walking around the city until I found myself on Coleman Bridge watching the bumboats, tongkangs and activity on the quays. Today the smell of spices mixed with rubber to form a strange concoction both pleasant and acrid at the same time.

I was lost in my thoughts when I saw a familiar figure cross the bridge ahead. She wore a dark blue trouser suit with a matching parasol. Despite the distance I knew at once it was Su Ling.

I jogged to intercept her and held up a hand. "Lunch?"

"It's not wise," she said, full of concern.

"I don't care," I said, and she hesitated before nodding.

We found a small backstreet place and sat in the shade.

"What's the matter?" she asked after ordering.

"We should get you away from Yipp as soon as possible."

After studying my eyes, searching deep within me, she said. "I can't go yet."

"Why not?"

"It's complicated."

"Yipp is still hunting your mother for what she did, for stealing his money."

"I don't…"

I placed a hand on her arm and she didn't pull away. "Your mother has been in touch—written another letter. She's in KL—or somewhere close. She's alive and well and wishes she could see you."

"Can you… Do you know where?"

I shook my head. "It's safer that way. Yipp sent men to threaten your aunt. He sent them after the war and again last week. The first one killed your uncle. The recent ones beat your aunt, but she doesn't know exactly where your mother is. It's better that no one knows, not until the threat has gone."

She said, "Is my aunt all right?"

I described her condition, said the physical injuries were minor but the incident had shaken her.

From her pocket, Su Ling pulled out the brooch I'd brought last time.

"Too garish to wear," she said. "I like to hold it for strength. Do you know what I mean?"

I nodded.

"You said a letter. Do you have it?"

"No, but I remember what it said." I recited the message while Su Ling smiled sadly.

The food was served but she only picked at it and I guessed her appetite had gone. She asked about my Penang case and I gave her an overview.

"You were very fortunate," she said. "I always thought the spirits were on your side."

"Perhaps they are," I said.

She stood. "I need to get back."

"Be careful," I said.

"You too, Captain Carter."

She kissed my cheek and was gone.

It wasn't until I paid the bill that I noticed something under her napkin. The brooch. Picking it up, I spotted a tiny clasp. It popped the brooch open to reveal two penny-sized photographs. One of Su Ling's mother that I'd seen before. The other was of an older couple. I'd not seen the woman before but the family resemblance was clear. The man's face was almost side on, like he was turning to hide something on his face. A mark or a dressing perhaps. He looked familiar.

If I'd studied it more closely maybe I would have realized it changed everything.

FIFTY-SEVEN

I stood at the reception desk on the twelfth floor of the Cathay Building. The receptionist smiled when I asked for a meeting with Mr Yipp. She placed a phone call and asked me to wait. But I stayed in front of her.

"Is Su Ling in the office?"

"No," a sweet voice said from behind me. I turned to see the assistant who had shown me the secret apartment. She smiled and I wondered again whether it had been her who had slipped into my bed on the first night. In the dark maybe I could have mistaken them. And it wouldn't have been hard to wear Su Ling's perfume.

I handed her an envelope. Inside was Su Ling's brooch.

"I'll make sure she gets this," the girl said.

Our eyes held for a moment and then we both glanced away. Yipp's hard man appeared, his face set, malice in his eyes.

The assistant slid away.

"Hello, Wang," I said, my voice calm and even.

"What are you doing here?" he asked as he stepped close, confrontation in his stance.

I smiled and held up my hands. "I want no trouble, Mr Wang. I would simply like to see Andrew Yipp urgently. He will see me."

"I don't think so."

"Please tell him that I have a business proposal for him."

Wang frowned, hesitated and then spun around. He walked swiftly along the corridor and turned back as if to ensure I hadn't moved. Then he disappeared into an office and moments later returned.

"You may wait," he said, and pointed to a meeting room I'd been in before.

The room was bare except for a large Chinese rug. I sat cross-legged on it looking through a window that faced north-east over the jungle and waited. A few minutes later a girl slipped silently in and placed a tea pot and cup in front of me and another where Yipp would sit.

I didn't have to wait long before Yipp came in from a side door and sat without making eye contact.

Someone else entered behind me and I guessed that Wang was standing by the wall. I didn't look.

Yipp precisely and carefully poured himself a cup of green tea. He took his time and sipped from the cup before replacing it delicately on its saucer.

I mimicked the gesture.

"I see your courtesy has returned, Captain Carter. I thank you for the respect," he said, looking at me for the first time.

I took another sip and looked into Yipp's eyes.

"I've been at Keppel Harbour," I said.

He nodded but gave nothing away.

"I know about your distribution business," I said.

"I have many distribution businesses, Captain."

"Medical supplies," I said. "Specifically morphine, which is in high demand."

"It is."

"I was told a story," I said, and relayed the tale of the man who passed the checkpoint each day with a bicycle. Each day the guards were suspicious but each day there was nothing illegal in his bicycle panniers.

"He was stealing bicycles," Yipp said, nodding.

"A classic misdirection. Hide a crime within another, less serious one—or in the case of the bike thief, just the suggestion of another, more serious crime."

Yipp let a smile play on his lips.

I said, "Originally I thought you were intercepting shipments and inserting your own. But it's much more clever than that. Almost foolproof. You make exact replica crates and items."

Yipp said nothing.

I said, "I witnessed a construction exercise in a village north-east of the city. Kallang Dua."

Yipp sipped his tea.

I said, "But that's not the clever thing. You take the goods to Keppel, store them and switch the crates there."

Now he spoke, his voice flat. "Switch the crates?"

"What comes off, goes on. I saw the Australian naval ship *Condamine* make a delivery. The papers were exactly correct. They delivered the goods, but miraculously they still had the supplies on board with the paperwork to prove it. The legitimate medical supplies are delivered and the fake ones take their place. Providing the original paperwork remains, no one is any the wiser."

Yipp raised his eyes. "The quality is good."

"The quality is excellent," I said.

"You will appreciate that it was the British who made Singapore a free-trade port. The way I see it, Captain, is that my operation is merely an extension of that original intention."

"That's an interesting argument."

"You've admitted the quality is good, so where is the crime?"

"Good doesn't equate to legal," I said. "But I'm more concerned about who is profiting from this process. Your distribution channel is the navy and probably elements of the army as well."

I stopped and waited. Let Yipp think. He signalled to Wang, and moments later our tea was refreshed.

I said, "The bicycle thief."

His eyes drilled into me.

"Like I said, it's the classic misdirection. The crime within a crime. You commit the crime of illegally supplying morphine. But it's excellent quality."

He said nothing.

I said, "No one would suspect it's the cover for your heroin smuggling operation. The quality is too good to be linked to heroin production. Therefore it is."

He still didn't comment, but I could see that I was right.

He drank some tea and indicated that I should do the same. When he finally spoke, he said, "We could have a different arrangement."

Greasing palms was just part of the everyday process but I thought I needed to tread carefully. However, he was more blatant than I expected.

"You could be on the payroll," he said. "You no longer work for the government or army"—he shrugged—"there doesn't appear to be a conflict of interest."

I said nothing and heard Wang shuffle his feet behind me.

Yipp said, "You shouldn't feel uncomfortable. Many people in authority do not have such a dilemma, Captain. Money is a magical oiler of wheels, and where money doesn't work, there is always fear."

I breathed in and out slowly, decided to be direct. "Did you use fear against Su Ling's aunt?"

Yipp's eyes showed surprise. "I don't know what you mean."

"Did you send someone to kill Mr Gao?"

He shook his head. "Now you are being rude, Captain."

I thought he was going to get up and walk away, but maybe the threat to his heroin distribution kept him there.

I bowed my head. "I apologize. I needed to know."

He studied me, and I could almost see the cogs spinning in his head, trying to figure me out.

I said, "You need to change your operation."

"A change would be good." Businessman Yipp was back.

"I can't replicate Keppel Harbour, but in principle can arrange a similar channel for transportation and storage."

"How would you arrange things? Tell me how the business would work. What would be the security and means of transport?"

Suddenly I was aware of my heart drumming harder with anticipation. It felt like I'd bated the line and cast it out. Now the big fish was ready to take the hook.

"I have it almost all worked out," I said. "For it to work we must take the utmost care. We must not be as blatant as before. Once the bicycle theft is known, it would be foolish to attempt a duplicate crime." I paused partly for effect, partly because of my racing heart. "I believe I will be ready to show you tonight. We must have utmost secrecy."

I turned around and exchanged stares with Wang. His body was full of tension, like he was just waiting for his master's attack command.

I smiled disarmingly and turned back to Yipp. "I have written the location I have chosen on a piece of paper." I pulled an envelope from a pocket and slid it across the floor towards Yipp. He didn't pick it up.

I continued: "We should keep this between us. If no one else knows our business then it will more likely succeed."

Yipp nodded thoughtfully, picked up the envelope and secreted it beneath his jacket. "You are very wise, Captain Carter."

"I simply want a fair reward," I said, "and I see no reason to jeopardize that. After all, there are severe consequences for me if this goes wrong, so secrecy and discretion are paramount."

"Very well." Yipp stood and bowed and I returned the gesture.

I thought he would say no more, but as I followed his henchman out of the room, Yipp said, "You had lunch with Su Ling."

"Yes."

"Her mother," he said quietly. "I did love her."

FIFTY-EIGHT

The Goodwood Park club didn't have its usual vibe, but then it was too late for lunch and too early for evening entertainment. The depressed atmosphere wasn't aided by a dreary number being played on the grand piano.

I took a stool away from the other three gentlemen at the bar and ordered water. It came with green olives in a bowl that I played with rather than ate. I thought about what Yipp had said. He had loved Su Ling's mother. Should that surprise me? She betrayed him and love can turn to hatred.

I also thought about Wang. He had accompanied me in the lift and to the foyer. There had been an electrically charged atmosphere between us and I sensed his body tense whenever I moved.

He said, "You know that Mr Yipp could just have you killed?"

"But he is a wise man," I responded. "He will deal with me because I have taken precautions should I die." I didn't explain what I'd done, I didn't need to. Yipp would work out that I'd have a contingency plan: information about his operation that would be delivered to the authorities upon my demise.

I saw Wang clench his teeth, undoubtedly frustrated that he'd have to find another opportunity to end my life.

The clock hand at the club did a circuit before the pianist changed and the music picked up. More people arrived and the level of background chatter increased.

By the time the clock had done another circuit the place hummed—in a discrete fashion—and that was when the German entered. He caught my eye and I joined him at a far table for two.

"You only have one more day," he said.

"That's all I need," I said. "It's happening tomorrow night."

"Where?"

"Pulau Blakang Mati."

His left eye twitched. "Why there?"

"Safe," I said. "Safe for your man, I mean."

"Why?"

"Not police jurisdiction. The island is controlled by the British Army. The old fort there is also a lure for Yipp."

The German processed this before nodding. "Clever."

I said, "Chen needs to be there. My debt is to him. I need him to release me from it before I hand Yipp over."

Again the German nodded.

"You'll guarantee he'll be there?" I pressed.

"Don't worry, Mr Carter. Mr Chen wouldn't miss this for the world."

I telephoned the Perak Protection Force in Batu Gajah and was quickly put through to Slugger Stevenson.

"Wow!" I said. "You really are connected."

"Only the most important people," he said with a laugh. Then more seriously: "Is this the call for help?"

"Yes."

"Will it be exciting?"

"I hope not."

"Then I'm not interested." He paused and I could hear his men in the background, their voices echoing around the wooden bunkhouse. Then he said, "Want to try again? Will it be dangerous?"

"Undoubtedly."

"That's more like it! When do you need me?"

"Now."

He laughed.

"Well," I said, "tomorrow night's the deadline."

"I can do that. How many men shall I bring? I can't spare everyone, but three or four?"

"Just you, Slugger."

"All right, Carter. I'll be there as soon as I can."

He arrived with five hours to spare and I told him my dilemma. I didn't want to be beholden to either gangster or start a war with them.

"But this Chen chap," Stevenson said. "He's here illegally…"

"Trusting the police is one thing. And even if I could, we'd need to catch him first."

Stevenson thought for a second. "Then we kill them both. Once they're on the island we've got them."

I shook my head. "But their men will know we've done it."

"What's your plan then?"

"It's not brilliant," I admitted. "We get Chen to kill Yipp and then arrest Chen."

"Tell me the detail."

So I walked through how I expected it to play out. And when I'd finished he pulled a face.

"You're right," he said, "it's not a great plan. We'll do it your way, but I still think we just kill both of the buggers."

FIFTY-NINE

Most of Pulau Blakang Mati was hilly with mangrove swamps, and the air was filled with the smell of decaying vegetation in the brackish waters. The night sounds were less intense than the rainforest of Malaya, but sporadic bird and animal cries added to a spooky atmosphere.

The British Army had built three artillery batteries to defend Keppel Harbour from attack in the Second World War. None of the island forts were occupied any longer, but their cannons and gun emplacements stood as an unofficial memorial to those who had defended Singapore from the Japanese.

Fort Siloso's strategic importance, guarding the western end of the narrow Singapore harbour, had led to occupation by the Japanese. After the war, the Royal Navy supported by the Royal Artillery moved in before handing it over to a Gurkha regiment. But then they had been relocated due to the communist threat from the north. Siloso had been deserted for about three years.

I stood by the howitzer that pointed at the small island of Pulau Keppel opposite. The panoramic view here was excellent. It had to be.

A full moon lit the coast and grassy promontory. Clear in the silver light, my dinghy was down there. A calm sea looked like mercury as it gently washed to and fro.

Thick jungle crowded in behind the fort and monkey cries pierced the night.

I waited.

At five to eleven, I heard a small outboard motor and then saw a single man inside an approaching dinghy. He tied the boat up beside mine, looked around and then began to walk up the slope.

I flashed my torch, causing him to veer my way.

He wore a suit and I suspected there was a gun underneath.

Fifty yards out, he stopped and looked left and right.

I flashed my light again. "Up here."

Andrew Yipp stood ten yards out and cleared his throat. "I do not like this place, Captain. Too many ghosts."

"The ghosts are inland," I said, based on nothing but hope.

"And I am here," he said. "I came alone, as you requested."

"Thank you." I turned and walked from the gun emplacement and then up the track towards the first buildings. I could hear Yipp behind, walking at his own pace. Not hurried. Light and cautious.

Two squat white buildings were coming up on my right. A storeroom followed by an engine room.

"Captain, where are you taking me?"

"The storeroom," I said, but he stopped at the railings on our right.

"What's this?" he asked, pointing down a steep flight of concrete steps.

"Most of the fort is underground."

"Show me," he said firmly, and I retreated to the steps. He followed me down to a thickly painted steel door. It was unlocked, and gripping the door handle I looked back. Yipp had one hand on the railing, a pistol in the other.

"No need for that," I said, lightly.

He ignored me. "Let's go in."

My torch illuminated a white-walled corridor. It was a few degrees cooler and musty air assaulted my nostrils. Two paces and I heard Yipp enter.

"What's down here?" he asked.

"Just one moment," I said. "You'll see why this place is perfect for your operation."

He grunted but I kept walking. Fifteen paces and I stepped right—a kink in the tunnel, put there for defensive purposes. We descended slightly for another fifteen and I stepped left—a kink back onto the original line. Fifteen more and I came to a room.

There was a metal gate across it.

I heard his footsteps retreat and turned around.

"I don't like the damp," he said as he disappeared around the kink.

I hurried out after him and met him on the steps.

"The tunnels then descend to the beach," I lied.

He reached the top and looked around, his gun ready.

"We're alone," I said.

"Tell me why I'm here."

"The island is under the control of the British Army. The Singapore police and Customs have no influence. And the army have left. They may own it, but they don't care. All this swampy island is good for is defence and trade. You get your goods here and you're away free. And I'm not just talking about the heroin of course."

He grunted and looked twitchy. I'd never seen him like that before. He seemed to spend most of the time looking down and to the right.

"It's deserted," I said, trying to reinforce my argument. "The army don't have the manpower or inclination today."

"I don't like the tunnels."

"Precisely, that's why I wanted to show you the storeroom. Leave the stock above ground and use the tunnels if you need to."

I was easing him onwards to the first building.

The heavy door was locked, and it creaked open when I turned the key. Inside was junk left by the Gurkhas, or maybe it was from earlier occupations. I flicked my torch over boxes and equipment.

Suddenly his gun was at my head.

"What's going on?" he snarled.

He glanced around, maybe spooked by animal cries in the jungle.

I ducked and a rifle butt slammed into Yipp's head. The old Chinese man spun, alarm in his eyes, but then he crumpled to the ground.

"Good timing," I said to Slugger Stevenson, who had been waiting behind the door.

"I figured he wasn't coming in."

I bent and checked on Yipp. He was breathing but would have a very sore head.

"You hit him too hard," I said, pocketing the man's gun.

"Hmm," Slugger said, looking at me with a cockeyed smile. "Really? You're complaining I hit him too hard when he had a gun at your head."

I snapped handcuffs on Yipp and we carried him deep into the storeroom. There was a cage there, like in the quartermaster's hut at Minden. Maybe it'd been an armoury. Now it served as a good jail.

I left him on the floor and locked the door.

"What are you doing?" Yipp asked, groggy from the blow.

I stopped and walked back to the cell.

"You've been hunting Su Ling's mother," I said. "You've practically kept Su Ling as your hostage."

"Not true," he said.

"So you didn't send men to beat up Su Ling's aunt."

"Why would I?"

"Because of the letters—because Mrs Gao might know where Miao Wei is."

"She's still alive?" There was hope in his voice.

I didn't answer. I'd already said too much about her. Instead I said, "Her aunt is afraid of you. You killed her husband and you killed her father."

"What are you talking about?" He was up now and staring at me through the bars. Even in the faint light I could see he thought I was insane.

"Are you denying you killed Su Ling's grandfather—not directly but by reporting him to the Japanese."

"I did no such thing!"

Then he fished in a pocket and pulled something out. Something the size of a small pebble. The brooch. The assistant must have given him the envelope I'd delivered.

"That's Su Ling's grandfather inside. On the right."

I shone my torch and opened the brooch.

"What was he hiding on his face?"

"He had a dressing on it," Yipp said, "A Japanese soldier struck him down for showing disrespect. He didn't die and I certainly never reported him."

I stared at the picture and said nothing.

He said, "He was a nice man."

" *Was*—so he is dead?"

"I don't know. He disappeared after the war. It was chaos after—people arriving, people leaving. That photograph must have been taken shortly before."

Suddenly it all clicked into place. Su Ling's grandfather. The scar. The lies.

"I'm sorry," I said to Andrew Yipp, then stepped out of the storeroom and locked the door. My head spun. I'd made a mistake.

I looked for Slugger, wanting to explain, wanting to let him know my plan had changed, but I couldn't see him. He would now be in the woods to my right somewhere.

I started in that direction but then heard the sound of another outboard motor. We should have had thirty minutes but Chen was early. However, no dinghy appeared and the noise stopped. I figured Chen must have travelled the long way round, approaching from the east and mooring before the exposed region.

I ran for the gun emplacement and flashed a signal, warning my partner and waited, watching the jungle to my left, listening hard. Blood thundered in my ears and suddenly my plan seemed crazy. I'd locked up the head of the biggest Chinese secret society and I had no idea what Chen was up to.

If this went wrong, I was a dead man.

SIXTY

"Where are you?" Chen's voice cut through the warm night air.

He was behind me, higher up, halfway between me and the storeroom but still close to the treeline.

I flashed my torch and he moved in my direction. The moonlight showed me he was wearing a long coat with a cowl over his head.

"Stop!" I shouted.

Chen stopped. He was about eighty yards away and I didn't like it. Not one bit.

"Where's Yipp?" Chen said.

"Safe."

"Let me see you."

I stepped away from the gun emplacement, with my hands up. I wasn't holding a gun.

Chen mimicked the no weapon gesture but didn't move.

As he did so, I saw the coat move. Perhaps a trick of the light, but Chen looked thinner and taller.

"Remove the hood," I called.

The hood was tossed back. In the moonlight I could see this wasn't Chen but his henchman, the German. In the same movement, the man swung a machine gun out from under his coat.

"Where's Chen?" I shouted.

"Here!"

I looked left and saw a man close to the engine room.

"Prove you're Chen," I called.

The man on the higher ground flicked a torch light on his face and off again. Clearly Chen this time.

I took two paces towards him.

"Stop!" the German barked. "Another step and I'll shoot."

"This wasn't the deal," I called to Chen.

"The deal has changed, Mr Carter. Now where is Mr Yipp?"

"Safe," I repeated.

"Not good enough!" Chen said and raised a hand.

The rat-a-tat-tat from a Sten gun sent me diving for cover. Bullets pinged off stone. I scurried to the low wall by the howitzer and raised my weapon. The German was running towards me, a zigzag route, blasting as he pounded up the slope. He was at the far side of the gun emplacement in seconds.

I got off a few shots and then he stopped and ducked down. I figured he was changing magazines and took the opportunity to run for the nearest trees.

As I dived behind a palm tree the ground kicked up around me and bullets thudded into the trunk.

Where the hell is Slugger? I thought.

And in that moment I heard another gun. But Slugger had a revolver and rifle. This was another machine gun. Jesus! There was yet another shooter out there. Chen might have brought an army.

But as I cursed my poor judgement, I realized the German was no longer shooting at me. He was firing at a man in the woods. I saw the other man moving between the trees, the sparks from his gun giving away his location.

The German stopped firing, repositioned and waited. As the new arrival came out of the trees, he blasted him. I saw the man jerk and dance as bullets struck home. But I wasn't just watching. I was running back up the slope, back towards the gun emplacement. Even as the new guy was being mown down, I was taking aim and shooting at the German.

A last burst spewed from his weapon and was silent.

I closed in quickly, my gun aimed at the man's head. He leaned against the wall, unmoving. Dead.

I took his Sten and made my way down the hill to the second guy. I could hear his ragged breaths twenty yards out.

"Wang," I said, recognizing Yipp's henchman.

He glanced at his weapon, just out of reach, and I picked it up before he could go for it.

"How bad?" I asked.

"Bad enough," he grunted.

"Stay there," I said, then shouted: "Chen?"

"Under control," Slugger called back from the top of the hill.

I walked up the path and found Slugger with a gun to the Chinese man's head.

"Tie him up," I said, and aimed one of the Stens at Chen's midriff.

As handcuffs were locked on, Chen snarled at me. "It all went wrong, didn't it?"

I shook my head. "Turned out all right in the end."

"What's your plan, Carter? Kill us both? Take over the drugs trade?"

I laughed. "You were going to kill me and Yipp, weren't you?"

He didn't answer.

I said, "You gave me a problem: owing you a debt without getting myself into deeper water." I nodded to Slugger. "Take him away."

Chen let an ironic smile light his face. "You're going to hand me over to the police?"

"No," I said. "I know you've got men in there who will get you away."

He frowned. "Then what?"

"Captain Robshaw of the military police is waiting at Empire Dock. He doesn't know why but he'll realize when we hand you over. First you'll be processed by the military police for damage to the fort." I couldn't trust the police but I knew I could rely on Robshaw.

Chen shook his head.

"Better to get the right man for the wrong crime," I said, replaying Chen's own words to me. "Then you'll be handed over to the police via the government's Internal Security. You've illegally returned to Singapore soil and won't be exiled a second time. This time you'll be incarcerated."

"What about the other two," Stevenson asked me.

"Chen's man is dead. Yipp's is badly wounded."

"Can I shoot him?"

Although it was tempting, I said, "No."

Stevenson shook his head. "You're no fun." Then I watched him drag his prisoner down to the jetty and loaded him into a dinghy, tying his hands to a stay.

I opened up the storeroom and found Yipp standing proudly, bracing himself for whatever might come through the door next.

Five minutes later I had Yipp and Wang in the second dinghy. I decided to leave the German where he lay since it worked well as evidence of Chen's attack on the fort.

Yipp said, "I trusted you," as we cut a path through the calm waters towards the harbour. I controlled the outboard while Yipp had an arm around his employee on the bench in front.

"And I trusted you," I said. "The agreement was to come alone."

"Good fighters of old first put themselves beyond the possibility of defeat. Coming alone wasn't an option."

I nodded, recognizing a quote from *The Art of War*. Of course, none of us had come alone.

"I am not your enemy," I said, repeating something Yipp had once said to me.

He was silent for a while and I listened to the engine, the splash of waves, and the groans from Wang.

Eventually Yipp glanced back and asked me about Chen, and I explained that the man expected me to repay a debt.

"You could have asked for my help."

"And become beholden to you instead?" I said.

My solution to the problem—my Pascal's Wager— had been to let Chen kill Yipp and then have Chen arrested. I'd blamed Yipp for all the bad things that had happened to Su Ling and her family, but I'd been wrong.

I didn't bother explaining to him how I'd misinterpreted the situation with Su Ling's mother. I'd realized he hadn't tried to kill her. He really did love her.

Yipp said, "So what will happen to my drugs business?"

"Generally, that's up to you. Specifically about the heroin? That has to stop. The morphine on the other hand is medicinal quality and there's a need for it. We should look for a legitimate deal with the army. I can do that."

"But you have conditions."

"Just one. I want the names of all military personal on the make. You give me the names in exchange for a contract with the army."

I let him direct me up Singapore River, strangled by the hundreds of boats tied up for the night and then on to Robertson Quay outside one of his warehouses.

Before we went under the fifth bridge, I undid Yipp's handcuffs.

At the quay his men rushed down and helped both Yipp and the wounded Wang out of the dinghy without asking questions.

I doubted Wang would survive and I didn't care either way. However, I was certain he'd get the best medical care possible. Yipp would make sure of that.

The head of the largest Chinese secret society stood on the quay and untied my rope. He held it in his hand for a moment as though it was of great symbolism. Maybe it was. Maybe he was showing me that he was the one in control.

He said, "I'll see you again." It could have been a friendly remark, but it wasn't. His voice was flat and full of implication.

I nodded and waved and he tossed the rope into my dinghy.

I glanced back as I motored away. Yipp was still there, watching me.

SIXTY-ONE

Before I left Singapore, I made some phone calls, and then I let Slugger Stevenson drive me up country. I did a lot of thinking and slept well despite being in the passenger seat of a Land Rover.

At Kampar, the stop before Batu Gajah, he dropped me off and we pumped hands.

"More excitement next time," he said.

"I'll do my best. And thanks."

He grinned. "Happy to save your life again."

"Save my—!"

He cut me short with a deep laugh, spun the wheels on the laterite and tore away, back to his role in the Perak Protection Force.

I had a long wait for the train, and once inside the first class carriage, I immediately fell asleep again. I missed the Kinta Valley mining area that I knew so well, Ipoh and the Perak River, and then the jungles and villages all the way up to the town of Perai.

The guard's "End of the line" call woke me, and still muzzy from sleep, I boarded the ferry.

Facing forward on deck, I let the cool sea air clear my brain. My mind went back to that first day when I'd been attacked by the Palestinian. Not long ago and yet it seemed like an age away. The mysterious deaths at the barracks had been solved. Harper was dead and the other crooks imprisoned. And back home, I'd dealt with Chen Guan Xi.

Just one more thing to resolve.

I watched the island of Penang appear through a mist, George Town and then Penang Hill looming up behind. I knew there was a funicular train that tourists took up to a botanic garden and considered taking a trip.

Back on land, I hailed a taxi and gave him the address outside Batu Feringgi.

Mrs Gao stared at me for a moment when I arrived at her door.

"I didn't expect you to return," she said. The bandage was gone and she no longer used the walking stick.

"Can I come in?"

She led me into the room with the fabulous view and photographs on the sideboard.

"I see that your injuries have healed. How are you now?"

She gave a minute bow. "I am well, thank you."

Although she hadn't asked, I said, "I'll have that tea, if you don't mind?"

She nodded, smiled and scuttled out.

In the ten minutes she was gone, I looked at the photographs and tried to imagine what it would have been like during the war—the oppression, the hardship, the stress.

Her eyes flicked from me to the coffee table when Mrs Gao returned with a tray.

"There are a lot of photographs of you and your husband," I said.

She sat and smiled and pointed to a chair.

I said, "One thing that bothered me was why there aren't any of your family—Su Ling, your sister, your parents?"

"Ah," she said as though it was an answer.

I said nothing.

"We lost them during the occupation."

"But your wedding photograph is here."

She glanced at it and smiled. "Luckily my husband kept a copy. Special."

I sat and she poured us both tea.

When she sat back, I said, "You haven't asked me about Su Ling."

"I was waiting for you to tell me. Is she all right?"

"Yes," I said. "I gave her the brooch."

She nodded.

I took a sip from my cup and let the silence grow.

Mrs Gao picked up her cup and I noticed the same shake I'd seen previously. She set it down again rather than drink.

"Are you nervous, Mrs Gao?" I asked.

She shook her head but made no eye contact.

I said, "Previously I assumed you had a condition, but now I believe you are simply nervous."

She looked at me, and I saw that I was right, although she shook her head again.

"I'd like you to explain," I said.

"Explain?" Now there was a tremor in her voice.

"Where did Mr Gao get his money to set up the carpet business?" Dr Suleiman had said that he had no knowledge of him prior to Penang. Also, Gao was no businessman.

When Mrs Gao didn't respond, I continued: "Was he a different husband or did he change his name too?"

"He changed his name."

"Why?"

336

"To make a fresh start."

I nodded. "When I first asked about your husband you told me stress had killed him. But he died as a result of the attack by the stranger." I paused and looked at her hard before continuing. "Why did you lie about that, Mrs Gao?"

She looked away. "I didn't know who you were. You might have been from Yipp."

"No," I said, "you mentioned the trouble and then tried to steer me away from it. I think you made a mistake and then your stories didn't make sense."

She said nothing.

"I thought the lack of family photographs was a little odd, especially since you were in touch with your sister, however, I missed the more obvious lie."

This time, when she looked at me, I thought her eyes looked moist as though she was on the verge of tears.

I said, "You told me Yipp arranged for the arrest and killing of your father. But you had already left Singapore by then. You have only been in touch with your sister. And she left at the same time."

In the silence that followed, I could hear her breathing faster. I took another sip of tea while hers remained untouched.

I said, "It was the brooch that was your undoing."

"The brooch?" She blinked, and a tear finally crested her eyelid.

"Su Ling put in two photographs. One of her mother and one of her grandparents."

She swallowed, and another tear ran over her cheek.

"Tell me what happened that night your husband was attacked, because the story he told the police was a lie."

At first I thought she was going to speak, but she swallowed again as though her voice won't come.

I continued: "It wasn't a stranger or one of Yipp's men who confronted your husband. It was your father, wasn't it, Mrs Gao?"

She wiped away more tears. "How did you know?"

I said, "During the occupation, your father was struck by a Japanese stick. He had a scar on his face and left upper arm. I saw that same scar on a photograph of the man who attacked your husband."

She nodded.

"I think your father tied up your husband and beat him. He wanted information, but your husband wasn't talking," I said. "But what I don't know is how things turned around."

"An employee—he owns the warehouse now—came back. He subdued my father and tied him up."

I nodded. It made sense. The man with the long grey hair and the bamboo furniture. It also explained why the man had been suspicious and a little nervous. He probably knew the truth about what had happened that night.

"Your husband didn't know what to do with your father, did he? I think he beat the old man and left him in the carpet warehouse and came home. I think he needed you to tell him what to do. It was your father after all."

"He wasn't supposed to die," she said quietly.

"I told my husband to reason with him, but when he got back... my father had untied himself and found a knife. They fought, my husband was stabbed... my father fell from the balcony. I don't know all the detail. It shouldn't have ended like that. He was supposed to talk." She shook her head and I wondered if she was reliving that night.

"An accident then," I said.

"Yes."

"But that was just one of many."

She'd stopped crying now and she just stared at a pattern forming on the surface of her cold tea.

"The attack by the men looking for your sister was also a lie, wasn't it?"

She said nothing.

"When I came last time, you checked who it was and then prepared yourself, putting on the bandage and picking up the walking stick. I checked with the local hospitals and you weren't treated by any of them. You said they were threatening because you were afraid I'd look for your sister and discover the truth."

She didn't comment.

I said, "It was a miraculous coincidence that the second time I visited you'd received a letter from your sister, thereby confirming she was alive and well. Again, to stop me looking."

She said, "You should have kept the brooch. I thought you'd realize it was a payment."

I ignored her and said, "I know the truth about your sister."

She looked up now, her eyes black and cold, defying me to be right.

I said, "The truth is, she's dead and has been for a long time. She never intended to steal Andrew Yipp's money, did she? He loved her. She loved him."

She took a long breath, like years of tension were being released.

I said, "It was your plan to take his money."

"My husband's. It was his idea, and once it started, I couldn't stop it."

"You killed her."

"It was an accident."

"Like your father's death?" I scoffed. "He came to Penang because he suspected the truth, and you had to kill him too."

She didn't deny it.

I took hold of her arm and stood. I walked her to the front door.

"What are you going to do with me?" she asked.

"It's not what I'm going to do, it's what you're going to do," I said. "You're going to confess to the police and you'll tell them where Su Ling's mother's body can be found. For her, that's the least you can do."

I opened the front door and ushered in the police. Old detective Noble was there.

I said, "I was right."

He shook my hand, and I could swear he had a tear in his eye. I walked away, leaving them to process the case.

I went back to the Palisades but didn't take a room. Instead, I sat in the bar, ordered a bottle of champagne on ice and read the newspaper as I waited.

About half an hour later, Hannah walked past, did a double take and bounded over to me. Her hug was tight and her perfume subtle.

"Wow!" she said. "I hoped I'd see you again, but didn't—" Then she noticed the champagne. "Is that yours?"

"Yes."

"But..." she started slowly, "you don't drink."

"Not much, but tonight is different. And I thought you could help me celebrate."

She was leaning on the bar, the nail of her little finger between her teeth. "I like the sound of that. What are we celebrating?"

"A satisfying end to a difficult case."

I signalled the waiter, and after popping the cork, he poured two glasses.

She drank most of the bottle and we went from there to a quaint restaurant outside of town where we downed another bottle. We talked of inconsequential things like being tourists, taking the train and visiting the gardens at the top of Penang Hill.

I don't think I took advantage of her, but when she insisted that I stay the night in her room, I accepted the offer. Then stayed for three. It seemed rude not to.

Acknowledgements

I would like to thank Ian Johnson (Capt.) for information about Penang and the army in the 1950s. I am also grateful to Stuart Fulling who provided photographs and cuttings about his father's (Lt. Jack Fulling) experiences in the army and Malaya.

Thanks to my wife, Kerry, and early reviewers: Pete Tonkin, Alex Jones and Lauren Babrook. Your support and encouragement is greatly appreciated.

Richard Sheehan, my editor, did another sterling job. Finally, I must express gratitude to my father who inspired the Singapore series.

Singapore Killer is next.

BLACK CREEK
WHITE LIES

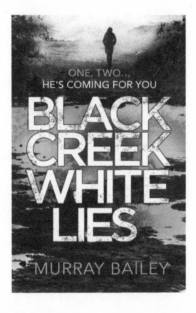

One night, Jade Bridger takes a dead-end path by the creek, and vanishes. Eighteen months after being wrongly accused of her murder, Dan Searle returns to Cornwall to rebuild his life and forget. But others won't let him forget.

He is quickly drawn back into the case and a dark and violent mystery; one that involved another girl years before. As the lies begin to unravel, Dan uncovers startling truths about his family and the past.

With dangerous people trying to keep their secrets safe, he must save those he loves - before time runs out...

DARE YOU TWICE

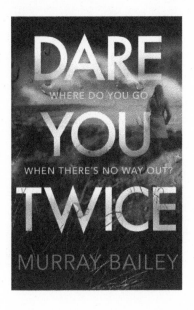

A teenage girl disappears from her locked bedroom. With no way out, and a trace of blood, the police conclude the worst. As Kate Blakemore investigates the strange case, she finds her own life threatened.

She goes into hiding only to find herself drawn into another mysterious case. On the Dorset coast, a young man has vanished without trace. Except for a cryptic message he seems to have intended for Kate.

Accompanied by her friend, Andrew and a British Detective, Kate follows the clues that take her from England to Paris, France. As the puzzle unfolds, Kate questions what she believes and whom she can trust. She has to work out what is really going on - or die trying.

Read the first chapter of the Egyptian crime-mystery:

SECRETS OF THE DEAD

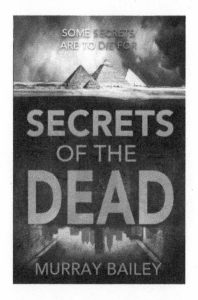

Atlanta, Georgia. When a body dump is found, FBI Special Agent Charlie Rebb thinks a serial killer has resurfaced. Called the Surgeon by the media, his telltale technique has everyone wondering why. But then the murders seem to stop again.

Cairo, Egypt. Alex MacLure is contacted by a student who thinks he's uncovered a conspiracy involving the pyramids. He asks for Alex's help to piece together a message using new discoveries. But the student disappears and Alex is arrested for a murder. Meanwhile, the special agent sees a sign that the Surgeon is now in Egypt.

MacLure links up with Special Agent Reed to track down the killer. As he decrypts an ancient story, MacLure realizes this is a race against time. The Surgeon must be stopped before he completes his terrible and startling mission.

ONE

Atlanta, Georgia

When he first saw flesh in the dog's jaws, Eddie didn't think much of it. His two hounds were often finding bones. Only this time it was different. The dogs had been running out by the church. And when he took the human hand from Deion's jaws, Eddie worried he'd be in trouble.

JJ was nowhere to be seen and didn't come when called, which concerned Eddie too. But first he decided to find where Deion had been digging and just replace the hand. No one would ever know.

Then he spotted his second dog, far too intent on his bone to respond to calls. But this one wasn't a bone, it was an arm. And that wasn't all. Eddie watched a lot of TV but he'd also seen the posters. This arm was distinctive with a Maori sleeve tattoo.

Eddie didn't think he was in trouble any more. He knew he'd found the latest missing boy.

Special Agent Charlie Rebb watched FOX News. She finished blending the super-greens smoothie and used it to wash down a couple of Advil. What was worse, the green gloop or the thumping headache?

Her phone rang. It was her partner, Peter Zhang.

"You watching this?" he said.

"Morning, Peter."

"Yeah, morning. Have you got the news on?"

"If you mean, am I watching the media circus at the church, then yeah. It's crazy."

"Five bodies they've pulled out of there."

"Hold on," she said. The pastor of the church was being interviewed. The display gave his name as Reverend Piccard. Behind him was a cluster of doleful members of his congregation.

"We are all deeply shocked," Piccard said. "The community is in shock. But at the same time, we must have faith in the risen Lord. The Son of Man must be delivered over to the hands of the sinners, be crucified, and on the third day be raised again." Piccard reached out and the people behind closed in and held hands.

Peter said something but she cut him off. "Wait, I want to hear this."

The reporter said, "Reverend, Mark Simmons had been missing from Georgia State University for forty days. There's been a state-wide hunt for him. And now we discover he's been under this church—under your church. Forty days under your church." She paused, adding weight to the statement. "Tell us how you found out about the body. How you learned about the other bodies?"

In Charlie's ear, Zhang said, "We don't know Simmons was under there for forty days! He could have been someplace else and been moved."

"Shush!" Charlie put the phone down on the counter so her partner couldn't interrupt.

Reverend Piccard repeated the story that everyone knew by now: a local man had found "the poor boy" while out walking his dogs. He said, "The man called the police and I got a call from them at home yesterday at around 10am. Of course, I came straight here and we have been praying ever since. This is a wake-up call." Reverend Piccard looked into the camera, speaking to the TV audience. "The human race is out of control and corrupt. Evil is abound. Greed and self-gratification have replaced God and godliness. We are being punished for turning our backs on the Lord. Only by accepting Christ can we hope for salvation."

"Has he said the words 'fire and brimstone' yet?" Charlie heard her partner scoff.

The reporter had managed to get a word in: "—and this morning the police issued a statement about there being multiple bodies under your church."

The reverend swallowed and nodded. A woman beside him closed in as though for comfort or protection.

The reporter said, "What can you tell us about those other bodies?"

Piccard looked like he was on the verge of tears. "Those poor boys… I've been told there are four more that the crime scene people have found. Five poor boys. We should all take a moment today and pray for their souls…" He paused. "I am sure we will learn in due course who they were, but for now I say, Father, into your hands I commit their souls. Christ our saviour rose on the third day. He will rise again. He will lead us from damnation and the serpent of evil will be driven out once and for all."

"This is crap," she heard Zhang shout. "Listen, I'll be there in fifteen to pick you up." He disconnected.

Twenty minutes later she was in his car and heading for the church in Dunwoody, north of the city.

He caught her rubbing her forehead.

"Headache, Chicago?"

She didn't respond. He knew the nickname wound her up and he kept using it. Just because she'd previously lived in the suburbs of Chicago. It'd been where her husband's job had taken him—before it all went wrong. Before she discovered what a two-timing little douchebag he was.

Zhang said, "That headache. Marcie says it's because you drink too much coffee."

Special Agent Zhang was a few years younger than Charlie. Maybe just the wrong side of thirty, although sometimes he could seem much older. He'd been married to Marcie for five years, and she always had an opinion. Or maybe it was just his way of expressing his own opinion. Charlie hadn't figured out which it was yet.

What she had figured was that Peter was struggling. Marcie didn't work and had health problems. At least that was what she claimed. Hypochondriac was what she appeared, and yet Peter would never say it. Her treatments for mystery illnesses were eating away at Zhang's savings. But worst of all were the sleepless nights.

Peter used to talk about her symptoms and insomnia. But not lately. It was like he'd resigned himself to the situation. It was never getting better.

As a good partner, Charlie knew she should be more understanding. But it was hard. Zhang was a difficult guy. Aggressive and sarcastic, he wasn't the person you let cry on your shoulder.

"Too much coffee," he repeated.

4

"Actually, it's because I need a goddamn coffee," she said. "I'm trying a health kick and there's more kick than health at the moment."

"Wow! So no coffee?"

"That's what I'm saying. Not for two days now. If this headache doesn't quit in another then I'm back on the caffeine."

They went through the centre of Dunwoody and took Mount Vernon Road before turning left.

He said, "Headache ain't so good for you know what."

Charlie thought, I guess you should know.

"And speaking of which," he said, "how is the new guy, Pablo?"

"Paolo."

"Close enough," he said. "About time I met him, isn't it?"

"No."

"Oh come on, Chicago!"

She pressed her thumbs to her temples. "Quit calling me that."

He chuckled. "Just winding you up. Getting under your skin. It's what partners do. Psych 101, that's all it is. Just be grateful you're not from some hick state like Kansas. Then I could have some real fun."

She turned to him, feeling a wave of despair. "For fu—"

"We're here," he interrupted.

The church stood proudly on a slight rise, with sunlight glinting off white shutters and a steeple. A giant white cross dominated the cut grass frontage. As they turned into the driveway, Charlie read the gate sign: "Church of the Risen Christ—New Beginnings". Beneath that was

Reverend Piccard's name. Charlie noted that it was on a removable strip. Maybe they didn't expect him to stay here long. Maybe after this he wouldn't anyway.

"I've not heard of this church before," she said.

"Fairly new," Zhang grunted. "They seem to be springing up all over the state."

"Doesn't look new," she said as they badged a uniformed cop and were waved through.

Behind and to the right were the media crews. They were penned off and well controlled. Ahead of them was the church parking lot. There were two police cars, an unmarked, an ambulance and a coroner's van.

Zhang stopped in the entrance.

"There are parking spaces," she said, but she knew why he did it, why he stopped here. It was like a statement: we're in charge because we can park where we goddamn like. She knew he played the same games with her. She was the senior and yet he liked to act like he was in control. It was the little things, like the nickname to wind her up. She'd come across it all the time from men in her career. But she suspected there was more to it from her partner. Maybe it was his way of compensating for problems at home.

They got out and both put on their FBI jackets. Zhang put on sunglasses, retro ones that he always wore for the image. She spotted the officer-in-charge, but for a moment Zhang was going nowhere. He surveyed the scene and then pointed at the church.

"You said it doesn't look new," he said. "You're right. I think they take over older churches. You know, ones that aren't doing so well. CRC seems to be doing all right."

Her brain took a moment to realize what CRC meant. Church of the Risen Christ.

She said, "You seem to know an awful lot."

"The internet." He smiled pointedly. "While you were watching TV, I was doing research."

They walked around the side towards the detective-in-charge. Charlie showed her ID and introduced them both.

The detective sighed like he'd been waiting for them to arrive and was a little pissed that he was losing the case.

"Detective Nick Garcia," he said. "Atlanta Homicide." He nodded towards the rear, where the uniformed officers were standing behind a media screen. "Just pulled out another one."

They quickly confirmed that all of the bodies were of young men. So far, only Mark Simmons had been ID'd, on account of his distinctive tattoo.

Number six was lying on the grass naked and on his front. The body was smeared with black mud.

"Caucasian male, probably early twenties," the detective said. "Obviously no identification. My gut says it's another missing guy."

Zhang beckoned the investigating coroner over. He introduced them both before saying, "Preliminary cause of death?"

"Of course, hard to say, but for the moment this one's strangulation. Ligature marks on the neck and wrists. A few lacerations on the body but they appear post-mortem. Looks like more than one animal got under there recently. Probably wild animals broke in before the two dogs found the hole." He nodded towards the church. The base had boards running around it, and at the rear they were broken.

"Would you flip him over?"

7

The coroner signalled to the uniforms and they carefully lifted number six and turned him onto his back. The whole procedure was smooth and respectful.

From the torso it was hard to tell the guy was white, there was so much muck. Charlie guessed they'd pulled him out by his feet, face down.

The ligature marks were less obvious on this side. His eyes were closed and his face looked peaceful, like he was just resting.

Zhang asked, "Had a look at the others?"

"Still only preliminary. This is the only one with obvious ligature marks. I'd say it's the second most recent."

"Mark Simmons being the most recent?" Charlie asked.

"Yes. He was also the only incomplete body. I don't think the two dogs tore off the hand or the arm. I can't be certain. The damage is all post-mortem, but probably a different animal or animals."

"Let's take a look at the site," Zhang said.

The detective and investigating coroner joined them as they knelt by the broken panels and looked under the church. Spotlights lit the otherwise enclosed area that was about twenty yards by six. It wasn't much more than an uneven crawl space—which explained why the body had been dragged out—maybe as much as three feet high in some places and almost nothing in others. Two investigators were at work, probing the space for more bodies.

Detective Garcia said, "None of the bodies were more than a few inches under the soil."

"So far," Charlie said.

Garcia grunted agreement.

She said, "There will be more."

8

Zhang said, "You can count on it."

He touched her arm and indicated they should move away. When they were out of earshot he said, "Did you notice?"

"Yes," she said quietly. Not because she didn't want the homicide guy to overhear, but because her stomach was knotted. It had been three years since they'd found anything else. Found any more bodies.

He said, "Looks like the Surgeon is back."

Secrets of the Dead is available now in paperback and as an ebook

murraybaileybooks.com

IF YOU ENJOYED THIS BOOK

Feedback helps me understand what works, what doesn't and what readers want more of. It also brings a book to life.

Online reviews are also very important in encouraging others to try my books. I don't have the financial clout of a big publisher. I can't take out newspaper ads or run poster campaigns.

But what I do have is an enthusiastic and committed bunch of readers.

Honest reviews are a powerful tool. I'd be very grateful if you could spend a couple of minutes leaving a review, however short, on sites like Amazon and Goodreads.

Thank you
Murray